TO ERR IS DIVINE

TO ERR IS DIVINE

by Ágota Bozai

ENGLISH VERSION BY DAVID KRAMER

translated from the German with
the close collaboration of the author

COUNTERPOINT

A MEMBER OF THE PERSEUS BOOKS GROUP

NEW YORK

Originally published in Hungarian in 1999 as *Tranzit Glória* by Tiszatáj Könyvek, Szégéd

Copyright © 2004 by Ágota Bozai
Published by Counterpoint,
A Member of the Perseus Books Group

Counterpoint books are available at special discounts for bulk purchases in the United States by corporations, institutions, and other organizations. For more information, please contact the Special Markets Department at the Perseus Books Group, 11 Cambridge Center, Cambridge MA 02142, or call (617) 252-5298, (800) 255-1514 or e-mail special.markets@perseusbooks.com.

Designed by Trish Wilkinson
Set in 11-point Adobe Garamond by the Perseus Books Group

Library of Congress Cataloging-in-Publication Data
Bozai, Ágota.
  [Tranzit glória. English]
  To err is divine / by Ágota Bozai ; English version by David Kramer.
    p. cm.
  "Translated from the German with the close collaboration of the author."
  ISBN 1-58243-277-5 (alk. paper)
  I. Kramer, David, 1948–   II. Title.
PH3213.B637T7313   2004
894'.51134–dc22   2003025393

04 05 06 / 10 9 8 7 6 5 4 3 2 1

1

My name is Anna Lévay, née Kuncz. I was born on the first of Septem-
ber, 1937. My mother was Fruzsina Major; my father was Tihamér
Kuncz, who was killed in the war. There were six of us children: four
girls—Éva, Kati, Zsuzsa, and I—and two boys—Laci, who lives in
our parents' house, and Pista, who was killed last year in an automobile
accident. I married in September 1956 and have been a widow since
November 1 of that year. I have a son, Péter, who turned forty this year.
He is a university lecturer in America. I completed my teacher certifica-
tion in Budapest and have taught Hungarian language and literature
in high school, and sometimes art history as well. I also have a degree in
library science, but I lost my job as a librarian when I was dismissed so
that the position could be given to the principal's mistress. I teach
twenty-nine class hours a week, two hundred seventeen students in seven
classes. Today is Wednesday, the twenty-ninth of October. I don't teach
tomorrow until the second period, so I can arrive as late as a quarter to
nine, room 12c. We are reading Kafka; my notes and class materials are
in the teachers' closet, on the second shelf, to the right, in a green card-
board loose-leaf notebook. It has been lying there since last year. Before
I take it down from the shelf I will dust it off, so as to avoid getting gray
specks on the white coat that I wear over my clothes at school to protect

them from chalk dust. First, I have to test Tibi Grün (what a dope that boy is!), whom in any case I cannot allow to fail the school year, since his father is a member of the municipal council and in charge of finances. That would only hurt the school. If I get everything ready on time, before the warning bell, I will have a cup of coffee in the teachers' room. If I buy some rolls in the morning, I had better be sure to keep twenty-five forints in change, which is the amount I have to put into the empty American salted peanuts tin next to the thermos bottle; the coins always clang loudly. The coffee is terrible. I could just as well make coffee at home, but it is too great an expense for me alone; my old coffeepot makes two cups, and there is only one of me. I do not drink very much coffee in any case; it would be a waste, and warmed up later, it loses its flavor; I would just throw it out, and I must be careful with money. So I drink coffee at school; what is important now is that before I go to sleep I must set the alarm clock, eight o'clock will do. Today, I can read till midnight. I am sure that it will disappear. Good Lord, why has this happened to me?

Not quite two hours earlier she had turned on the taps, first the hot, then the cold, even though she had learned that it is safer to do it the other way round. But she had become accustomed to doing it her way. Before she ran the cold water into the bathtub she poured some bath salts and bubble bath directly on the spot where the stream of water would hit, so as to maximize the quantity of foam. For a long time she used to consider bubble bath a waste of money, until her colleague, a physics teacher, explained to her that foam is a heat insulator; by preventing the water's warmth from escaping it allows one to stay longer and more cost-effectively in the tub. She always poured out exactly one capful, of the cheapest sort. On the shelf was a bottle of American bubble bath that her son had sent five years ago at Christmas, along with other small presents and an airline ticket, together with a letter: "Dear Mother, don't delay. Come! How I long to see you!" And since then, he wrote only at Christmas.

At Christmas and on her birthday and on her son's birthday, too, she indulged in the American bubble bath. But today was a normal day: not a weekend, not a holiday, no famous person's birthday; it was just another ordinary twenty-four hours like many, many others.

She screwed on the cap to the bath salts and noisily set down the bottle on the glass shelf that was attached to the tile wall with a cord and two anchor bolts—a shelf that she carefully wiped down every other week. Then she took off her hand-knitted sweater, the good old wool skirt that once was white but now was gray from many washings, and the nylon slip—fifteen years old at least, but in those days they made things to last; you buy something today and it falls apart in no time—and rolled down her pantyhose, carefully, lest they should tear; the prices they charge these days for a simple pair of pantyhose. But the cuticle of her right index finger, despite a careful manicure and the application of hand cream, was rougher than it might have been; blame it on chalk dust. But whatever the cause, a stitch in the fabric tore, and the stocking began to run with destructive abandon.

She quickly reached for the bottle of clear nail polish lying on the shelf below the mirror, with the result that the plastic cup in which she kept her toothbrush tumbled down. The toothbrush landed in the tub, but that was of small import. The run must be stopped as quickly as possible. Later, when she was through with her bath, she would put on her warm bathrobe and sit on the arm of the sofa in the room where her son had once slept; that was where the light was best. She would put on her glasses and use thread rescued from pantyhose that were beyond repair to mend the run so that even a trained eye would hardly have noticed it. And what if someone did? If only someone would notice! It must be at least ten years since anyone had looked at those shapeless legs. But her mother had always said, "A tear, not a patch, brings shame." Young people today no longer value things. Their attitude is that it is better to spend than mend. The young woman next door, for example, throws away things every other day that could easily be repaired. They don't value what they have, and then they complain that they don't earn enough money.

She applied a drop of nail polish to the end of the run, carefully laid the pantyhose on the washing machine, and took off her brassiere. Her breasts had long since become slack, and she had recently noticed the first wrinkles in them. She had feared that it was cancer, but her physician, an old acquaintance—they had spent quite a bit of time together at the university in Budapest—had reassured her; it was just the natural aging process, though that was hardly a comfort. Nor had she noticed that she had put on weight until the remarks of old acquaintances had led her to divine that her figure had changed. More and more frequently she was greeted with, "My, you appear to be in full bloom!" or "You've become quite well-rounded!" and when she finally stepped on the scale, she discovered that she had gained fifteen kilos that she would be happy to lose.

She opened the door of the automatic washing machine and threw in the brassiere. Every day she put on a clean one, for she had a tendency to sweat, and she hated to think that she might be emitting body odor, which to her was such an intimate matter, almost as if one were walking around naked. It had been five years since the last traces of menopause had departed. Quickly she pulled her underdrawers down to her knees. She did not allow them to drop all the way, because the floor, which she washed every other day, she considered unclean. She removed her left leg first, then the right, while holding on to the edge of the bathtub to avoid becoming dizzy. The underpants quickly went the way of the brassiere. She had bought them, as she had the brassiere, from the Chinese merchant, ridiculous what it would have cost in another store. To be sure, they were of poor quality, but if treated with care, they would last a long time, and anyhow, where else could you get ones like these, with extended legs whose elastic didn't cut into your thigh.

She turned off the cold-water tap, checked the temperature—it was just right—and plopped into the water. When the waves subsided, she reached for the remote control that lay on the edge of the sink and switched on the television. The large screen of the apparatus, which stood in the anteroom, could be viewed easily from here. She waited for the movie to begin. The commercials were still running their course. It was the same on the other channel. She didn't switch to any further channels; they were of no interest, and there was nothing else she wanted to watch. So as not to miss the beginning of the film she switched back to the first channel. The commercials were still playing. All they show, she thought, is nice girls and women whose common characteristic is their ability to attract a man: By using the advertised product they become beautiful, alluring, or seductive, or else, if they have already won their matrimonial campaign, they spoil their husbands with the whitest shirts and underwear, the tastiest dishes, and the most dazzling cleanliness. That is how it is.

Advertisements are one thing, real life something else altogether. Where do you see a commercial message to the effect that most housewives do not always prepare healthy and glamorous meals and do not always consume the "right" products because they cannot afford them, and they have, and wear, articles of clothing that are stained because the stains won't come out, and even if they did, that one might have better things to do with one's time? After all, most housewives are capable of wearing a dress that might have a spot on it; perhaps they don't have the washday product that could rinse it away, or they haven't the energy to do daily battle with the household chaos, even if the cleansing agent with the euphonious name were as good as advertised. And what's more, their homes are not always sterile, and they manage just fine with the odd bacterium or speck of dust. Perhaps they console themselves by citing Freud, who said that behind an exaggerated mania for cleanliness lies a repressed, unsatisfied sexual longing.

Thus did the teacher philosophize to herself. Then she heard the theme music announcing the beginning of the film, to which she now turned her attention. Years ago, in the mid or late sixties, she had seen this film at the cinema, with whom, she no longer remembered, perhaps with a man, perhaps with a female colleague, it no longer mattered; the theater had been dark and cold—so cold that you couldn't even remove your overcoat.

The bath water was warm; the foam retained the heat; in the course of the film, and it was a long one, she had to replenish the hot water only once. During the less interesting parts she amused herself by scooping up a rainbow of soap bubbles from the layer of foam, trying to lift them out of the water without breaking them. Sometimes, she squeezed some foam between her hands, formed a thin film of the soapy suspension between her thumb and forefinger, and attempted to blow bubbles. Occasionally, she met with success. She thought of her childhood playmates; who among them was still alive, she wondered, and what did they look like now?

She lay her head on a towel on the edge of the tub and drank the chamomile tea that she had prepared; it would soothe her strained vocal cords. She had gathered the chamomile herself during the summer vacation, elderberries and blueberries, too. In two weeks it would be time to gather rosehips. A neighbor woman had once told her that her kitchen looked like a witch's pantry, and she didn't dare to mention that she had also put up wild mushrooms in oil for the winter.

The film came to an end, the foam was dwindling as the next wave of commercials began. Not wanting to run more hot water, Anna Lévay slid deeper into the tub and soaked her hair. She rubbed it thoroughly with egg-yolk shampoo until she had worked up a thick lather, and then began to slide even deeper into the water to rinse off the suds. That was when she noticed it.

It was as though her head had grown. Her careful calculation of distance, refined over many years, was now inadequate for the necessary submersion maneuver. Yet she did not feel that she had bumped against the tub. It felt rather as if she had grown a hump on her foam-bedecked head. She corrected the motion, rinsed her hair, quickly soaped herself under her arms and on her neck, chest, and stomach; then she knelt in the tub and let the long-handled brush play across her back, then carefully washed the most hidden part of her body, just as the gynecologist had recommended, from the front toward the back. Finally, she stood up, washed her legs, quickly showered with cold water, and stepped, dripping wet, onto the soft bathroom carpet. She reached for the towel to dry her hair. The hump was still there. Energetically, she rubbed her body dry with a linen towel from her trousseau, just as her mother had always dried her when she was a girl. Then she went to the steamed-up mirror, but the more she wiped it, the more blurred the image appeared. She took the hair dryer, switched it to high, and blew at the mirror until she could see herself.

It is a climacteric delusion, she thought, or perhaps only an optical illusion.

It was only recently that the eye doctor had increased the strength of her glasses by a full diopter, and she was not yet used to them. She suspected that what she was witnessing amounted to nothing more than an anomaly of refraction. She quickly dried her hair, lifting up a few strands at a time with the nylon brush and blowing warm air over them. She felt a mild resistance as she turned the brush in her hair, and she was unable to bring the hair dryer closer than twenty centimeters to her head. Perhaps, she thought, I am suffering from a loss of muscle tone, or simply weakness in the arms, or more likely both at once, for such are the wages of old age.

Her hair was almost dry. She was working on the strands at the very top of her head when she observed the purple brush handle disappearing—and the black nylon bristles as well—as if behind a column of light, but then it must be a reflection, not refraction, but from where? She threw on her bathrobe and hurried into the bedroom, to assure herself under better light that her eyes were deceiving her, that it was really only an optical illusion.

But her eyes were not deceiving her; it was not an optical illusion.

She put on her bifocals, the cheapest kind, distributed by the National Health Service. First, she looked at it with the top half of the lens, the part for distance viewing, and then with the bottom half, which were her reading lenses.

There was no doubt. It was there. A halo.

At the nape of her neck, just a bit above, began the edge of the circle. It rose above her ears and the top of her head; the degree of luminosity was indeterminate, but it glowed with an even light.

Impossible, she thought; there is no such thing; I do not believe it; these are the first symptoms of insanity. And as proof against madness she recited aloud her personal attributes and her program for the next day: "*My name is Anna Lévay, née Kuncz. I was born on the first of September, 1937. . . .*" She was relieved that she could perform the recitation in a logical and organized manner, and this calmed her down somewhat. Perhaps she should ask her neighbor whether she could see what she herself saw, but she dismissed this thought at once, for it dawned on her that she would thereby precipitate an avalanche of gossip. But what, on the other hand, if she went on some pretext, to borrow some mustard, for example? She could act as if she hadn't noticed anything, and if the neighbor mentioned it, she could feign surprise. But it was already past ten o'clock, and there were only young married couples on her floor; by now they had put their children to bed and were occupied with each other.

She pulled on her flannel nightgown. She had to unbutton one more button than usual, but she got into it without difficulty. Then she buttoned it up to the neck and set back the heat to fifteen degrees, night temperature. Gas was expensive, and given her tiny salary she could count herself lucky that she could supplement her income by taking on private students, which paid the utility bills so she wouldn't have to freeze to death, which is what had happened three years ago to a pensioned colleague of hers. She turned down the featherbed. It had been part of her trousseau, and all these years she had treated it with loving care, never taking it out before All Saints' Day. But this year all signs pointed to a cold winter, and so she had allowed herself this luxury. She sat down on the edge of the bed. To pray? No, not that exactly, although the featherbed reminded her of her mother, and how every evening she would hear her prayers.

My eyes, dear Lord, begin to close,
While you keep watch and never doze;
O Father, guard me while I sleep,
My parents, brothers, sisters keep
From harm throughout the dark of night.
Until the morning sun so bright
Turns down to us his smiling face;
Then joyfully we all embrace.

But then times had changed, and praying before bed was no longer permitted, and in school you had better not even think of mentioning prayer.

Carefully, she raised her legs onto the bed, one after the other. To protect her spine, she supported herself on her elbows; she then reached for the switch on the reading lamp on her night table, and picked up *A Hunger Artist*. She was looking forward to her bedtime reading; it was not just that she was planning on discussing the story in her lecture the next day; she liked Kafka, and in any case, she could not sleep without reading. It is a habit of intellectuals, she thought. She took the volume and sank back into the pillows. A moment later, she was sitting bolt upright. The halo, extending above her head, had hit the pillow first, sending a sharp shooting pain into her scalp at the point of attachment.

She went to the mirror, but without switching on the light in the anteroom, for she simply hadn't the energy to go to the other door, and so she looked upon the apparition in the shadowy half-light of the room. An attempt to touch the halo met with stiff resistance, as if she had tried to grasp a magnet of like polarity while wearing a magnetized steel gauntlet. She couldn't bring her hand closer than ten centimeters.

The halo was warm. Not knowing what else to do, she went over to the medicine cabinet, took out the digital thermometer that she had received as a present from the last class for which she had been the form-mistress, and held it as close to the halo as she could. If it is a hallucination, she thought, this instrument will prove it;

after all, I can still see; my eyes won't lie. After half a minute she looked hopefully at the liquid crystal display. The thermometer showed forty-three and one-half degrees Celsius, way above body temperature. No longer in any condition to separate fact from fancy, but nonetheless making use of her reasoning ability, she observed that such a temperature was not hot enough to start a fire; she could return safely to bed, in the hope that the halo would disappear by morning; one should act as if nothing had happened; it simply will not do to let oneself be driven crazy. A person who lives alone can easily lose contact with reality; it would be best not to think about it.

She repeated the ritual of lying down, but this time she stuffed a small, hard pillow behind her neck, just big enough that the discomfort could be comfortably tolerated. She read until midnight and then switched off the reading lamp.

She could not fall asleep; the room was too bright, and the snow-white embroidered cotton pillow intensified the light. She turned on the lamp again, walked quickly to the bathroom, and grabbed a dark-brown bath towel, which she placed under her head; then she spread a blanket over the featherbed, the one with the ugly tiger stripes that her sisters had given her so that she could cover her feet when later, after her retirement, she would sit in her rocking chair among her lovingly cared-for house plants and knit in the sitting room next to the balcony window that didn't close properly.

She lay down again. Again, she turned out the lamp. It was still too bright. She got up and put on her sunglasses, which reduced the glare of light but pinched her uncomfortably behind her ears, so that it was a long time before she was able to fall asleep.

2

The alarm clock rang at eight o'clock the next morning. Anna Lévay might well have forgotten about the events of the previous evening were it not for the sunglasses on her nose, the blanket on top of the featherbed, and the bath towel upon the pillow. She sprang out of bed and rushed to the mirror.

The halo was still there. She frowned. The creases in her forehead became deeper than usual. She attempted to move her scalp, but a point just about in the middle of her head seemed paralyzed, as if in her sleep it had gotten itself stuck to her skull.

She dressed quickly, making an effort not to think about the whole business. She went into the kitchen, spread some margarine on a slice of bread, then applied a thin layer of rosehip jam. She preferred homemade jam, but there was none left, and it would be mid-November at the earliest before she would be able to gather this year's rosehips and make a fresh supply. Then she made herself a cup of tea. She breakfasted slowly and with great concentration. She then stepped once more in front of the mirror. The halo was still there; if anything, it was even more pronounced. Anxiety slowly overcame her. She selected a long, steel knitting needle and stuck it with full force into the halo. For three seconds she was able to hold it there, but then the force of the energy field ripped the needle from her hand, and it sped, point first, like an arrow, right through her only winter coat, coming to rest in the wall of the anteroom. A hasty damage assessment revealed that the needle had caused no serious harm. She brushed the wool coat with a stiff brush. At the time she bought the coat she had struggled with her conscience over such an expensive purchase, but it had now turned out that the more expensive choice had been the better value, for a synthetic fabric would have been left with an irreparable hole. She straightened the thick lining, held it fast, and sealed the hole from behind with a drop of nail polish.

With this thing on my head I cannot take the bus, she thought, and she rummaged about for her greenish-white rabbit fur hat in order to conceal the uninvited ornament under its flaps. It was only when she had lifted the hat up above her head that it occurred to her that the halo had earlier resisted her hand as well as the knitting needle, and so it should not tolerate the hat either. But for some reason, it did. A small corona of light could be seen escaping from around the edges of the hat, but it was so small that anyone who saw it would surely register it, if at all, as an artifact of refraction. There was still time to get to the high school on foot. That way, she thought tactically, fewer people are likely to see me than if I travel on a public conveyance.

She lived in an upper-middle-class neighborhood, where one did not generally travel on foot, excepting the joggers, of course. If one had an errand to run, one set out in a fancy car or on a breathtakingly expensive bicycle. The bus was a mode of transportation left to the domestic help, and to wives and children, though the latter only on the way to school. At the end of the day they were picked up and chauffeured home.

Anna Lévay set out. On the street, she met no one she knew. She had to go past the "caterpillar," an ugly building about fifty meters long, with numerous wooden columns and a corrugated aluminum roof, a remnant of the last years of the previous political

system, when shops were increasingly being leased to private entre-
preneurs. The voice of the people had dubbed it the "caterpillar,"
and "caterpillar" it had remained. Later, the creature that had given
its name to the structure materialized as an unattractive drawing on
the building's advertisement-encrusted façade. Across from the
caterpillar were the hospital and the outpatient clinic. As was to be
expected, at this time of day the only people at the clinic were those
from out of town who had come in by bus and were waiting outside
for the clinic to open. Now there was only the gas station to get
past, and there no one paid any attention to pedestrians, and in any
case, a hedge separated the station from the sidewalk. Then came
the crosswalk, the back wall of the McDonald's—the dining area
with the plate-glass windows was around the other side, and any
students who might be sitting there before the start of the school
day would be unable to see her—and then the bridge over the four-
lane road. There were trees next to the two ten-story apartment
blocks, which also showed their rear walls to the street, and so from
the ground floor it would be difficult to see her even from the side
with windows, and from the upper stories one could see only what
was on the far side of the gas station. The leaves had not yet fallen.

She decided to enter the school through the rear door. Therefore, she had to turn right, past the bar with the English name,
which was where the truants hung out after they had gotten friends
or relatives to write a note saying that they were sick; at some time
or other she had said to her class that they should feel free to hang
out in the pub, she would bring them their homework assignment
there. Behind the bar she had to turn right into the next street,
which led behind the school, where the expensive cars belonging to
the students were parked, so many and so close together that teachers arriving too late, generally in old cars that hailed from the Socialist period, found themselves without a parking space.

The janitor was working on a crossword puzzle and paid no attention to who came and went. Anna Lévay closed the heavy double door behind her, but so softly that she might have been a tardy

underclassman. It was just five minutes after eight-thirty. The teachers' room was empty. She took off her coat and with great care hung it on a hook, together with her hat. In the mirror over the coffee machine she could see that the halo was still there. The day was cold, but the sun shone more brightly than usual into the room. She quickly went over to a table and sat down, hoping that no one would notice anything. She had the good fortune to have chosen a spot directly in front of a window, through which the morning sun shone. *Ex oriente lux,* she declaimed, trying to see the whole affair from a humorous point of view. But that was not going to be easy.

The first to arrive was one of the biology teachers, who greeted her and then directed his attention to the coffee machine. According to an unwritten rule of the collective, whoever drank the last cup of coffee had to make the next pot. The coffee was bitter, of the cheapest sort. To drink the stuff you had to be either very addicted or very tired.

The second colleague, a former pupil, a German teacher fresh from the university, let her glance rest on Anna Lévay somewhat longer than was absolutely necessary, so long that she felt the blood rush to her head. But the young woman appeared not to have noticed the unusual apparition, or if she did, had put it down to the play of the morning light on her gray hair.

The teachers' room began to fill. Class registers were taken to the closet and tossed onto the shelves, each with a loud thump. There were nineteen classes, and in theory there should have been nineteen thumps. She counted. Someone switched on the long fluorescent lights. Another colleague, the Hungarian teacher, arriving after the lights had been turned on, steered herself directly to the place next to Anna Lévay, who responded by blushing a deep red. Her face was red with fear, her heart was beating in her throat, and she thought about the explanation that she would have to give after her public unmasking. The colleague slid into her chair. She had passed right alongside her and had certainly noticed the unusual warmth. But no, apparently, she had not noticed it.

The bell rang. Children's eyes are sharper than those of adults, she thought. Children are also much more critical, and more merciless. Even if they did not actually see the light, they would not fail to detect their teacher's nervousness. Between class periods the word would spread: There is something very odd about Mrs. Lévay. And from then on, all the students would be keeping a watchful eye on her, scrutinizing her every motion and gesture, her every intonation. She shivered. Not because students might gossip, but because her colleagues might become aware that something was amiss.

She was one of the last to leave the teachers' room. Slowly, she walked over to the shelf on which the class registers lay and took the register for 12c; it was easy to spot, being covered with checkered self-adhesive paper. She then walked with her customary measured step to the teachers' closet. She opened the door, removed her notes from the shelf, wiped the dust from the pile, just as she had planned the previous evening; that recollection reminded her of the discovery of the halo, and her brow darkened. She walked to room 12c. She did not test Tibi Grün, the dope, after all. For the entire period she lectured with academic thoroughness on Kafka. She enjoyed the sound of her voice, which filled the room, resounding off the two bare walls, one paneled in wood and the other consisting of a row of windows. Chalk dust and menopause had worn out her voice, which was now immediately recognizable on the telephone as that of an old woman; but after forty years of classroom practice its intonation had been perfected.

Her scalp began to itch, but she dared not attempt to scratch it. What if something happened like what had happened with the knitting needle? She patiently continued her lecture, slowly, so that not a single student would ask to have anything repeated and thus look up at her. In this way almost forty minutes passed. At the warning bell, five minutes before the actual end of the period, she quickly bade the class farewell, so that they would have no time to come to their senses. She promised a tough quiz for the next class, raced out of the door, and fled into the teachers' bathroom. She did not worry about the arrogant principal's predilection for lurking in the hallway to catch those who cheated the clock; the principal, a loathed, melancholy Cerberus, was also a former student of hers.

The renovations to the school building were not yet complete. On the ground floor the bricklayers were still pounding away. One frequently was unable to hear oneself speak in the classrooms above. The English teachers in particular, for whom the subtleties of pronunciation were of special importance, complained and cursed at the incompetent laborers who were unable to complete their work on time. At least the toilets were fully functional, even if poorly designed, for behind the entrance door there was a little alcove the width of the door, where there was a built-in cabinet for the cleaning materials, which formed a right angle with the door of the inner sanctum. Moreover, the outer door opened inward, and the inner door outward, so that a person could hardly get through. Nevertheless, Anna Lévay made her way into the inner premises, laid the class register and her notes on the toilet lid, locked the door, and stood on tiptoe, for the mirror was set for a man's height. The halo was there. Her scalp continued to itch.

Since she expected that what she was about to do would produce noise, she flushed the toilet. Now she had only a few moments, the time it took for the water to swirl down the drain and then refill the tank. She removed her watch from her left wrist, fearing that its metallic parts might disturb the force field, since she was convinced that the phenomenon must have an electromagnetic basis. She quickly washed her hands and then reached for the halo. She approached it cautiously, as one might an unfamiliar dog: First, you must bend down to it, then let it sniff your hand, and if the beast doesn't pull away, you must then lightly touch it on the chin, then stroke its cheeks and ears, and only then pat its head. Before she had touched it, she felt its warmth. Nothing unpleasant, just a tingling sensation that made her hairs stand on end. Feeling no resistance, she moved her hand effortlessly into the light. It was as if she had reached into a pot of honey that had been warmed, ready to mix into the dough for honey cake. She scratched her head. Her hair was fine, and it had once been light brown. Beginning when she was thirty, it had gradually become blond, though that was really just the invasion of gray, which made her hair seem lighter. Despite all the well-meaning advice of friends, she had never dyed, curled, or permed her hair. At the hairdresser she demanded the most puritanical of cuts, and then always dried it herself, always straight, the way it grew. At sixty her bloated face was ringed by a scanty pageboy.

As her hair turned grayer, her porcelain-blue eyes became more and more prominent. Her students were afraid of her. Not because she was particularly strict—in fact, her teaching was rather liberal—but she always demanded that they actually learn something. She graded consistently, showed no favoritism, and was not opposed to laughter, in moderation, in her classes; indeed, at times she even provoked laughter to relieve the tension. She never spoke about herself, and thus was considered unapproachable. Small wonder her students found no human frailty in her that they might ridicule. With her piercing gaze she could bring even the most ill-behaved class into line.

But there was one occasion on which she had shown her feelings, a few years ago, on October twenty-third, the anniversary of the 1956 uprising. In her Hungarian class she had told the students about what the state security apparatus had done to György Faludy. At that time, in 1956, she was still a student. She had been sitting on the wide marble steps of the philosophy building reading an article in the newspaper—written as one could not have written before or afterward—ten heads behind a single newspaper, and all reading together. At the first joke they all giggled, and then they almost rolled down the steps with laughter. More than forty years later she remembered it verbatim: "György Faludy, the well-known poet and translator of Villon, had long been a thorn in the side of the regime. Therefore, the state security apparatus was given the task of fabricating an indictment against him. Faludy, who for decades had been a member of the labor movement and knew well the methods of state security, was aware that at his arraignment he would have two choices: confession or torture. Therefore, he declared at once, 'I would like to make a statement. I wish to confess.' Then he explained that in 1941, in New York, three functionaries of the American secret police had sought him out—their names were Edgar Allan Poe, William Blake, and William Shakespeare. They recruited him to spy in Hungary for the imperialists. Since then he had been working for the Americans. Faludy's most heroic achievement at this hearing was that he did not start laughing. The officers of the state security carefully and seriously wrote down everything he said. One of them even mentioned that Faludy should be whipped if for nothing else than because the American officers with whom he was in contact had such difficult names, but in the end they allowed him to sign the statement. His sentence was fifteen years in prison." Then Anna Lévay mischievously added that she was telling them all this only because it might someday be of use to one or another of them. Despite their clamoring, she would not be drawn into providing the students further details.

Then she accompanied the students to the auditorium in the cultural center for the twenty-third of October commemoration. The city had given the schools the responsibility for the official program, and the schoolchildren now made up the audience of the dress rehearsal for the ceremony. From the way her students were conducting themselves Anna Lévay could see that the spirit of '56 had faded. She recalled how in many years, on the twenty-third of October the state increased the size of the police contingent on duty, the railway stations were more carefully monitored, informers were put on full alert, and a mood of unbelievable expectation hung in the air.

The event was accompanied by historical film footage that had been disseminated by the so-called Institute 56 just before the changeover in the political system. Anna Lévay did not look at such films: Under the old system it was because of the commentary, and then later it was because it had become uninteresting to her. She took care not to look at the white sheet set on a wooden frame in the middle of the stage that served as a screen. Instead, she observed the faces of the students, the direction of their gaze, the adolescent hands touching in the dark, the bored yawns.

The videocassette recorder had been lent by a neighboring industrial concern. The teacher who had organized the event was not allowed to touch the expensive apparatus. She nodded to the operator when another clip was to be shown, and he pressed the button. Once, the operator accidentally pressed the reverse button. Anna Lévay heard laughter. Everyone was watching the screen. She searched for the cause of the laughter and saw the teacher in charge waving desperately to the operator of the videocassette recorder, who was taking no notice of her. Then she noticed that the revolutionaries in the archive footage were running backward; the flash of guns died out; bullets found their way into the barrels of rifles; saliva flew back into mouths. She saw destroyed house walls blown upright by grenades that were healing themselves; lethal firearms eased themselves into the hands of their owners and secured their safety catches, and in the following clip all the guns nestled together in their wooden box. And then, dear Lord! she saw the blood flow back into the open chest wound of a body lying on the ground; the shattered ribs and torn blood vessels knitted themselves together, the blood began to flow again in arteries and veins; the entire person, to the last bloody scrap, was again covered with skin and hair; the medical orderly next to the body buttoned up the man's shirt, stood up, and ran away backward; the dead man began to move, then he stood up on the screen as large as life; on its own, his shirt spit out the bullet, the cloud of smoke dispersed itself, and there stood Dr. János Lévay, fresh out of medical school. He was muscular, with thick black hair. He took a step backward, then two; a smile played over his face; thirty-two healthy teeth gleamed; behind them was his tongue, which half an hour earlier had been wandering between his wife's lips, and so he went, backward, into the door of his aunt's house,

waved, and disappeared into the dark, where shortly after they had
begun to make love he had gotten up; for the noise of battle, which
had begun at the moment of penetration, could be heard in the
room, and driven by feelings of patriotism he had rushed out to join
the other revolutionaries, or, as they were called for a long time afterward, counterrevolutionaries.

Anna Lévay had felt sick that time in the cinema room of the
cultural center. She had run to the lavatory and let cold water run
over her wrists. And even after she had calmed herself somewhat,
she stood still in the small room, which reeked of smoke and urine,
and looked blankly at her reflection in the dirty, clouded mirror.
She had then run home as if pursued—without eating the lunch she
had paid for in advance—taken two sleeping pills, drawn the curtains, fallen into bed, pressed her head into the pillows, and cried
like a young girl in the throes of first love.

The next morning she had awakened in a sweat; the sheets were
soaking wet. But she had pulled herself together and—contrary to
habit—drunk two cups of coffee, the entire contents of the coffee
pot. She had put the quilt and pillows out on the balcony to dry
and stuffed their covers into the washing machine. Then she made
another pot of coffee. After that, it was still two hours before the
start of the workday. She had gone walking in the park alongside
the harbor, sat on a bench, and stared at the birds flying overhead.
She had wanted to stroke a cat that was snuggling up to her leg
from behind, but with a sudden leap it had sprung away from her
and then remained a distance away, still in view, crawling about in
the fallen leaves that came up to its neck. Anna Lévay had waited
until seven-thirty and then crossed the bridge over the railroad
tracks, over the promenade full of small shops, past the cafés that
she had frequented in the sixties and seventies, across the market
square to her place of employment. On that day she had been particularly somber.

Just as at the time of that incident she now stood before the
mirror in the lavatory, which today reeked of disinfectant, and

asked herself what she might have done to have merited a halo. All right, then, she had been a widow for forty-one years. But that was nothing special; there were plenty of others. She had certainly not received it for being pure; so much was certain, admitted; János Lévay had taken her innocence; he had even rejoiced in the child, that is, he could rejoice only in the news of a child, for the child had been born after his death. There had been a problem at the registry of births; they had demanded a declaration of paternity; they suspected her of wanting to crown the fruit of her immorality with the name of a fallen counterrevolutionary, for at that time they had not yet moved in together and were living in separate dormitories. But she had almost upturned the desk into the official's lap: Damn it, why don't you shut your filthy trap and look at the marriage certificate, she wanted to say, but she restrained herself and said only that she had been raised as a good dialectical materialist and was quite certain that the Holy Spirit had not visited itself upon her. And when was her legally espoused husband supposed to have signed a declaration of paternity? Certainly not as his blood was flowing onto the street, and furthermore, the lady comrade official may well believe that if she, Anna, had wanted to leave the country, she could easily have asked one of her friends who had fled abroad to declare himself the father, but she had not done so; as a pregnant widow she could also have climbed aboard one of the trucks that was heading for Austria, but that, too, she had not done, so could one please just let her live in peace? And that is how it remained.

So virginity was not at issue. But what, then?

She had not, it would seem, broken the Ten Commandments. She had not taken the name of the Lord in vain, even though it was currently the fashion to do so at every suitable or unsuitable opportunity. She did not even tell off-color jokes, and if she heard one, perhaps she smiled, but she considered even that a sin. She might even jokingly inform the perpetrator that he was risking damnation, but since that was spoken in jest, no one ever took her seriously.

She did not go to church. Or perhaps it would be more accurate to say that her only motivation for entering a church was to visit it as a cultural or historical monument.

She belonged to no political party. In the past, she had taken part in political gatherings—at the time they had been obligatory—but in compensation one had amused oneself, in exactly the same company, outside of any formal organization, by joking about the sad state of Hungarian Socialism.

Today, that was considered a point in one's favor. The success of these member meetings was surpassed by only one event. Once, a well-known specialist, a physician who answered questions on popular science in what was then the most widely read magazine for young people, had chosen the high school as a venue in his cross-country sex-education lecture tour. The lecture was drawing to a close. The birds had built their little nests, the bees had buzzed among the flowers, and the unicellular organisms had been fruitful and multiplied each according to its kind and in its own way, as is usual in such lectures. In short, the doctor had mentioned everything that all the young people already knew, and now, since there was plenty of time left in the allotted hour and a half, and he had to do something more to earn his honorarium, he began to hold forth against decadent behavior, in particular, the coarse terminology for all things sexual that had become so prevalent. How different things had been in earlier times. In folk culture, discussion of sexual matters had taken place in a civilized and polite manner. Back then, one did not say "screw," but "flower," that is, to flourish in the enjoyment of life. Now, wasn't that more expressive? The harangue came to an end, and the requisite, "Are there any questions?" was intoned in such a way that one would have had to have been quite out of one's mind to have raised one's hand. But within the mind of one student, a girl who planned to study literature at the university, her deconstruction of the doctor's muddying of the semantic waters had piqued her little gray cells, and her hand floated aloft.

The room became deathly quiet, for this girl was renowned for her dreadful puns. In response to the question that she asked, she received a warning from the principal, but only a verbal one, since a written warning would have required him to write a lengthy justification. Her question made this girl, normally an outsider, even, one might say, a young woman on the edge of ostracism, extremely popular. At that time, the first signs of cracks in the Socialist edifice were just becoming apparent, and for an entire minute the assembly had audibly groaned in anticipation. "Doctor, sir, may I ask a question?" "Why of course, young man." (Her breasts were nothing if not prominent, and so a new wave of amusement spread through the audience.) "I wanted only to grant you that we young people employ truly contemptible expressions, but if we were to follow your counsel and use 'flower' to mean 'screw,' how should we understand the popular slogan, 'Long may Socialism live and flower'?" The teachers had not dared to laugh. The history teacher, a poker-face by nature, stood up and shouted at the students, "Stop it at once. You will get cramps in your stomachs!" But the laughter would not, did not, stop.

The above-mentioned former student was at the moment in classroom 9b explaining the formation of compound tenses in English, for she had finally succeeded in being admitted to the university, after the four-year suspension imposed on her for her question. Her voice could be heard all the way over in room 12c, and those of her students as well, who must have found something amusing in one of the model sentences—her colleague appeared to have retained her pleasure in words—for they were laughing loud and long.

The bell rang. Anna Lévay waited a bit, leaned with her back against the door, took a deep breath, and walked out into the half-darkened corridor.

For her next class she searched among her papers in the teachers' closet for a class exercise and decided to give her students a surprise quiz. For this, she had to go to the secretary's office to fetch the key to the duplication room. The secretary pressed the key mechanically into her hand. Anna Lévay walked with it to the other end of the corridor, and although there was a large notice on the door warning that running the copy machine with the door closed could be hazardous to one's health, she closed the door behind her and, in fact, locked it. The thick wall of glass tiles that separated the duplication room from the office allowed pale light to filter into the chamber's tiny confines. The walls were draped in uniform shadow, against which the glow of the halo could be seen. She became convinced that she was not hallucinating.

The copier was set in motion. Twenty-nine copies at two pages each spewed out of the machine. When she was done, she turned off the apparatus, closed the door behind her, returned the key to the secretary, and hurried through the assistant principal's office into the teachers' room. She wanted to pick up her class register in time to be able to hand out the quiz precisely when the bell rang. Her colleagues were still chattering away as she left for class.

Her wooden clogs clattered on the hallway floor. She had to avoid the students who were sitting here and there. Because she was so short she was often simply not noticed. More than once she had been almost mowed down. At times, she feared that a student's elbow would bang her in the head. But she managed to get to her classroom unharmed. At once, she switched on the bright fluorescent light over the blackboard, so that she was brightly illuminated while her students sat in semidarkness, due to the pine trees in front of the building. The windows opened to the east, but sunlight never penetrated into the room.

She distributed the quiz papers to the first three rows, with instructions to pass them on back. There was no point in attempting to cheat, she said; they were getting essay questions, and so there would be nothing to gain from cooperation. Furthermore, each student was required to write the names of his neighbors to either side on the test paper. After the complaining died down, she turned on the rest of the lights and sat down in the last row. When the students were taking a test, she usually read the weekly literary journal to keep up with current developments, but today she felt no desire to do so. She entered the day's class period into her register, stared at the slim backs of the students and the refined movements of their hands, and listened to the scratching of their fountain pens. She had taken care that she would not be disturbed with questions. At the end of the class period she asked the students to lay their papers on her desk, and then she quickly left the room. Meanwhile, the light had changed in the teachers' room. As she entered, she noticed at once that in the vicinity of the place she had earlier occupied there now hovered a dangerous shadow, and so she hid herself behind the morning paper, which she took from the common reading table.

In the third period she had planned to watch a video with the class in 10c. It was dark in the viewing room, so she would just have to get there before the class arrived; then she would pop in the cassette, sit in the back of the room against the window, and push the curtain a bit to the side, so that the contrast wouldn't be so sharp. It would be necessary to tell the students to get settled as quickly as possible, for the film ran exactly forty-five minutes. Clearly, the editor who cut the film to this length had never been a schoolteacher.

All went according to plan. Again, she looked at the bent backs, imagined the bored faces that belonged to them, and paid no attention to the notes that were being passed back and forth. But when a girl bent her head on the lap of her neighbor, her boyfriend, Anna Lévay could not help warning her to be careful when standing up, God forbid that her earrings get caught in his zipper. There was considerable laughter, but above the din she managed to inform the class that when next they met, they would be given a quiz and an essay to write about the video they were supposed to be watching with focused attention. Then there was silence till the end of the lesson. She gave them their homework assignment and dismissed them.

The long break between class periods began. The school's public address system made the announcement to the accompaniment of music of deafening volume. To Anna Lévay it was noise, composed of nothing but aggressive rhythms without a trace of melody. Music, she thought, was something that one could enjoy, and who could enjoy this? She returned to the teachers' room by a circuitous route.

Her colleagues were drinking coffee; some were eating homemade sandwiches or other snacks. There was not yet a snack bar in the school. In the chaos of the half-finished building there was no place for one. Anyone who was hungry could go across the way to the elementary school. One colleague was collecting money for the faculty lottery fund; another was organizing stamps for the philately club; a third was reading the newspaper. The school had subscriptions to two national newspapers and one sports rag. The last of these was always picked up by the gym teacher as soon as it arrived and taken into the smoking room; for the rest of the day one would have to look for it there. The two other newspapers were spread out over an entire table, the one usually occupied by the newspaper readers. Anna Lévay spent these fifteen or twenty minutes motionless at her place and trembled in anticipation of the next period, in which she was planning to show slides of ancient architecture.

She had the fifth period free. She could have eaten fried liver with mashed potatoes in the cafeteria, but she did not yet dare to appear in such a crowd. She decided to put off her meal until after the seventh period, when the cafeteria would be less crowded. She feared most the employees of the municipal council, who took their lunch in the school cafeteria and among whom she had many acquaintances.

The municipal officials always lunched between twelve and one o'clock. They wore elegant dresses and suits, which they apparently could well afford, though what they spent for a single outfit was equal to about two months' wages for a high school teacher just out of university. Most of them were arrogant. Among them were many of her former students, from the lowly typist to the departmental head, who wielded power over life and death and whom she had helped to prepare for the entrance examination at the Faculty of Law. One or two such specimens were enough to cause her to worry about the long-term effects of the moral education provided by the high school.

On this day, instead of eating her lunch, Anna Lévay went to the secretary's office, which at the moment was empty. The ugly gray

door to the principal's office was closed, as was that of the assistant
principal; and Marika, the secretary, was probably in the bathroom.
Anna Lévay sat down in a worn-out green armchair, a remnant of the
1970s, picked up the telephone receiver, and dialed the number of
the father of a student who had graduated the previous year, a neurologist and psychiatrist at the municipal hospital. At first, no one at
the hospital switchboard picked up the phone. "Stupid idiots," mut-
tered Anna Lévay, and it amused her greatly when the woman who
finally answered could not refrain from saying, "Who the devil is it
now?" and then after transferring the call forgot to press the mute
button, so that instead of the usual background noise Anna Lévay
could hear the woman chatting with a colleague about her sexual es-
capades. She was about to yell something particularly pleasant into
the telephone, a choice comment that would give the woman something to think about, but the doctor was already at the receiver.

When they had been talking about five minutes, Marika re-
appeared. It would have been awkward to continue the conversation, so she told him that she had to go; in any case, she said that
she had called only to find out how his daughter was doing at the
university, knowing that the doctor would respond to her interest
with an invitation to visit: "Look in on us on your way home, dear
Mrs. Lévay," he would say, and she would accept his invitation at
once. They agreed on eight o'clock that evening, and with that the
conversation came to an end. She registered the fact of the call and
its estimated duration into the registry book. She would pay for her
calls at the end of the month when the secretary added them up.

She was pleased that she had been able to accomplish her mis-
sion without calling undue attention to herself.

During the sixth and seventh periods she was supposed to give a
talk on psychological drama to an elective class. She began to assemble the materials, but then decided to plead hoarseness and present
the students with printed copies of the information and show a film
instead. She checked whether the video room was available, bor-
rowed a film of *Crime and Punishment* from the library, took the key

to the duplication room, tramped down the corridor with the red concrete slabs, thinking that if the floor had a checkerboard pattern, she would walk only on the white squares, out of superstition, as she had done as a child. The key turned stiffly in the new lock of the new door, and she entered the tiny room. In the greenish twilight she again saw the halo. She thought of her upcoming meeting with the doctor.

She returned the key to the secretary, stapled the pages together, and went through the assistant principal's office into the teachers' room. Twenty minutes until the bell. The teachers' room was rather full. She did not want to engage in conversation, and so she laid the pile of papers on the table and fled into the smoking room. She felt nervous and sensed a particular quivering in her stomach that generally reduced her tolerance for putting up with any sort of idiocy. The least additional strain on her nerves and she could have burst into tears or begun to howl or even bite, if the rules of polite behavior had allowed it, but since polite behavior was the rule, she held everything inside and thereby became even more nervous. There was only one cure: either to get a sedative from Marika or to give the students an unannounced written classroom exercise.

In the room, permeated with cigarette smoke, she felt unwell. Moreover, it was dark here. Newspapers lay on the table. She began to read, but had not the patience to plow through the longer articles; anyhow, she knew what most of them were about from listening to the radio, and so she read only the headlines. In one of the newspapers a cigarette packet had been used as a bookmark, and in the packet was a single broken cigarette. Perhaps its owner had abandoned it intentionally, since real smokers stick with cigarettes of normal length. Each puff is calculated, and anything less than a whole cigarette simply won't do. Anna Lévay had never smoked. Absentmindedly, but conscious of what she was doing, she removed the cigarette, handling it as Eve might have cradled the apple. And what about the serpent? She put the thought aside. A snake is a phallic symbol and therefore not appropriate for a widow. No one saw how she carefully rolled the cigarette between her fingers, as she had seen smokers do. She had no idea what the purpose of such a maneuver was, but she simply had to do it. If it was simply a ritual, well, then, good. She reached for a lighter as if she were not doing it for the first time, struck fire, and then looked long into the flame, until it occurred to her that the gas could run out, which would not please the owner of the lighter. And furthermore, the fact that a nonsmoker had been in the room might arouse suspicions and lead to gossip.

The first puff was unpleasant, and she suppressed a cough. She did not inhale into her lungs; she wanted only to taste the smoke. The nicotine will penetrate the mucous membranes of my mouth, she thought; I must just try once more to see whether it is really as calming as my colleagues say. Just as she registered the taste, she thought she heard rain beating on the windowpanes. She stood up and walked over to the window.

She could see her reflection in the ground-floor window of the elementary school. Surrounded by smoke, the aureole around her head was even more noticeable.

Just as when a ray of light penetrates a dark room through a knothole in a shutter and its contours are made visible by the floating motes of dust, so the paler regions on the edge of the halo began to emerge from the background into which under normal light they merged. She quickly stubbed out the cigarette, opened the window carefully, so as not to be seen, and then moved along the wall to open the door to create some cross-ventilation. The light around her head followed her shadow. If she held her head erect, exactly parallel to the surface of the wall, then only a small strip of light was visible, but if she tilted her head a bit to one side, then the light appeared as an oval disk, as if a flashlight were circling the room. Since all the ashtrays were empty and she didn't want to leave any evidence behind, she put the remnant of the cigarette, which for a habitual smoker was unusually long, in her pocket.

She wanted to return to the teachers' room. She was already in front of the door, her hand on the knob, when an idea came to her.

Propelled into sudden motion by her thought, she hurried in a tempo that put the lie to her age, tripping down the steps, past the janitor's room, right through the swinging door, and then, making a sharp right, into the physics teachers' office. She knew that at this moment her physics colleagues were teaching. If there had been anyone there, she would have said that she had come to make herself some tea, since only the physicists had an operational teakettle. But the room was empty, and so she was saved the trouble of the lie. For security she shut the door behind her, opened the glass doors of the cupboards, and began to rummage. She had ten minutes. Soon she found what she was looking for, but first she had to climb up on a chair to open the cabinet, and then climb down to fetch the apparatus from the lowest shelf. She switched it on and stuck the counting tube as far as it would go into the halo. She put her ear close to the loudspeaker, just as a cancer patient in the last stages of illness might strain to listen to a mumbled diagnosis in Latin. Not a sound was emitted. When the tube was held in the air the speaker ticked once or twice, but in the area of the light it was completely silent. Geiger counters don't just break, she thought, but just to be sure she decided to test it. In the cabinet, carefully protected in a lead box, lay a piece of radioactive uranium ore from a Hungarian mine. One of the teachers had brought it to school the previous year, a frustrated old biddy who compensated for the miseries of her private life by moonlighting as a newspaper columnist. She had allowed the piece of ore to sit for two days on her desk, until the physicists measured its radioactivity and locked it up. Heedless of the danger, Anna Lévay carefully removed the rock from the box. The Geiger counter crackled. She repeated the measurement several times. It appeared, then, that within the halo reigned a complete absence of radioactivity. To make absolutely sure, she held the counting tube in front of her forehead and turned so that the piece of ore was behind her back. Silence. The radioactive particles seemed to be completely blocked by the halo. Carefully, she put everything back in its place.

As she made ready to go, it occurred to her to measure the halo's electrical characteristics. Removing a voltmeter from its shelf, she held one terminal in the air and stuck the other into the light. Zero volts. She had established, so it would appear, that the phenomenon was not an electrical one. She then attempted to bring various magnets close to her head, but she felt neither attraction nor repulsion. At the sound of the warning bell she quickly opened the door, for she feared that one of the teachers might pop in early; she sneaked into the little preparation room that adjoined the classroom. Through the door she could hear the voice of the physics teacher, who always went into overtime; pity the poor students. He was speaking about the laws of inertia. In the preparation room she saw a collection of prisms; she picked up one of them and held it in front of her forehead. The light that came out was no different from the light that went in. She checked this several times, because she couldn't believe her eyes. Under normal circumstances the light must, as she knew, be refracted into a rainbow of colors. She finally gave up; it was a mystery that she was unable to solve. She stood for a moment, puzzled and spellbound.

She dashed out of the room, and to reach safety before the bell rang for the break, she bolted up the stairs to the teachers' room two at a time. Buried in her books, she awaited the bell for the next period, and then she waited another five minutes to be sure of meeting no one in the corridor. She hurriedly got through the elective class. Normally, she was not so slipshod, but now she simply did not have the strength to speak. The students seemed to have noticed nothing.

The thought of the coming lunch period filled her with dread, dread not that the halo would be discovered, but that in her nervousness she would somehow make a fool of herself. In the cafeteria, hungry students were jostling each other in the food line, and no one paid any attention to her. She made use of her teacher's prerogative and proceeded to the head of the line; the kitchen staff served her at once, wished her a good appetite, to which she usually

answered that she already had a good one, unfortunately; one had
only to look at her circumference to see that whatever she may be
lacking, it was not appetite, to which the servers always replied that
having a circumference was fine, as long as she was healthy; whoever
didn't like it didn't have to look at it, and then they would laugh.
Anna Lévay pushed her tray along toward the salads and napkins,
but the tray got caught on the poorly assembled grid, and she almost
spilled her soup over her blouse. With a sigh, "It seems not to be my
day today," she carried her tray with shaking hands to one of the
reserved tables. As she began to eat her soup, she broke into a sweat,
but she was determined to act as though nothing were amiss. "May
I sit here?" asked a colleague as she approached the table. The question was a mere formality; a reply in the negative would have required a lengthy explanation and drawn unnecessary attention. So
she attempted to smile pleasantly, though at that moment she would
have preferred to see any prospective interlocutor go to the devil,
and she added that there was really no point in asking, since they
had been having their lunch together for ten years. As she pushed
the soup bowl to the side of the tray in order to devote herself to
the main course, the colleague looked over to Anna and cried, "For
heaven's sake, what's wrong with you?" which caused Anna Lévay to
sweat even more profusely, now that her gloriole had been discovered. "Wrong? What should be wrong? Everything is fine," she
replied, prepared in the worst case to deny everything. "Why, you're
sweating like a pig. Aren't you aware of it?" the woman replied and
added that if she were not feeling well, perhaps an ambulance
should be summoned; many heart attacks begin with just such an
outbreak of cold sweat. "Nonsense! Just a hot flash. It's menopause,
or maybe I'm just awash in joy; damned if I know." Relieved, she
added that it had been years since even a little flu had kept her
home, and they both chuckled over the joke that even disease had
no desire to drag women like them—no longer in their first youth
but not yet properly aged—into bed.

When they had finished eating, they took their trays to the
drop-off point, placed their silverware in the red plastic container,

put glasses, soup bowls, and dinner plates each in their place, and finished off the familiar ritual by tossing their crumpled napkins into the trash can. These were routine movements, as ritualized as the sentences that accompanied them: "Thank you so much, it was delicious yet again," and "You feed us like the prize hogs in the stalls of Nagytétény," to which the kitchen women would reply, "Tomorrow will bring sunshine, since you ate everything on your plates." "If only that were what determined the weather!" said the teachers, before making way for the next diners with their trays.

Then Anna Lévay walked with her colleague in the direction of the teachers' room. They had to take a detour, since the corridor that joined the main building to the cafeteria was still under construction. To get to the rear entrance of the main building one had to go out into the courtyard, and from there through the passageway with its freshly plastered concrete columns. A crowd of hurrying students swarmed through the narrow door. The two women waited a moment, but since the flow of students did not diminish, they carved a way for themselves through the multitude. They had to do battle for a while before space was finally yielded to them. The teachers proceeded in the direction of the lavatory.

Anna Lévay remained another hour or so in the school building, correcting papers. At three-thirty she suddenly stood up, put on her coat, left her heavy bag behind, and walked to the public library. To get there, she had to traverse the underpass beneath the main street, and she was surprised that its name, Soviet Street, had survived the change in the political system. There seemed to be no law that determined which names were changed back to what they had been before and which were simply given an entirely new name. It passed through her mind that Vak Bottyán Street had been renamed Vilma Street, about which the whole town was chuckling: Why was the name of the blind Bottyán not good enough any longer? Certainly not because the Austrian tourists, who came to the town in droves, might not wish to be reminded of the famous Hungarian general who had led the rebellion against the Habsburgs. This recollection was interrupted by the sharp stench of ammonia, which could indicate nothing else but a decomposition product of urine. Anna Lévay looked about, but she saw only the graffiti in the pedestrian tunnel, which had only recently been completed. The previous year, she had almost broken her ankle on the crumbling steps. It had taken an accident and a suit for damages before the money for reconstruction had been found. The new walls were immediately covered with graffiti and posters of all sorts. Particularly repulsive were several placards that, judging by their graphics, were unambiguously and extremely right-wing oriented and against which the police could do nothing. It was like Prometheus's liver: What was scraped off by day had grown back by morning. "After all, we can't post a guard on every corner," is how the city fathers defended themselves on local television. But they ought to be able to do something about the pissing, the teacher thought, not shying away from the idea that those caught urinating in public should have their hoses chopped off; for of course, the perpetrators were all men, of that she had no doubt; a woman doesn't so easily squat down in a public place. Another possible solution would be to supply the metal gutter running along the wall with a weak electric current that would run up the stream of urine and create a painful short circuit in the perpetrator's apparatus.

As she ascended the steps she was feeling practically jovial, and she hummed to herself the melody "Rejoice greatly, O daughter of Zion" from Handel's *Messiah,* which she had sung in many an amateur concert, as a student the soprano part and then, with ripening years, the alto. Thus she reached her goal. One of the two doors to the municipal library was always closed, and for years now she had tried the wrong one at least twice a week. This time, too, she chose the wrong one. Entering the library, she exchanged a quick greeting with the woman in the cloakroom, who like all the others noticed nothing, and then she cast a glance into the journal reading room, which was separated from the other room by a glass wall. There, one could read the daily newspaper, and it also served as a room where one could go on cold days to get warm. She had often observed visitors drowsing over their reading matter. To her relief she saw no acquaintance whom she would have to greet. She surrendered her coat, took the coat check in exchange, and went to the reading room on the second floor. After murmuring the obligatory greetings that politeness demanded, she told the librarian in charge that today she was going to be neither a borrower nor a lender, for she needed only to use the reference collection. Then she hurried by the counter. The haste was unnecessary, for no one took any notice of her, but Anna Lévay saw in the glass wall that the halo still floated about her head.

In the room with the new parquet flooring, the "sanctum," as she called it, readers were sitting absorbed in their books, among them some of her students. Outside, it was already dark, but nevertheless, only the fluorescent ceiling lights were burning. Municipal funds for reading lamps had been deemed "insufficient." Once, she had asked the librarian how many members of the municipal council had library cards, and he still owed her an answer. But why should he have answered? There were laws protecting privacy, and moreover, the library was financed by the municipality. But he did smile knowingly and say, "Not as many as there could be. . . ." Anna Lévay had certainly never run into any of them in the library.

Without thinking, she turned right and passed the shelves on which the librarians had wisely set out required reading for students, crime novels, esoterica, collections of cartoons, and other books of general interest so that readers whose taste ran to these more popular items would not get themselves lost in the labyrinth of loftier literature. Once, she had advised one of the librarians with whom she was friendly to shift the location of this shelf every month, so that the parquet floor in front of it would not suffer too greatly. In the library, the space between the shelves was so narrow that two readers of even moderate girth would not be able to get past each other. The planned alterations had been postponed for years, since something more important, in the eyes of the municipal council, always intervened, such as costly measures to shore up the sagging tourist trade.

In the reference room she quickly gathered the books that she required and looked for a suitable place to set them down. The room was empty except for the attendant, but all the tables stood between the window and the glass wall near the staircase, so that in the gathering gloom the aura surrounding her head, whose golden shimmer was clearly distinguishable from the cold light emanating from the fluorescent tubes, would be reflected as in a mirror. Furthermore, it would be visible to anyone coming up the stairs. Therefore, she told the attendant that she was working on a comparative interpretation requiring additional materials, and she carried the books that she had selected into the room where the circulating collection was kept. There, she set herself at a small table between one of the catalog cabinets and the beginning of the literature section, and in such a way that a shelf standing perpendicular to the window completely hid her head. She found it necessary to shove the table a bit to the side to achieve the necessary angle, but finally, she was ensconced in safety. She had chosen for her researches the least-used part of the library.

She set to work on her stack of specialist books and wrote down the relevant information in the notebook that she had brought along for the purpose. The first fact that swam into her ken was that there is a naturally occurring *gloriole,* a sort of interference phenomenon that can take place when the sun is low on the horizon. If the observer stands with his back to the sun with his shadow projected against a foggy background, then a faint glow of colored concentric rings can sometimes be seen around the shadow of the observer's head. The gloriole arises from the refraction of light rays as they strike the observer. The term "halo," or "Cellini's halo," is used to denote a bright white ring surrounding the shadow of the observer's head on a dew-covered lawn with a low solar angle of elevation. It is caused by the complete reflection of the light rays in the dewdrops.

In her apartment, where she had first observed the apparition, there was neither a foggy background nor a dew-covered lawn.

In Latin a halo is called a *nimbus,* which means "cloud" or "fog," but can also mean "renown." I had no idea that I had a nimbus, she thought, although a short while ago it had pleased her when a clerk, who knew only her name, when they were introduced cried out, "Oh, you're Mrs. Anna Lévay; you are a teacher of great renown." She quickly skimmed through the Latin terminology, where she learned that the phenomenon was also called an *aura,* which can mean holiness and sunlight. Another term was "glory," or "gloriole," from the Latin *gloria,* which denotes "adoration" or "splendor." In Greek it is called *haloa,* the corona, or halo, that surrounds the sun or moon. And in Hungarian it was a *dicsfény* or *glória,* a circle of light, an aureole. She thought of Árpad Tóth's poem "Evening Aureole," which she had been teaching for thirty years; she might have laughed if she hadn't been the object of the joke.

Soon, she had assembled a small typology of halos and related phenomena. According to her sources, the original form of the halo is that of the aureole. Only God wears a triangular halo. A round halo with a cross in it is an attribute of the Holy Trinity, so God the Father must decide whether He feels like putting on a triangular halo or a round halo with a cross. Does He change them according to His mood? she wondered, and her eyes flashed contemptuously. The Virgin Mary wears a halo studded with stars and pearls. In Heaven the saints and angels are allowed only a simple disk, rarely one that emits rays of light. In the Eastern tradition saints sport a square gloriole while on Earth, an affair that looks like a foil candy wrapper arching over their heads, for the square symbolizes Earth, while the circle represents Heavenly perfection, which is not, of course, a suitable symbol for one who is mortal. Therefore, there is a rule that when a living saint returns his immortal soul to his creator, it is not the size of the halo that changes, but merely its shape. Even while the soul is in flight—or, at the very latest, at the outskirts of the Pearly Gates—the transformation of square into circle takes place, which considered from a mathematical point of view might be seen as representing a solution to the classical problem of squaring the circle, though here in its converse form of circling the square, so to speak. But all of that is just theory, she thought, for in all of recorded history there is no proof that anyone has actually *seen* a genuine, authentic, holy halo.

At this point she rose and walked over to the employees' washroom, disguised with the inscription "OFFICE." As a regular customer and high school teacher of long standing, she could claim the privilege of being spared the effort of going down the flight of stairs to the readers' lavatory. She also had special privileges when it came to taking out books: She could check out as many as she wished, and she never had to pay a fine. A thin yellow plastic strip on her library card alerted the frequently changing librarian trainees to her special status. Now, too, a nod sufficed for her to be granted admission to the "OFFICE," whose true purpose was hidden from the uninitiated.

The heating pipes were of an unusually substantial size, and a muggy, stuffy heat held sway in the small chamber. The last time she had visited the place, a cockroach had crawled out of the toilet paper roll and crawled up her arm. She had screamed, and the cleaning woman, who happened to be passing, had opened the door to see what had happened. The two of them had enjoyed a good laugh. This time, Anna Lévay remained standing in the tiny anteroom, raised herself so that she could look into the mirror, and examined her own, authentic, halo. But the mirror was too clean, and she was unable to see the halo's contours. Therefore, she took the cigarette butt out of her pocket and lit it with a match from the packet that had been left on the porcelain table, apparently forgotten by one of the secret smokers on the library staff. She covered her crown of light with smoke the way a beekeeper smokes a hive. There was no doubt about it; her gloriole was round. It sat directly over her head, just as it might appear on the head of a dead saint.

Suddenly, her blood pressure rose so high that she had to lean against the wall to support herself. The cold of the tiles brought her somewhat back to her senses, and in an attempt to get a grip on herself and the cryptic nature of her situation she tried to recall what she had read about such occult matters. She thought of astral bodies, which she knew about from books on ethnography; she thought about Plato, and about her husband, whom, she believed, she had seen, physically, shortly after his death, forty-one years ago, the last time on the fortieth day after the day on which he was shot.

Perhaps she should just leave everything where it was, walk home, and, without revealing her identity, call the police and the ambulance service and ask whether an accident had befallen one Anna Lévay, née Kuncz, said person having not returned home the previous evening. Or perhaps it would be more efficacious simply to place a phone call to herself. If the line were busy, that would be proof that she was still alive, since it would mean that she was at home, holding the receiver in her hand. If she called herself from the public telephone in the theater lobby using her phone card and heard herself picking up the receiver at home, then she would have evidence that her physical self and her astral body had separated, and each was traveling along its own path.

Her mind raced as she pondered the various logical permutations of this telephonic experiment.

Suddenly, she felt the desire to urinate. While she was relieving herself in the inner chamber, she observed the thick yellow stream of her urine breaking against the industrial porcelain of the toilet bowl. With great relief she drew the conclusion that she was most likely alive on the physical plane. Perhaps, upon arriving home, she should eat fish and honey, as Christ had done after the resurrection.

Returning to her pile of books, she continued her researches, discovering references to halos in the shape of a rhombus, as well as to the hexagonal variant, which was associated with figures in religious allegories and was also the basic type in Islam, where it was usually represented as fire.

A gloriole's light usually ranges from a warm yellow to a rich gold, but that of the Virgin Mary, the queen of Heaven, is often represented in the colors of the rainbow, and even Judas had a halo, though his was black, which suggests that the halo was originally a symbol not of goodness, but of power. In the art of primitive peoples only gods wore halos. In India, it has been in use since the end of the third century, most probably a result of Greek influence. The sun gods Helios, Apollo, Mithras, and all the gods of the constellations wore an aureole, as did the Roman emperors. Because of its heathen origins, not to mention halos being rendered unto Caesar, early Christian art avoided the halo, but then Christians, too, needed a symbol of spiritual privilege: In pictures of Christian rulers one sees a simple circular gloriole. In official Christianity, the halo makes a relatively late appearance. Since the fourth century Christ has been thus marked as a king, and since the end of that century as the Lamb of God as well. Thereafter, the halo's exclusivity diminished, for in the fifth century every angel was given a halo, and the elect among mortals were granted them as well. By the sixth century the halo had become rather an everyday sight.

In the early Renaissance the halo was represented by Giotto and Fra Angelico as a disk or ring. Certain Florentine painters painted the halo as a disk physically attached to the head of the saint. Later, this disk floated not behind the head, but above it. Michelangelo and Titian rarely depicted a halo. In this same era the Flemish painters began to depict rays of light instead of a halo, which was then redis-covered by the Italian painters of the Counter Reformation. In the Baroque, the halo became simply a field of luminosity. Tintoretto represented the halo realistically, as light emanating from the head.

That was about all there was to be learned here on the subject. It was better than nothing, but not enough to explain the phenome-non at hand. To answer the question as to whether promotion to sainthood with the concomitant bestowal of a halo was a prerogative of ecclesiastical authorities or Heavenly powers, she examined a de-scription of the rules governing denial of sainthood, paying special attention to Catholic sources. She hoped later to be able to engage in further research on this topic, and thus she wrote out a list, first of the mortal sins, then the venial sins, and finally, the Ten Commandments. But she was unable to concentrate, and she wrote the words mechanically, each on a new line, with a dash after each one, as she had done long ago in lectures at the university.

She decided to begin with the Ten Commandments as the more familiar list of what thou shalt and shalt not. She was on safe ground with the first commandment, not having prayed to any unauthorized gods. Nor had she made unto herself any graven images, and so there was no way that she could have bowed down to them or served them. Nor was she in the habit of taking the name of the Lord her God in vain. If she wanted to curse, she was more likely to mention His diabolical opponent. As for the sabbath day, she worked six days in the week, or, more accurately, five days in school and one at home, and kept the seventh for her own diversions. That day did not fall on Saturday, but on Sunday, and though she couldn't vouch for her son, there were otherwise no difficulties with that commandment, for she had neither daughter nor servants, nor had she cattle, nor any other animals, nor had she received any strangers within her gates who might have violated the prohibition against work on the day of rest. She also had no problems with the commandment on honoring one's father and mother, even if it were only that her days might be long upon the land which the Lord God had given her. She had not killed. Adultery gave her pause, and she thought awhile about the correct definition of that transgression, but finally, she decided on her innocence to the extent that one took the Old Testament as a standard of behavior. She had not stolen. She had not borne false witness against her neighbor, at least not officially, for she had not once in her life been involved in a judicial proceeding. She did not covet her neighbor's wife, no problem, since her tastes did not go in that direction. Had there been anything in the commandments about coveting thy neighbor's husband, then she might have had a problem. Many years ago, love had led her into temptation, but she had stood fast. Since then, however, it had given her pause, and sometimes in her evening reading, when she came upon an erotic passage, she wondered whether it had been right not to have given in to bodily desire and to have kept her relations with her neighbor's husband strictly on the level of mental gratification. She did not covet her neighbor's house, neither his manservant nor his maidservant, and neither his ox nor his ass. If that was all there was to it, she had a clear conscience.

The *Catholic Encyclopedia* treated the matter of sin in a lengthy excursus. It stated that in primitive religions sin consists in offenses against magical forces or taboos. In cosmic and polytheistic religions it is insults to supernatural beings that are regarded as sins. In the Old Testament sin represents a turning away from God—idol worship, for example, or blasphemy or traffic in magic—while in relation to mankind, sin is connected with a lack of respect for one's parents, with murder, adultery, sodomy, tormenting of the needy, and the refusal to pay for work that one has had performed.

Augustine describes sin as the absence of moral goodness.

At this moment it occurred to her that she was actually an atheist. Her family had left the Church after their house had burned down in 1940 and her father had driven away a member of the parish who had called on them to collect the church tax, which that person had demanded even among the still-smoking wreckage of their house. Her father was standing on the sooty ruins. He pulled a charred burner of what had been their stove from under the ashes and let out so loud an oath that all the neighbors rushed over to see what had happened. She could not remember ever having gone to a regular church service. The Bible appeared in her literature classes, of course, and from that and her evening reading had come whatever little knowledge she had of Church history and dogma.

The wall clock struck quarter to six, the library would soon be closing. She quickly returned the books to the shelves, easily locating their places, since each time she had removed a book, she had by habit pulled the book to its right out a few centimeters to mark its place. One was not supposed to return books to the shelves, but she did not want the librarians to see what had interested her. She exchanged her coat check for her coat, spoke a few words with the attendant in the journal reading room, and then stepped out into the October evening. She returned to the school for her bag, but she did not wish to go home. She did not like the four-lane road, with its ten-story buildings, that led to her apartment block; those buildings seemed better suited to serve as a backdrop to an antiutopian film scene than as human habitation. She lived in a similar building, of course, but at least it possessed the virtue of having only four stories.

As on every other evening the concrete walls now reflected thin, barely audible, nerve-wracking sounds, something like the chirping of crickets. What got on her nerves was that she knew the source of the sounds and that the audible portion of the sound was only the top register beneath which a deep underlying animal communication was hidden, that the inaudible sounds were also reflected from their bodies to the pavement, and that the bats living in the cracks in the walls knew that she was too large for prey, but not dangerous.

She hated the police station, and the canal with its rancid smell, the fast-food restaurant—that red-and-gold temple to consumerism—the gas station, all lit up, whose construction right in the middle of town in the immediate vicinity of the hospital had been managed, so one heard, through threats, pleas, and shady business arrangements between certain multinational corporations and the municipal council. When she wasn't in a hurry to get home, she preferred to take a detour through a small street in the town center.

Instead of turning left into the four-lane road, she directed her steps to the right. She crossed the fountain—named for the last president of the Central Committee and popularly known as the concrete sink—in the middle of which was a basin clad in blue faience containing two standing figures of naked girls that were sprayed with water when the fountain was turned on. Previously, a modernistic steel structure had stood there, but popular opinion had found it so repulsive that it had been removed. She passed the building site in the market square, through the crosswalk, under the arcade of the "House of Lords," which had been built for former employees of the municipal council, down to the promenade, disfigured by countless kiosks and small shops. In front of the cinema she turned right. The railroad barrier was closed. She waited a few minutes, and then decided to go through the underpass that led to the bank of the canal. Having arrived under the bridge, she was assaulted after a few steps by the penetrating stench of urine and feces. She held her nose and thus managed to cover the distance to the opposite staircase. In the off-season this out-of-the-way corner was taken over by the town's homeless. In the evenings of earlier summers it had been used by couples as a place for sex. At this time of year a respectable woman did not venture here at all, and even in September it was not advisable to be wandering here after dark. But Anna Lévay had nothing to fear. Her corporeal dilapidation was such that she was not afraid of sexual attack, and she carried no objects of value. This was not quite accurate, for she was looking forward to tomorrow, October 31, with just under three hundred forints, though that was just small change. The second of the month was payday, but that fell on Sunday, and so she would be receiving no money until Monday, the third. Fortunately, the cupboard was full, the gas bill paid, the electric bill still a way off. The telephone bill fell due on the eighteenth, but she could pay as late as the twenty-eighth, and by then she would have had private students, and that would give her enough money to pay for the phone. Her winter coat did not meet the standards of current fashion, and her handbag was old-fashioned as well, but it was a practical object, constructed of rawhide and divided into two compartments, with an outside pocket that you closed with a buckle, filled with student papers and her own notes, practical but worthless.

She climbed the steps, past the former House of the People's Health, which now provided space for offices and courses in financial management, but later would be renovated and turned into a music school for the private profit of the mayor. She then proceeded along the canal, past the water police, past the sluice gate, arriving finally at the harbor. By now it was completely dark. Off to the side she saw ships hulking along the dock. The wharf for passenger ships was empty. There was nothing left of the summer crowds. Not a single bar was open; the windows of the pavilions were shuttered. The leaves now lay ankle deep where that famous stall, beloved by fishermen, had served fried fish and wine. It had recently been torn down. The rustle of leaves pleased her, and she waded through them until she reached the rose garden. There the grass began, so she returned to the path. She was astonished by the swans swimming in the cove. The first had come more than twenty years ago. Since then, they had multiplied with such determination that people were already discussing ways of reducing their numbers. In winter, she often fed them with breadcrumbs. Many families brought along entire loaves of bread and collected an entire flock around a single child. On such days the swarm of swans took no notice of a few meager crumbs in the hands of a lonely old lady.

She walked slowly along the breakwater. She decided that she would go as far as the lighthouse and then go home. Anglers had cast their lines from the end of the breakwater. They were unaware of her approach. Lost in contemplation of their bobbing floats they did not even turn around as she walked by them. The water was high; the waves reached the concrete edge of the breakwater. At several places she had to walk through a thin pool of water. She looked across to the lights of the town on the opposite shore and to the pale lamps of the sailboats in the middle of the lake, out for the evening to fish for pike. She heard waves break on the rocks, slippery with algae, and then, their force broken, slap against the reinforced concrete of the breakwater, and she became lost in thought.

Suddenly, she was aware of a change in the rhythm and melody of the water's movement and then of the agitation among the anglers. Fish were splashing about, more and more of them. They beat the water with their fins, poked their heads out of the lake, and leaped about with their slimy, slippery bodies. The water seethed; the fresh air smelled of the cool of the deep. Anna Lévay looked out over the parapet and saw millions of wet scales reflected in the light of her halo.

She quickly drew back, turned around, and made ready to slip away. Behind her she heard loud oaths. Respectable citizens encouraged unspecified persons to excrete digestive byproducts, while others invited unnamed individuals to make use of their tongues in unusual regions. Others merely expressed a wish that something would go to the devil. She couldn't follow all that they were saying. Besides, she knew that the cursing was not meant for her. Nonetheless, she saw her terrible suspicion confirmed, and she hastened her steps to get out of that place as quickly as possible. As she reached the rose garden she heard a slapping sound reverberating over and over from her left: Hordes of slim zander, mighty pike, fat carp, delicate common bream, white bream, and twenty-kilo catfish clattered against the breakwater. Many of them were driven by their frenzy onto the shingle of the promenade; some had a fishing line, tangled up with other lines, dangling from their mouths.

She began to run, for the anglers had also begun to run away and were shining their powerful flashlights from afar. She took care to remain in the shadows. To keep the beams of light from reaching her she ran to the right, on the small strip of land between the trees and the water. She was running along the harbor when suddenly, she heard a dull thud, as if someone were banging a Chinese gong with a raw veal cutlet. The swarm of fish was beating against the sluice gate. Innocent beasts, she thought, symbols of religious obedience: The wrath of God, which had called forth Noah's Flood, had spared the creatures that dwell in water. If fish had been sinful, there would have to have been a Noah's Ebb, too.

She looked back and saw that the anglers were attempting to gather the booty into their fishing nets. One of them had retrieved his car from the nearby parking lot—free of charge out of season— and was throwing the more valuable specimens into the trunk of his sinfully expensive automobile, carefully choosing only the best from among the many varieties. Anna Lévay was already at the railroad barrier when that representative of the town's newly wealthy drove by, a pink trail of bloody water dripping from the trunk of his car.

It was six-thirty; she had better hurry. She accomplished the remaining kilometer and a half in under fifteen minutes. She thought of the dinner of breaded fish and bread and honey that she had planned while in the library, which led her to recall that there was a pike filet in the freezer, the present of a thankful parent whose daughter she taught, but mindful of her upcoming visit to the doctor, she decided that the smell of fried fish would hang in her clothes and hair, and that might induce her hosts to look more carefully into the cause of the odor, and put her under closer scrutiny than otherwise. She did not want scrutiny. Therefore, she stopped in at a grocery store near her home to buy one hundred fifty grams of inexpensive cheese. She definitely wanted to have eaten supper before going to the neurologist at eight o'clock. It is not a good idea to pay a visit on an empty stomach. It only makes you nervous, and then against your better judgment you eat more of the snacks that they offer than is proper.

It was very bright in the store, and she could look for what she wanted with confidence, without worrying that anyone would notice the halo. She considered whether to buy smoked cheese or Edam and finally decided in favor of the latter. She was already at the register and was waiting for her change when she heard a shrill voice. Her neighbor's nine-month-old infant, who was nestled in its mother's arms, was reaching for Anna Lévay's head and emitting loud cries while attempting to grab the halo. The child's babbling consisted of the repeated vowels "a" and "o," and Anna Lévay was terrified that the infant would cause others to notice the halo. "Excuse me, Mrs. Lévay," said the mother, visibly pained. "It's nothing," said Anna Lévay, and then she turned bright red.

At that moment the teacher saw her gloriole in the convex surveillance mirror above the head of the cashier. She found the image amusing, for the halo looked like a poorly trimmed monk's tonsure. She staggered out of the store without waiting for her change. The cashier, with her hand left dangling in the air, looked back and stared with open mouth at Anna Lévay, but she could detect nothing in

particular. "The poor woman is at the end of her tether; she's working herself to death in that high school," she said sympathetically,
and to bridge the gap of silence she added, "On top of which, when
she gets home, I have no doubt that one of her private students will
call. I'm really worried about the poor creature."

Anna Lévay ascended the stairs. To put it more precisely, she
skulked up the stairs. She had not turned on the light, and anyhow,
most of the bulbs were burnt out. But she had no need of the light:
Her own light lit her way. She wondered whether this was how it
was with the unbaptized wise men in Dante's *Purgatorio,* who were
lit by the light of their own souls. How lovely, she thought deri-
sively; if I decide to spend evenings standing on a pedestal, I will be
performing a civic duty by providing the festive lighting that the
town has been wanting for so long. But that was nothing but gal-
lows humor, and she knew that humor was not going to solve her
problem.

She had already arrived at the first landing when the neighbor's
intractable dog, just returning from a walk, came running up to her.
She did not like this dog. It was a mongrel with a treacherous gaze,
an opportunistic brute that bit everyone that his owner didn't like.
The owner happened to be a member of the town self-governance
committee, the worst kind of bureaucrat, a sniveling lickspittle and
toady. On the assumption that dogs take after their masters, and con-
versely, she had once avenged herself on the cur with a powerful swat
of her umbrella on its nose after one morning it had plunged across
the stone entrance hall and ripped her only intact pantyhose. Since
then the beast had always growled at her.

Yet now it sidled up to her like a cat. She could hardly get by. At
last, she was standing in the doorway to her apartment, ready to enter, but the dog suddenly lay down right across the doormat. She
stepped over him, closed the door, set down her coat and bag, and
proceeded into the bathroom to wash her hands.

She looked up at the mirror; it was the mirror in which she had
first seen her halo. Then she went into the kitchen, put on the water

for the noodles, and had begun to grate the cheese when she heard the voices of the man next door and his wife as they tried to pull their dog off her doormat. The dog whined; his owners called him an ungrateful wretch, reminded him of the excessive quantities of expensive dog food he ate, demanded that he show the respect and gratitude due to his master and mistress, and then threatened to disembowel him if he would not obey. The tirade ended with an angry bang of their door.

The noodles were ready. She sprinkled the cheese on top along with the remains of a mushroom ragout. She hastily spooned it down. Her conscience pricked her—she really should be eating with a fork—but she hadn't the patience to spear the spindly little objects, a procedure that netted only three or at most five noodles at a time. It was already after seven-thirty. She quickly brushed her teeth, grabbed her coat, and left. On the threshold she stumbled over the dog. Since she was already walking at a fast pace, she must have delivered the dog a hefty kick in the ribs, but the animal did not reply by biting her leg; on the contrary, it greeted her with a gentle whimper and then snuggled down into the doormat. She had to bend over the beast's recumbent body to close the door. Not a growl was to be heard. Although Anna Lévay had not exchanged more than fifteen minutes' worth of conversation with these neighbors in all the years she had been living there, she now decided that tomorrow she would ask them politely to show her the dog's rabies vaccination certificate; she found the animal's sudden change in behavior highly suspicious.

The doctor lived two streets away, in a neighborhood of large upper-middle-class houses. A moment after she rang she was ushered into the house and offered a seat in an enormous leather armchair. Orange juice and delicacies from a pastry shop were brought in. For half an hour they chatted about the progress their daughter was making at the university, items in the day's news, the town's political affairs, the performance of investments, new clothes, seaside vacations, and other such small talk. For lack of a better topic, and just to have something to say, they also reported on what they had been doing that day. The doctor had written a report on a pyromaniac (what crazy things some people do!), made his rounds at the hospital, finished up some paperwork, and then seen patients at his office. The doctor's wife, a homemaker, had driven her husband in her car to the hospital and then had gone shopping, after which she had instructed the maid on how dinner was to be prepared, and then gone to the swimming pool and after that to the beauty salon. In the afternoon she had picked up her husband at the hospital, and they had gone together to their favorite café. The teacher then mentioned that after school she had gone to the library and then for a walk in the harbor to get some fresh air; after rushing about all day one had to discharge all that tension, and there was nowhere really to go; culturally, there was nothing going on. After all, there were really only two or three decent cultural events in the entire year; the rest were cheap musicals. For a long time, now, the movie house had been showing nothing but action films for teenagers; there was no social life; her circle of friends had long since broken up; there were no longer even the party meetings that one had been obligated to attend. Somehow, one had to find a way to kill the time. Now that they had navigated through all the topics of conversation, the situation was becoming awkward. At that moment the maid summoned the neurologist's wife to the telephone.

When the two of them were alone, Anna Lévay asked the doctor for a tranquilizer for her overwrought nerves. The doctor asked for her symptoms, and the teacher revealed only that she felt weak and sometimes saw bright flashes of light in front of her eyes. The doctor asked what sort of flashes they were, small rings or pulsating beams, and whether they remained in one place or moved about, whether they were associated with a particular object, and when they made their appearance. She answered that she could not observe them precisely; she only felt their presence, and if she attempted to observe them, she became uncertain and no longer knew for sure whether they were really there. She feared that this anomaly was the result of stress; she was even afraid that she might be hallucinating, and if it wasn't a hallucination, that would be even worse. The doctor looked at the teacher, who sat tense in the leather armchair, back bent, legs crossed, hands folded on her knees. He knew that he was looking at something unusual, but he could not determine what it was. He knew only that something unnatural was in his field of vision. He listened to the teacher attentively until she was finished; then he said to her that without an examination he could not form a diagnosis; she must come to the hospital, where the necessary tests could be made.

Anna Lévay took fright. No, no, she didn't think that it was anything so serious, no, not the hospital, not for anything, that would just cause gossip that she had been seen in the neurological department, which is why she had wanted to see the doctor at home, so that she wouldn't have to show herself there; she knew that it wasn't only the mentally ill that were seen there, but nonetheless, she did not want any gossip. After some hesitation the doctor agreed to give her some mild tranquilizers, and if the symptoms continued, she should certainly let him know; it could be arranged for the examination to take place when he was on night duty; then no one would know except the nurses, but he wouldn't be on night duty until the following weekend. He rose to fetch the medication from a cupboard. He then noticed that his expensive tropical fish in the five-hundred-liter aquarium behind the armchair had positioned themselves so as to form a perfect circle around the teacher's head. He said nothing. After giving her the packet, he sat down again and watched to see when the first fish would break out of the circle. None of them moved. But fish have to swim, for otherwise, they can't breathe. On a pretext he stood up, walked over to the aquarium, and stared at the fish. Their scaly bodies—red, gold, orange, blue and green, black and white—hovered motionless behind Anna Lévay's head, far from the circulating pump. Only their gills pulsated. He concluded that perhaps the fish were sensitive to light and were being disturbed by the large chandelier overhead, which was seldom lit; they had become used to the small table lamps and their own light, and so he switched off the chandelier and switched on the light attached to the aquarium, but the fish didn't budge.

Anna Lévay took the doctor's getting up a second time as a signal that it was time for her to go. So she took her leave. At the urging of her hosts she promised to come again another time. It does one good to converse a bit, said physician and wife in chorus; intellectual company is rare here. What were there now but a bunch of useless riffraff, superfluous characters who had completely ruined this charming resort town, and then the new cultural philistines who order oysters in restaurants, the self-important moneyed class, cheap little Mafiosi! What had become of the good, respectable middle class?

Anna Lévay walked home. She closed her apartment door behind her, drank a glass of warm milk, brushed her teeth, removed her dentures, undressed, slipped her nightgown over her head, took two of the pills that the doctor had given her, and climbed into bed. It was eleven o'clock.

3

Although the events had transpired late in the evening, the next morning, all the daily papers provided extensive coverage. They wrote that cadets at the police academy, who in the early evening hours were carrying out exercises in front of the police administration building, had become aware of an automobile coming from the direction of the harbor that had passed them three times at elevated speed. The fourth time, they stopped the car and noticed a bright red liquid oozing from the trunk. At once, they commanded the driver at gunpoint to place his hands behind his head; they pushed him up against the car, frisked him, demanded identification—just as they had learned at the academy—and then instructed him to park his car in the administration building's enclosed courtyard.

A thorough search of the automobile revealed that the trunk was full of half-dead fish. One of the policemen was wounded when he carelessly took hold of a zander from the wrong side. Another officer had to be taken to the hospital emergency room after being bitten by a pike. The wound was not serious, however, and he was soon released.

Under questioning, the driver of the car testified that while fishing he had become aware of a large number of fish swimming along either side of the harbor, and when the fish on the left side reached the red basalt blocks of the breakwater, signaling the end of their path through the harbor, a large number proceeded to cast themselves on the shore, while those on the right side continued further, until they crashed against the closed sluice gates. The driver continued his narrative, reporting that he then used his mobile phone to notify his friends of the phenomenon. They arrived a few minutes later, and the men then carted off the fish as best they could. He went on to say that they had attempted to throw back the undersized fish and those whose capture was forbidden, but these immediately threw themselves back on the shore, as though acting out in reverse the fairy tale about the fisherman and his wife. He had nothing further to relate. He stuck to his story and confirmed it by signing the transcript of the interview.

The police proceeded at once in full force to the scene of the action, but when they arrived, they found the place deserted. The section of shore parallel to the rose garden was completely empty, with no trace of any dead fish. But on the wet ground of the park they found automobile tire tracks. A series of plaster casts would determine whether they belonged to one or a number of vehicles.

A search of the driver's residence uncovered about three hundred kilos of fresh fish of the choicest varieties. The woman of the house appeared already to have washed and sorted the cadavers in preparation to scaling them before placing them in the freezer when the commando team arrived. There was clearly prima facie evidence of theft and destruction of public property, and so the gentleman in question was taken into temporary custody. The police announced that any witnesses to these events should come forward. It appeared certain that the suspected perpetrators could not possibly have caught fish in such quantity with the rods and nets that were found in their possession, and thus the investigation was extended to include a search for illegal fishing equipment. At the same time, the fishermen's association was notified about the case and told that it was to suspend the suspect's fishing license until the investigation was completed.

The newspaper editors were of varying opinions as to whether the story should be run under the police blotter or in the section on local news. The tabloids chose the former and compensated for a lack of hard information with stories of illegal fishing from their files. In any case, due to the late hour at which the story broke, there was not much space to be allocated for this sensational account. Among the political dailies, only those with the highest circulation reported the affair, and then with only a few lines among other events.

It was after the papers had all gone to press that the head of the water police reported that there had been a number of alarms in the early evening, all of which appeared to be related to strange movements of fish. In the eastern part of the lake an illegal angler was reeling in a prohibited pike that was at the end of its strength when it suddenly shot off in the direction of the harbor named by the alleged perpetrator in his statement. At the same time, a large fish of undetermined species had crashed against the heavy wood and metal pier belonging to the former Socialist Party's holiday residences, causing it to collapse. In addition, the crews of private sailing vessels out on the lake engaged in fishing for zander, equipped for the most part with sonar, reported that at the time in question their equipment had reported large movements of fish traveling in the same direction.

The lock-keeper had reported the strange event at about seven-thirty that evening. He had entered it into his notebook and then informed his superiors by telephone, who, seeing that a leak was not at issue and the hour was late, did nothing other than order an official investigation the following morning.

Anna Lévay awoke at exactly twenty-five minutes after five o'clock. For decades now her biological clock had been set to this time. She got out of bed, stretched, and on autopilot went to turn on the radio. Usually, she switched on the set just in time for the news.

This time, however, she had miscalculated. They were still broadcasting advertisements. She had a phobia against the insistent, deafening drumbeat of the consumer society, and so she switched off the radio and waited until, according to her reckoning, the commercials should have ended. At this point she recalled the doctor's words from the previous evening, the fishy adventure at the harbor, all the events of yesterday. Perhaps, she thought, it was all just a hallucination. She hastened to the bathroom mirror and looked at her reflection.

The halo was still there.

She noticed that her hairdo was well past its prime. She would have to make an appointment, this afternoon at two o'clock if possible. She was well aware that her hair would look ridiculous in any case, but it was time, and already yesterday she had planned that late in the afternoon, to avoid the weekend crowds, she would go to the cemetery to honor her deceased husband's grave with the usual three chrysanthemums.

She felt a bit embarrassed at the thought that her preparations were as though for a secret rendezvous. She had not been to the cemetery since May. She thought about what she should wear, and finally decided on a short dark-blue woolen suit, which she wore only to convocation at the start of the school year, graduation, and those occasions on which a former student received an advanced degree. It was so plain that she need have no fear that her colleagues would ask why her manner of dress was different from the usual. She always placed her clothes in her dresser neatly ironed, but the creases from lying about with other clothes were plain to see, and so she ironed the accompanying blouse once again, and since the iron was already out, she ran it over the skirt as well. Then she hung everything on the arm of the kitchen chair, to be put on later. She was about to spread some rosehip jam on her bread, which she had already spread with margarine, when the six-o'clock news came on, with a report on the mysterious movements of fish, the call by the lock-keeper, the arrest of a suspicious citizen, and the unusual fish kill.

Her blood pressure shot up. Since she still had time, she lay down again and pulled the covers over her head, just as she had done when she was a child and had longed to return to the safety of her mother's tummy. She wanted to shut out all thought, to have complete calm, to close her eyes, surrounded by darkness, merge into nothingness, to float along on a stream of consciousness. And so she switched off the light.

It was after 6:30; the hair salon would be open. She reached for the phone. She did not have to reach far, for it was on the bedside table. When the telephone line was put in (in those days it was by the grace of the government), only one phone jack was supposed to be installed. But Anna Lévay tipped the workers to get an additional jack in the bedroom; this was very important, since in her old age she might become disabled. Who thought of cellular phones back then?

The apartment block in which she lived had been built at the end of the 1970s. It was a flimsy affair, quickly thrown together, badly soundproofed. One always knew what was going on with one's neighbors. In decades of living side by side one came to know the musical preferences of the others, their favorite television programs, the words they used in argument, and in lovemaking. One knew when a plate broke or a door slammed.

The tenant above her was in the bathroom, for the contents of the toilet could be heard swirling noisily down the outflow pipe. It must be the husband who had been relieving himself, for his wife could be heard setting the kitchen table for breakfast. Chair legs were scratching along the floor like chalk on a blackboard. Food was being warmed in the microwave, which always announced the termination of its regime with three heartrending squawks.

Anna Lévay felt a rumbling in her bowels. She hastened to the toilet and shut herself in. She put down the seat and sat for a quarter of an hour in the darkness in her nightshirt, with her legs braced against the door. She then relieved herself, of which, given the condition of the plumbing and the construction of the walls, the neighbors in their turn would now be aware, and then proceeded to the sink to wash her hands. She switched on the light, but within two seconds the bulb had burnt out. A second switch operated the fluorescent lamp over the mirror. Normally, she never turned on this light, partly to economize, but more because she hated the fluorescent glow.

But the fluorescent lamp appeared to be out of order.

The light from the anteroom will suffice, she thought, and as she soaped her hands, she again saw the halo in the mirror. She batted at the apparition like one who tries to brush away a pesky housefly, until finally, enraged at her lack of success, she simply banged her head with full force against the wall. The halo fended off any contact between her head and the damp tiles; the effect was like the meeting of two magnets of like polarity. When she came to, she found herself seated on the carpet, hands folded, her elbows resting on her splayed knees. As she opened her eyes, she observed how the light from the halo illumined her lap, and she sensed its warmth. She then showered with alternating regimes of hot and cold water. In one of the cold phases, with her inner eye she saw Jacob, locked in conflict with the Lord; then Jonah in the watery interior of the whale; and finally, on account of the tingling in her lap produced by the heat of the halo, Miriam's wonderment at the Annunciation. That was all.

She quickly dressed, deciding against the high heels, choosing instead a pair of shoes that were ten years old and long out of style, what were euphemistically called "slippers," which made her look even more like an old lady. She felt that she just wouldn't have the nerve to pull off a whole day in dressy shoes, and in any case, they would be impractical at the cemetery; the pointed heels would easily sink in the soft earth, making holes like a garden dibble between the grave mounds.

At quarter past eight she walked out of the door. Crossing the threshold, she heard a soft whimpering, and then walked right into the neighbors' dog, who had apparently spent the night on her doormat. The animal pulled itself together and proceeded to follow Anna Lévay as she returned to her apartment, took a piece of sausage from the refrigerator, and offered it to the dog, which then followed Anna Lévay down the staircase, she in her agitation, and despite her age, bounding down the flight of stairs to the ground floor. But the animal instinctively grasped the situation, and quickening its tempo made a dash for the door, and then lay sprawled across her path, wagging its tail. By now Anna Lévay had reached something of an altered state of consciousness. She opened the door, but instead of leaving the building, she blocked the exit with her broad back and began to stroke the dog's fur, first on the back, then the ears, and finally under the snout. While the animal was basking in her attentions, she popped out the door and pulled it to. She looked back and saw the poor creature pawing at the glass.

Arriving at the crosswalk in front of the hospital, she stepped out in front of an approaching car, a red luxury model. Its occupant was the neurologist, deep in thought about the events of the previous evening. He suddenly noticed the pedestrian in his path and engaged the brake pedal with full force. As the automobile screeched to a halt he touched with his left forefinger the button of the electric window opener, ready to shout at the troublemaker, "You stupid asshole, are you tired of life, or are you trying to kill me?" But all that issued from his lips was, "Good morning, Mrs. Lévay, how are you feeling today?" Anna Lévay paused a moment, replied with a smile that all was well, and continued on her way.

The hospital guard did not move from his place as he raised the barrier with his remote control to admit the doctor, who eased his car into its parking space. The neurologist stepped out and walked to the rear of the vehicle to retrieve from the trunk his thick briefcase, which served not so much as a means of transporting medical volumes and patient records as for inspiring in others a feeling of awe at his importance. He closed the trunk and walked up the steps cut into the small hill on which the hospital stood. He looked around as was his custom, taking a last long gaze, one that would have to last the entire workday, at his red steed, and with manly pleasure pressed the button on the remote control for the central locking system. It was not until the three tiny beeps had sounded to admit him and he was turning with a feeling of satisfaction to enter the building that he noticed that his car's bumper, which was made of a hard composite material, was cracked exactly in the place near where Anna Lévay had been standing at the moment he had braked. He had not felt an impact, and the teacher hadn't wavered in the least. He was certain that his automobile had been intact when he left home. Every morning, after closing the garage door, he would look with satisfaction at the manufacturer's trademark, for he had thought long about purchasing a different make entirely, but in the end he was satisfied with his decision. Thus he concluded that somehow, Anna Lévay had been the cause of the damage.

He hurried into the building. He would have liked to run, but that would have put too great a strain on his dignity. He found himself in the predicament of the marathon walker who with only a slight increase in speed slips into a run and is thus disqualified. With an iron will he held himself back. He did not wait for the elevator, but took the stairs three at a time to get as quickly as possible to a telephone.

First, he called the police to report the accident, namely, that in consequence of running into Mrs. Lévay his bumper had cracked. The officer on duty answered only after the fifteenth ring and connected him with an individual at the traffic bureau, who proceeded at once to admonish him that he should have remained at the scene, identified two witnesses, and waited for the arrival of the police. Hadn't the ambulance staff informed him about the procedure? As it was, the situation was now very complicated, for he had committed an offense and should be charged, but perhaps one could do something for the good doctor. The official told him that if he believed himself responsible for the accident, he should seek out the injured party and work out a settlement; there was no need for a legal proceeding. The doctor replied that no one was injured, but he was quite certain that the pedestrian had been the cause of the accident. He had known the officer when he was still walking a beat;

several times, he had brought mentally disturbed citizens who were a danger to the state to the police station: drug addicts, attempted suicides. The policeman was possessed of a great simplicity that caused these disturbed individuals to respect him. This officer respected the physician mostly because of his profession and rank, but since he considered what had just been uttered an impossibility, there escaped from his lips the words, "But Doctor, just think how much force it takes to break a bone and how much to break the bumper of your big car. I simply cannot believe that the pedestrian escaped without a scratch. If I didn't know you, I would suggest that you have yourself examined, a joke, of course, no offense. Are you insured? Just tell them that someone ran into you in the parking lot. That would be better for all concerned."

After being greeted by the doctor, it occurred to Anna Lévay that she still needed to buy flowers for her afternoon visit to the cemetery. She planned on going to the flower shop in town, right after her visit to the hairdresser, but then it occurred to her that it would be crowded there, and furthermore, the best varieties of flowers were more expensive in the center than elsewhere. Flowers were truly inexpensive only at market, but she considered it unworthy of the sacred memory of János Lévay to buy flowers for his grave on the cheap, even though she knew that the flowers would not lie there long, that at nightfall they would fall victim to graveyard thieves, who would sell them the next day to be placed on another grave. But for her it was all merely a gesture to maintain her spiritual equanimity, and she would not be bothered by trifling material concerns. And so shortly after she had returned the doctor's greeting, she turned back in order to purchase three chrysanthemums at the flower kiosk near the hospital parking lot. What a morbid idea, she thought, to sell flowers for the dead right here, considering that it was highly unlikely that visitors would present such flowers to their convalescing friends, but since they were here, one must take advantage. She paid 150 forints. She had no use for decorative paper. That left her exactly 120 forints for coffee. That was the extent of her purse, but she would have something this evening, when her private student came at seven o'clock and paid for an hour of her time. She carried the three yellow flowers through the town, as if she had been given them at a rendezvous, the blossoms on top, pressed against her overcoat, shielded from the wind.

Having finally arrived at her school, she went directly to the teachers' room, removed the class register for 12b from the shelf, and took it to her table. She placed the flowers in the communal vase, sat down, and took a deep breath. No one else was in the room. The conscious portion of her brain prepared for the coming class lesson, hands and eyes searching for her notes, while the unconscious part tried to understand what had occurred. In this she had no success. She concentrated with all her energy on her lesson. Normally, she didn't have to prepare for her classes, but today she wanted to leave nothing to chance, so that no one would notice anything unusual about her. Her strategy was to flood her students with dates, which would keep them busy taking notes. Where there had not been a quiz recently, there she added one to the lesson plan. For one class she prepared a list of thirty literary terms that the students had encountered, for which they would have to supply the precise definitions. For another class she prepared a worksheet with the title "What's the Difference?" A third would have to write on a topic of their own choosing related to the Baroque period. In the seventh, elective, hour she had arrived at the theme of "life and literature." A nice little topic. In the first part of the hour she would immediately launch a discussion as to whether literature had contributed in any way to progress in the world. She thought of the role of the writer in Central Europe as a force for political change, on the influence of works of literature on politics, but she had no intention of limiting the discussion to contemporary issues, and therefore she determined to begin with the Enlightenment, with Diderot's *La Religieuse*. In the second part of the hour she planned on considering the effect of some specific works as well as a book's impact on the reader, and finally, the theory of catharsis. This would all be divided, of course, over several class periods, so that there would be time left in each class for student reports on their reading, which, as she already knew, would be abysmal.

Everything went as planned. She took great care to arrange the lighting and went as seldom as possible into the teachers' room, spending instead the greater part of the time in the washroom and along the corridor, where the students paid no attention to her. She was effectively disguised as a hall monitor, since the teacher supposed to be fulfilling that duty was nowhere in sight. Tactical considerations led her to abandon the white coat that she had been wearing for years, with the excuse that she had spilled coffee on it. In reality, what had happened is that it had occurred to her, when she was still alone in the teachers' room and had brewed her first cup of coffee, that dark colors absorb light, while light colors reflect it. So she took off the coat and poured the last drops of her coffee not into the thermos, but onto the front of her coat. Over her black silk blouse she put on her dark-blue jacket, and to render an explanation unnecessary, she hung the soiled coat over the back of her chair.

In the middle of the fourth period the secretary arrived and called her to the telephone. Such a thing had never happened before. As she hastened along the corridor to the office she tried to imagine who the mysterious caller might be who had been able to get past Marika's refrain, repeated a dozen times a day and brooking no discussion, "I'm sorry, she's in class, please call again when classes have been let out." She didn't want to ask in front of the students. A hot pang shot through her head: Had she perhaps forgotten to pull out the plug of the iron? Had there been a fire in her apartment? A burst pipe? Or had her son unexpectedly arrived from the New World?

It was the neurologist. Of course. The town's chief citizen, drinking companion of all the local worthies, privy to all their secrets, member of the municipal council. He was calling from the mayor's office, just across the four-lane highway, with the request that the teacher meet him at once in the café at the cultural center. She replied that seventh period would end at one-twenty. After that, she was going to eat lunch, which was another twenty minutes, so she would be available at one forty-five. At the worst she would be late to the hairdresser. If the matter was brief, perhaps it could be taken care of in the pause between two periods. The doctor did not say what he wished to speak to her about. Since one forty-five was unavailable to him due to a private consultation that could not be postponed, and he believed that the matter would take some time to discuss, they agreed to meet in the evening at eight o'clock, and to make it easy for Mrs. Lévay, the doctor would call on her.

After lunch, Anna Lévay hurried through the underpass that led beneath the four-lane highway, across the market square, and along the main road with the fashionable boutiques until she reached the hairdresser in the "House of Lords." The shop belonged to the industrial collective, which was somehow still around from the previous political system. A glance at the setup gave an impression that everything there had been left untouched since the seventies. Those orange lamps made of plastic, those chairs covered in light-brown artificial leather, those metal footrests!

The mirror-lined wall was long enough to accommodate eight hairdressers. During the time of massive tourism the women had had to wait in long lines in order to have their coiffures spruced up in anticipation of a night on the town. The entire operation was like the last stage of an assembly line: Its processing completed, the production unit smiles, offers a tip, and is then shipped out of the factory. Most of the hairdressers spoke German, and some had even gone so far, in deference to the nationalities of the clientele, to learn a few words of Czech or Polish. The cleverer among them had put together a little phrase book of the terms that couldn't be explained in sign language. A few yellowed copies were still to be found buried in the recesses of a cabinet, though the stream of tourists was now long gone with the winds of change.

Anna Lévay had been coming here for thirty years, and for all of those thirty years to Terike. Terike and her colleagues all wore heavy shoes to ward off varicose veins. Most had a sagging stomach, thick arms, and a double chin, which fused the neck and head into one undifferentiated rectangular block. Their hair, however, was always in finest fettle; every day it was freshly curled, combed out, and sprayed. A hairdresser's head is her calling card. A hairdresser must know whether and about what to speak with a customer. These women seemed to have at their disposal a limitless supply of gossip, anecdotes, and jokes provided by and about their customers. Once, they performed an experiment to see how long it would take for a piece of news to spread among this town of twenty thousand inhabitants. They figured that a customer hearing something at the hairdresser's would pass it along to two of her acquaintances that very day. And in fact, a customer's slip of the tongue mentioned on one day was reported back to them the next.

Terike was presently occupied with a customer who had shown up late for her appointment, and begged Anna Lévay to be patient a bit, offering her a seat and several colorful women's magazines, and then returning to the head at hand, which she was in the process of blow-drying. Every now and then the comb would get stuck in the shoulder-length hair, and the teacher was curious as to whether the customer would evince any sign of pain. Suddenly, her eye fell on the drying brush, whose bristles were made of metal. In a flash it was clear to her that her hair would also have to be dried, and she recalled her morning adventure with the knitting needle. The mirror gave back a clear image of her halo.

Her experience thus far indicated that no one had noticed the apparition, not even the most observant, nor those standing but an arm's length away. But now she feared that Terike would notice it, would sense it with her brush, and she could imagine the commentary on such an extraordinary occurrence that would soon be broadcast to the salon's clientele. Anna Lévay abruptly stood up, took her overcoat, and walked out without a word. When she put her hand into her coat pocket, she realized that a great embarrassment had been spared her: She had completely forgotten that after having paid for two coffees in the teachers' room and three chrysanthemums at the flower kiosk—and even if she hadn't paid for them—she had not enough money with her.

She strolled back to the school to fetch her flowers, planning to proceed at once to the cemetery. She looked in the shop windows, as she had done as a child when instead of going to school she had gone to visit a friend who secretly had stayed at home. Times had changed. Today, she thought as she observed her reflection, together with the halo, in the window of a travel agency, a café closed for the winter, a bakery, a china shop, a second-hand shop, a bazaar, and an insurance agency, one searched for the truants in the surrounding bars and game halls.

As she passed in front of the green bureaucratic building of the town hall, she was overcome with nausea. Her overtaxed nerves seemed about to short-circuit. Her stomach was preparing a rebellion against the cauliflower soup and roast beef with onions that had been placed within, plotting in anger to return them whence they came. She recalled the neurologist's phone call of that morning. She felt even worse on encountering the stench of urine in the underpass. When she came out again into the open, she took a deep breath and prayed that she might arrive at the school without incident. Praying was not something with which she had much experience. She could not very well fold her hands in public; after all, everyone knew that she was an unbeliever, and it would make quite a spectacle. It was really just a very small prayer, in which she asked God please, if He would not explain her absurd situation, He might at least make it halfway bearable.

She arrived at the school door, nodded to the custodian, and then turned to the left, the image of a respectable teacher, back straight and steps leisurely. She closed the door of the teachers' toilet behind her and gave back her lunch.

At two-thirty, she entered the teachers' room, plopped herself down at the newspaper table, and began to read; that is, she acted as though she were deeply absorbed in the newspaper. The lines of type swam before her eyes, and although her eyeballs moved, her brain absorbed not a word of the printed text. Nor was she thinking about anything. She simply floated along in a dull mental state, as if groping about in a fog. She returned to herself when a colleague spoke from the immediate vicinity: "What will you be trying next, Anna!" She was reading the sports paper, upside down. As a student she had worked as a typesetter at a printer to add to her stipend, and there she had acquired, out of sight of students, that secret art, as well as the ability to read inverted text fluently. That she was reading the sports rag, however, was something definitely unusual. "Oh, I was so far away," she said, and gave the defense that she was just keeping her old skills in shape, it didn't matter what the text was, she had just sat down to catch her breath, she was on her way to the cemetery, since she did not want to land in rush-hour traffic on All Saints' Day. Visiting a grave was an intimate matter, and it bothered her that many made it a social event, following the visit to "their" grave with a walk through the cemetery as if one were at a party, gossiping and taking note of who had how many flowers and candles and whether there were any at all. Then they would hold forth the rest of the day about whom they saw, how they looked, and who looked as if they would soon be following in the steps of their deceased loved ones. Anna Lévay could not bear this gossip, nor was she pleased when someone stared her in the face while she was conversing with the soul of her late husband.

She carried the vase in which she had placed the three chrysanthemums that morning to the sink, took out the flowers, and gently shook off the water that clung to the stems and lower leaves. Then she emptied the vase with a quick movement, rinsed it out, and returned it to its place. That accomplished, she wrapped the flowers carefully in their paper and lay them on the table while she put on her coat. It was a good two kilometers to the cemetery, and no bus traveled there. Perhaps one would do so next year, perhaps not.

Every year, Anna Lévay went to the cemetery on foot; for her it was a pilgrimage, and this time she suffered the pangs of conscience because the thought of the journey gave her no pleasure. She would probably meet some old women who always have time and whom courtesy would not permit to pass by in silence, and the thought filled her with anxiety. She knew everyone in the city, and she could not let her behavior provide any cause for gossip.

Her colleague, the only daughter of a family belonging to the newly wealthy—though one who had fallen far from the tree—who even without working knew where her next meal was coming from and who taught merely because it gave her pleasure, this colleague now offered to drive her out to the cemetery. At first, she put up some resistance out of politeness—gasoline is expensive and she would manage in any case on foot, she had plenty of time—but then she accepted the offer. This was the colleague who had been responsible for the organization of that memorable celebration on the anniversary of the 1956 revolution. Anna Lévay resented her for this, though with no good reason, since her colleague had not known János Lévay and thus could not suspect that the operator's error that had resulted in her husband's resurrection would drive her into a deep depression. Her colleague was not the least to blame, and she had revealed neither to her nor to anyone else why she had felt ill, nor had anyone noticed that she had left the room.

Together, they walked to the exit and into the courtyard. At once, the cold hit her in the face. The next moment something collided with her legs. It was the dog, who greeted her with a wagging tail, having spent the day waiting for her in the courtyard, loafing about among construction workers, buckets of mortar, and cement mixers, because this morning she had entered the building through the courtyard door. She had already been once again in the courtyard during the day, on her way to lunch, but at that time there had been quite a crowd. Perhaps, the creature had not dared to approach her, assuming, of course, that it had even been there. Apparently, it had gotten out of the building with one of the tenants. Anna Lévay pretended that she was unacquainted with the animal.

Her colleague, who was known as a great friend of dogs, attempted in vain to stroke the dog's shaggy russet coat. She consid-

ered the smell of a dog, particularly a wet dog, particularly masculine and erotic. She had no idea why, but she made a sport of
stroking the fur of dogs she encountered, thereby collecting an as-
sortment of dog smells. She would let the scent remain on her hand
as long as she could, washing it off only under the compulsion of
dinnertime. The cheap after-shave lotion of her first lover had had
a similar effect when in an excited state he reached a certain level of
adrenaline and sweating. She had often detected the scent during an
embrace in the rose garden, in the Jókai park, in the tunnel under
the railroad tracks, and on the bank of the canal, even at the cemetery where she would now be taking Anna Lévay and where their
first and only coupling had taken place, which ended in an abortion
at the other end of the country. Her parents had protested against
that "déclassé element, outside of Party and society," who became
a news reporter and then—at first prohibited, then tolerated—a
writer, and finally an apostle of the change in the political system.
She often thought she recognized herself and their common mem-
ories in his writing. In such cases she would become depressed for
days and share her sorrows with the dogs. But this dog withdrew
from her. And why she was telling all this to Anna Lévay, she did
not know, but she told it nonetheless.

It was warm and dry inside the comfortable, sleekly contoured
automobile. From the radio, or rather, from a cassette, classical music issued forth. It was a slow, dignified, splendid Baroque melody,
not one of those classical hits, perhaps Telemann, and the volume
was not too soft. This unmarried colleague, a lively and joyous free
spirit, always listened to such music, and always very loud, as counterpoint to the deafening roar that poured forth from the other automobiles. The music rang out from the car, whose motor was
relatively quiet, although the body was not completely soundproof,
and when she would stop at a traffic light, pedestrians and other
waiting drivers would stare at her like profaners of a shrine.

The music made Anna Lévay quite calm. When she got out of
the car at the cemetery, she was in such awe of the expensive machine that three times she closed the door too gently. Her colleague

promised to be waiting for her in front of the gate in an hour, she needn't hurry, she herself would sit in the car as long as necessary, but now she had to hurry into town to shop, to prepare for a rare evening visit from her current lover. She giggled.

The row of urns filled Anna Lévay with disgust. Not that she would have opposed the modern energy-saving variant of the age-old method of cremation, she even considered it reasonable, for a grave must be taken care of, flowers planted, an expensive grave-stone of marble, granite, or concrete installed. And then one had to pay again for the plot every twenty years and set out candles on All Saints' Day; otherwise, people talked. But that was not really the is-sue. What disturbed her more was the thought that behind, beside, below the wall of her urn would lie the ashes of strangers. Who knows, perhaps there are souls that return to their containers of ashes, somehow they must communicate with each other, perhaps they are loud, or have disgusting habits, and then even in death she would feel as if she were living in a community of prefabricated houses. In that case it would be better to scatter the ashes. Or—a mad idea, which she had read about in a glossy magazine at the hairdresser's—to have the finely pulverized ashes installed in an hourglass.

Once she remarked to an acquaintance that when she died she wanted to be cremated, for burial had become terribly expensive, but she wished to end up neither in a wall of urns nor on a shelf, better to take the ashes to the nearby explosives factory, use them as filling in a large firework, and then shoot it out over the lake. Then at least there would be some truth to those texts in the obituaries, usually drenched in crocodile tears: She was an explosive talent, who flared like a comet, her eyes brightened her surroundings, and now she has become a shining star. Not a bad idea. One could make a business out of it. Those of us about to die could perhaps, while they were still living, select a star; a red one, or orange, blue, many would perhaps want a white one, or multicolored, according to party affiliation, devoted patriots would want red–white–green; one could request, say, to be shot over the Danube during the traditional fireworks on Constitution Day. At one's own expense, of course, that is clear, and if such a thing were to become fashionable, it would be a boon to the fireworks industry.

That is what she was thinking when she almost collided with a child who was playing catch with his friend among the shrubbery. Indeed, the cemetery was unusually lively. Before it became dark, grandmothers were bringing their grandchildren to grandfather, and housewives who thanks to the money they earned in summer now took it easy at home in the off-season made the obligatory respectful visit to the deceased members of their families. They were mostly women, except for a well-liked surgeon who was accompanying his wife on his day off. A television crew were walking among the graves, and a woman production manager in a violet coat busied herself in the vicinity of the delicate cameraman.

Anna Lévay was walking along the main path directly toward the stone cross when she saw that the camera was pointed at her. She darted among the grave mounds, anything to avoid being filmed, and then took a detour to the final resting place of the mortal remains of János Lévay.

She had to sit down; otherwise, she would have toppled over. The dwarf arborvitae that she had planted at the edge of the grave had all been stolen, but that wasn't what upset her. In the middle of the small plot, there dangled from the sturdy stalk of the now fully grown plant that she had obtained as a seedling from her neighbor, dear God, there dangled, like two limp purple testicles, two well-developed eggplants, frozen in the recent frosty nights. She had seen, in a horizontal variant, something similar in the Museo Nazionale in Naples, on the marble pedestal of the bust of the Pompeiian banker Caecilius Iucundus, upon which, cast in bronze, had been erected the entire organ, in rest position, complete with worked-out pubic hair and testes, as a sign of respect for the spirit and sexual power of his ancestors. The tourist group that she was with had amused themselves considerably over the delightful art object, and she, too, had smiled; the more demure of them—according to their own testimony—never even looked at it.

She began to tear out the plant by the roots, but suddenly she felt an abhorrence at disturbing the earth under which her husband was decomposing in his by now long rotted casket, down to which the delicate roots of the plant stretched. So she simply broke off the thick stem in the middle and took the heavy mass that remained in her hand, hidden under her coat, to the dumpster.

She did not take the shortest route, for she wanted to know whether her neighbor had given her the plant out of naiveté or malice. The neighbor, in turn, had obtained the plant from a Transylvanian relation, who, in spite of his Hungarian descent, was a gardener in the presidential residence in Bucharest. The rest of his family despised him for this and seldom saw him, maintaining a cool reserve when they did. The seedlings that he sent them every spring were, however, not sent back. Perhaps this man had been playing a joke on his relatives, or maybe the family thought that their member who had emigrated to Hungary would have noticed the joke, or else they simply had not dared to tell her, or not considered it important. Anna Lévay and her neighbor had been at the cemetery together in spring and had helped each other out with garden implements. If it had all been a mistake, there should be such eggplants growing on the grave of the neighbor's deceased relative.

In fact, the neighbor was at this moment standing before the burial mound, legs apart, grasping two purple fruits, one with each hand, carefully, from below, as if they really were testicles, but in contrast to Anna's treatment, she twisted them to try to remove them. Finally, she began to pull on them, but they would not tear off. So she set her legs even wider apart until finally, above the dust of the dead one's loins, she crouched down as if in a saddle and managed to pull the plant out by the roots.

Anna Lévay had no desire to speak with her. At best, she may have wished to have a good laugh with her neighbor about the whole affair. Perhaps her friend, with her piercing gaze, would see the halo, and she had no wish to arrive at such a point. And furthermore, she was concerned about the disappearance of the arborvitae. They had been expensive. She had planted them the previous year, so that they would grow over the entire mound, and she then would not have to bother any longer with flower seedlings. In any case, Doctor Lévay, being allergic to pollen, was not particularly fond of flowers.

In town it was said that unscrupulous thieves sold dwarf firs, complete with the root ball, as Christmas trees, but not with the best goodwill could she imagine what use they might have for arborvitae. Perhaps they sold them to a nursery. And the cemetery attendant defended himself with the assertion that he was not a guard and could not be running around outside every day, and anyhow, what was he to do if he actually caught the thief?

She returned to her husband's grave and there spent the remaining time until her colleague's return. At precisely four o'clock she walked to the exit and got into the car. They drove slowly through the town. A stroll by car. She paid no attention to her colleague, who spoke to her ceaselessly. She could see that her mouth was moving, but she was incapable of ordering the sounds into phonemes, words, sentences, coherent thoughts. She stared straight ahead and came to herself only when they stopped in front of the only hotel in the center of town that was open in winter. Her colleague got out, went around the back of the car, helped her get out, and led her into the hotel café. This was an expensive spot, not a place for high school teachers. The communication must have been rather one-sided; in any case, she had no recollection of having said anything, but she must have responded to her colleague's questions and ordered something, for a few minutes later a large cup of hot tea and an enormous portion of fruit salad were placed in front of her. At the bottom of the bowl swam almond-stuffed prunes in liqueur, cherries, and slices of peach and apricot. On top was a thick layer of whipped cream, upon which, to her horror, lay an entire bright yellow slice of pineapple, looking like nothing less than a halo floating on a cloud. The fibers of the fruit ran out from the center like the rays of a gloriole in a painting of the early Flemish Baroque. She looked for the first time at her colleague, who had ordered for herself the house special chocolate torte.

"All right, finally, listen to me, Anna, dearest," she said, and although this sentence penetrated her consciousness, Anna Lévay still could not concentrate. She considered whether her colleague had seen something or whether the pineapple symbolism was a chance occurrence. Mechanically, she spooned in the whipped cream delight and from time to time cut off little pieces of the fruit ring with her teaspoon by pressing them against the wall of the bowl. She ate like a ministrant on stolen Host.

Her companion frequented this hotel, going often to use the swimming pool or the sauna to keep herself in shape, and after swimming, she generally put in an appearance at the café. Since she was a regular customer, the staff took special care to supply her guest with a double portion of almond liqueur in her fruit salad, which Anna Lévay distractedly spooned down to the last drop. Then she drank the large cup of hot tea, and since she felt herself affected by the alcohol, was thankful for her colleague's offer to drive her home.

In the quiet of her apartment Anna Lévay put herself back in order. She washed her face with cold water and drank the coffee left over from the morning. Then, in anticipation of the doctor's visit, she made the necessary preparations for baking cottage-cheese tarts, for she had no money left to buy ready-made sweets; furthermore, after the incident the day before she had no desire to go into the shop. What she really wanted to do was meditate, as she called it, quietly to herself before the arrival of her visitor, so she kneaded the dough, rolled it evenly with the rolling pin inherited from her mother to the thickness of a finger, cut out circles, placed them on a baking sheet, turned on the gas oven, shoved in the sheet, which gave forth a loud screech, washed up, and sat on a stool and waited. Fifteen minutes later, she took the finished tarts out of the oven, placed them on a dish, aired out the room, laid a clean tablecloth on the kitchen table, and put her books and notes in order, for soon her private student would arrive.

At five-thirty the student knocked. She planned to study law, just like the others whom Anna Lévay tutored. It was a fashionable subject. Those of her students who studied law at university and graduated earned about ten times as much as a high school teacher just short of retirement. And this girl, too, she thought, would fail to recognize her ten years hence when as a pert young lawyer she drove by her old teacher in her sports car and splashed water all over her coat.

Along with the girl, the shaggy, dirty dog pushed its way into the apartment through the crack in the door. Anna Lévay bent down to him, petted him, and looked into his eyes, through which she seemed to understand him; she liked him very much, he was a good dog, but now he must go home. She rang the neighbor's doorbell. He thanked her for bringing the dog home; they had been worried about him and had no idea where he might be. Anna Lévay did not reveal that he had followed her, saying only that he had come in with her student, most certainly because of the smell of the tarts. He loves them, said the neighbor, and the teacher saw how the dog stared at her until the door was shut.

Her private student was a difficult case. No aptitude for analysis. She could lose herself in the spirit of a work, and if one loves a text too much, one cannot look at it with detachment, examine it in detail; one behaves with it like a mourner over his deceased relatives: One is shocked at the thought of dissection; one loves the thing as a whole, unscathed, indivisible. "You should be an actress, my dear," she had said more than once to her student. "Then you would be concerned only with synthesis, not with analysis." But then her parents, a bank director and a physician, would immediately reduce her allowance to force her back onto her ordained path.

"I don't think that you are cut out for this profession, my dear. You are not such a tough cookie. If you gather thistles, expect

prickles; you may soon become bitterly disappointed!" This is what
she wanted to say to her, but never did.

She addressed her students formally, as she had been by her own
teachers. This seemed to her the best means of maintaining distance
while showing respect for them. Some of the students considered it
unfriendly, and even a bit ridiculous, for teenagers to be addressed
as though they were adults. She reminded them that formal address
was a tradition in the most exclusive British public schools. It was
not until the graduation ball that she addressed them informally.

She never had any private students whom she was currently
teaching at school. It was not because of any prohibition by the unwritten ethical code, but because other students would be carefully
watching whether such students were being favored. They might
have suspected her of disclosing the topics of tests well in advance,
at the private lesson. Although she would never do so, she did not
want to be involved in such conflicts.

The student left at seven, and while Anna Lévay waited for the
doctor, she noticed—perhaps it was an excess of chalk dust, the excitement at the cemetery, possibly even the cold fruit salad—that
her neck was swollen. When her sister called, she could hardly
speak. She turned on the television. By pushing a button on the apparatus several times (the battery in the remote control was dead)
she tuned into the local station. Then she sat down and stared, motionless, at the moving images, this against the fear of silence, which
is why she always turned on the radio when she was alone, even the
one in the teachers' supply cabinet, it didn't matter what was playing, just so that it was not silent. She had neither dog nor cat, no pet
at all, and only the green plants that she received for her name day
or birthday symbolized the living world. To keep from going mad,
then, she needed some form of communication, even if one-sided.

There were people on the other side of the television tube; the
announcer and several reporters were speaking in turn; from the studio located in the vicinity of the high school the ether was transmit-
ting these visitors to her, too. She observed that their mouths were
moving, and even heard voices, but her mind was incapable of con-

verting the sound waves into meaningful utterances. A ceremony for All Saints' Day caught her attention: emotional music, a deep contralto voice recited the first part of a well-known Hungarian dirge, and in the process left out a word, from which Anna Lévay concluded that she would have given her a failing grade; with a sigh she made note that in the local media talent counted for nothing. Then the voice mentioned the theological explanation for death, original sin, whereupon the teacher, responding to an inner voice, switched on the video recorder to record the program. Later, she watched this program several times. The camera showed in turn various gravestones, devotional objects, and meditative images of nature, accompanied by a shaky voice that at the last sentence finally cracked:

Today is All Saints' Day. The first of November is the day of the dead. This custom was promulgated in the tenth century by the Benedictines, but its roots stretch back into the pre-Christian era. For November, the month of the scorpion, was held by many peoples in the ancient world to be the month belonging to death. Nature dies, halfway between the autumn equinox and the winter solstice. The Celts believed that on this day the laws of nature are suspended and time stands still. The barrier separating the living from the dead collapses, and the spirits of the departed leave their grave mounds and wander freely among the living. In Hungary as well, it was earlier the custom on this night to leave food on the table for the returning spirits, and in the entire Christian and Jewish world it is common to light candles. The flame, climbing toward heaven, symbolizes the soul. In the Anglo-Saxon realm the darkness is illuminated by pumpkin lanterns. According to Catholic teaching, the faithful, both living and dead, are joined in the eyes of God. This is the community of saints. Those still living represent the church militant *(ecclesia militans);* the dead in purgatory, the church suffering *(ecclesia patiens);* the glorified, the church triumphant *(ecclesia triumphans).* On All Saints' Day the church militant celebrates the church triumphant. The living faithful commemorate the glorified, those

whose saintliness was not recognized in life and who therefore
were left unrecompensed on Earth.

Anna Lévay saw herself as a spirit at the edge of the television
screen. She saw how, upon seeing the eggplants, she had sat down on
the high concrete enclosure of the neighboring grave, nervously
looked about, and grappled with problems of the meaning of existence. They must have caught her with the telephoto lens, she
thought; how fortunate that they didn't see the eggplants, even so, it
was a disgrace that one wasn't left alone even at the cemetery, one is
being observed even in mourning, it was almost like slipping a camera into your bathroom. Anyhow, she was only partly in the picture,
way over to the side, as though by accident, as if the cameraman
hadn't seen what he was shooting: In spite of the tripod the picture
shook, he probably wasn't paying attention; nonetheless, it seemed to
her that the figure sitting on the grave, even if only in profile, was
clearly recognizable even to outsiders. One should call up the program director, Anna Lévay considered, and demand compensation,
but then it occurred to her that this would only call more attention
to her. And anyhow, the cemetery was public property, they had the
right to work there, even though one could condemn what they were
doing on ethical grounds. She then went on with a sense of malicious
pleasure to see whom among her acquaintances she could make out
on the screen, but she saw only the cemetery gardener, who had been
summoned to give a demonstration of his work and was pulling a
cart with rubber tires upon which lay some downed branches, styl-
ishly draped over a coffin-shaped wooden box. The report came to an
end, and there followed some blaring music, which was unendurable.
She crouched down over the video recorder and watched the program three times more from up close. She wanted to cough, but no
sound came from her throat, and a cup of herb tea had no effect.

After his conversation with the policeman, the doctor telephoned
the insurance company. Busy. Later on, it was still busy. While he
was waiting, he leafed through the newspaper. In the local section,

which was generally filled haphazardly with news of crime, he skimmed through a report on the events at the harbor, but found nothing further of interest. A nurse brought his morning coffee. In his nervousness he dropped the container of cream, even before he had opened it. The liquid sprayed out of the paper. He liked to read the newspaper when eating or drinking, and it annoyed him that the fluid had covered some of the text. Overcome with fear of loss, he wiped the mess up with a tissue from his pocket and read the article, now somewhat smeared, once again. Then he lay on the sofa to wait until the nurse informed him that he could begin his rounds. In this excited state he began to reason things out.

While he was doing some shopping that morning, a young intellectual who lived in the area had discreetly asked to make an appointment with him, because her daughter was behaving strangely. She seemed to detect signs of perceptual abnormalities or even hallucinations, and on top of everything, the child had been bothering a universally liked teacher. It was very embarrassing; nothing like this had ever happened in the family, but now the child would simply have to be examined.

Anna Lévay, around whose head the fish had aligned themselves the previous evening and after whose departure had managed only with great difficulty to resume their normal swimming patterns, had mentioned that she had been at the harbor in the late afternoon.

He turned on the radio, where the details of the unusual fish kill were being reported on the eight o'clock news.

And then there was the mysterious automobile accident involving the teacher.

After doing his rounds, he rushed to the town hall to report on these events to the mayor and to make it clear to him that in the event that the phenomenon should turn out to threaten negative consequences, then all necessary steps must be taken to avoid any harmful effects on tourism, for even now planning was underway for the next season. On the other hand, if it turned out to be positive, then they should figure out how to turn the situation to their advantage.

Considering the confidential nature of the affair, they instructed the secretary not to admit anyone and not to put through any telephone calls. First, the mayor demanded that Anna Lévay be subjected to a thorough psychiatric examination. The doctor considered this impossible, since such examinations could be ordered only in case of a crime or other danger to the community. One could not prove that she had lured the fish out of the water, and to do so would serve no purpose, and would simply rob the town of the last vestiges of its good reputation. They agreed that the doctor would make use of his personal acquaintance with the teacher to arrange a meeting with her as soon as possible for the purpose of delving into these matters.

He then telephoned from the mayor's office. After making the call, the doctor said to the mayor that it would in fact be better if he visited her in her apartment; these intellectuals are smarter than average, and she would sense that something was afoot if merely on account of a simple case of exhaustion he were to start carrying out all kinds of personality tests on her, but in her apartment he would be able to draw conclusions from small telltale signs.

Then the mayor and the doctor had themselves driven in an official car to the harbor, which they could have reached on foot in five minutes. They noticed a large crowd gathered by the sluice gate. Journalists, television reporters, and photographers from all the print media in the country, sent here in a great hurry, were observing the dead fish, which were still floating about in the harbor, no cleansing tide having yet appeared. Farther off, on the island between the piers, members of a cleanup squad, dressed in protective suits, were busy packing the dead creatures into plastic bags, while divers were having a closer look at the ones that were floating farther from the shore. With his telephoto lens the photographer from a Budapest tabloid observed signs of external injury on the bodies of the dead fish. "My God, as if they had raced at top speed into the wall!" he cried. The cameramen, who all trained their objectives on the cadavers, confirmed this, and the mayor felt compelled to order that the fish be removed from the plastic bags and spread out in plain view. Few of them had head injuries, but on closer examination, it became clear that something had occurred to them en masse: Gills were burst, scales were rubbed off in patches the size of a man's hand, fins had bored deeply into eyes, smaller fish had had their entrails pressed out over their scaly skins like the flesh of wet lemons. Apparently, this calamity involved not chemical, but physical, means. The fish, which had voluntarily crowded into a small region of water, were simply suffocated, there was no room to breathe. It all must have been like the rush of well-informed small investors a half hour before the official announcement of a bank's insolvency.

There was plenty of speculation. A pompous hack spoke of neurotoxins. Another made the witty observation that perhaps in connection with the NATO maneuvers that were taking place nearby, the Loch Ness monster had come on an official friendship visit, and the fish had fled from the monster in panic. Someone else, more objectively, assumed the presence of an unknown large predator and asked his boss, the chief editor of a commercial broadcaster, for permission to rent a large sailboat equipped with fish-seeking sonar, or perhaps a motorboat, which, though officially prohibited on the lake, would be easy to obtain. He was granted permission, and he raced away together with his cameraman.

Considering the awkward situation—the travel agencies were already planning for the transportation needs of the coming tourist season, and accommodations and program planning, as well as the associated advertising campaigns, were in full swing—the mayor came to the conclusion that an international scandal was not precisely what the town needed most. It was only recently that foreign countries intent on undermining tourism in Hungary had engaged unscrupulous journalists in connection with the mass dying of eels; they had written negative articles and published defamatory reports in the more important journals to the effect that it was hazardous to one's health to swim in the lake, accompanied by a photograph of a rusty sign in the harbor on which was written, in three languages, "SWIMMING STRICTLY PROHIBITED." This was topped off with the observation that the Hungarian authorities had long been aware of problems involving pollution of the lake. The mayor therefore decided to explain his unexpected appearance at the harbor in a press conference.

What he really would have liked to do was to impose a gag order on the press, but that was no longer the fashion, and moreover, it would simply have increased the general curiosity. Furthermore, after the news reports, everybody already knew about what had happened. One can at best hope to use one's skill to influence the unfolding of future events, he thought, and he instructed his secretary, by cell phone, to organize a buffet in a nearby restaurant and invite a number of experts to appear. When the secretary reported that his instructions had been carried out, the mayor invited the representatives of the media to the restaurant, and there the speculation continued.

The expert on fishing arrived out of breath. He voiced the hypothesis that poachers had employed a new, universal, hitherto unknown bait, which explained the great variety of species of fish among the cadavers. Therefore, an investigation had been ordered among the anglers who had been fishing in the harbor at the time in question. Extensive information on all this had already been collected, an indictment against persons unknown had been issued; he had just come from police headquarters and could state that the authorities would begin this very day with house-to-house searches. Chemical or biological influences could be ruled out, based on observations already made, but one may rest assured that the entire catch of the angler who was now under arrest had been confiscated and carefully frozen until the samples, which had been dispatched at once to the laboratory, had been analyzed.

When the assembled company had been provided generous portions of alcoholic refreshment, the mayor cautioned his colleagues in the press to consider carefully just what news they pub-

lished so that no false alarms should be generated and no panic in-
stigated. Upon returning to his office, he telephoned, one by one,
the chief editors of all the media outlets represented, and informed
them with measured and friendly words of his concerns. He explained that he himself had been on the spot and had met with the
reporters who had been sent to cover the story, and he added that
certain elements that were less than fully interested in objective reporting were spreading negative stories. An investigation was underway that could last several days. Until then, they should refrain
from spreading any kind of panic; the moment that any new information came to light, he would inform at once his most esteemed
editor in chief, and first of all, of course, the one to whom he had
just been talking. Because of the confidential nature of the matter
he gave them the number of his private cellular phone, that is, of
one of his cellular phones. He had such a phone precisely for this
purpose, and when difficult situations arose he would leave it
turned off for days at a time or give it to his secretary to deal with.

The doctor was still with the mayor.

They drank a good deal of coffee and agreed that they would
tell no one of the inferences they had drawn from Anna Lévay's visit
to the harbor and other signs.

Upon his return to his consulting room, the doctor examined
the professional literature on hallucinations. The suspicion came
over him that the teacher may have been under the influence of
drugs. Perhaps she had taken LSD, which, in the case of a sufficiently large dose, could induce waking optical hallucinations and
indeed the feeling of omnipotence in which, for example, the person taking the drug believes himself capable of walking on water or
flying through the air. In some situations such experiences appeared
as an aftereffect, only weeks after the drug had been ingested, and
the symptoms were easily confused with psychosis. So that everything should be properly documented, he took a cassette recorder
with him in the pocket of his suit jacket. He placed a ninety-minute
cassette in it and planned that after three-quarters of an hour, or

perhaps earlier so that the clicking of the machine would not be heard, he would go into the washroom to turn over the tape. In this way the teacher's every word would be documented.

With these preparations complete, precisely at eight o'clock the doctor was standing in front of the teacher's door. He turned on the tape recorder and knocked. It had now been half an hour since Anna Lévay had lost her voice. She heard the knocking and admitted the doctor, but it was clear to him by looking at her that her thoughts were elsewhere. During the formalities of removing his coat, the following dialogue ensued in the darkness of the hallway:

"How are you?"

"*I lead in the way of righteousness, in the midst of the paths of judgment.*"

"Are you feeling well, Mrs. Lévay?"

"*This is the Lord's doing; it is marvelous in our eyes.*"

"Do you see it now, too?

"*Unto the upright there ariseth light in the darkness: he is gracious, and full of compassion, and righteous,*" she added, pointing to the problematic point on her head with her index finger three times in rapid succession.

"But Mrs. Lévay!"

"*We see not our signs: there is no more any prophet: neither is there among us any that knoweth how long. The light of the body is the eye: if therefore thine eye be single, thy whole body shall be full of light. But if thine eye be evil, thy whole body shall be full of darkness. If therefore the light that is in thee be darkness, how great is that darkness! There be many that say, Who will shew us any good? Lord, lift thou up the light of thy countenance upon us. I will walk before the LORD in the land of the living. Take therefore no thought for the morrow: for the morrow shall take thought for the things of itself. Sufficient unto the day is the evil thereof.*"

"God damn it! Can't you say something sensible?" The doctor had lost his self-control, convinced that the teacher was deliberately leading him astray. As if someone had pinched her arm to see whether she was dreaming, with a sudden jerk, Anna Lévay returned to the level of ordinary discourse and politely invited her interlocutor into the living room, without any reaction whatsoever to his angry question. He was as embarrassed by this as if he himself had been caught in a hallucination.

"Well, now, how are you Mrs. Lévay? How was your day?" he asked, figuring that the woman would speak uninterruptedly for at least five minutes, and then he would attain, according to the Gottschalk–Gleserschen method of content analysis, additional information, even if not in a quite legal manner. He was not disappointed. The teacher mentioned having bought flowers near the hospital, and that she had actually wanted to go to the hairdresser's but she had forgotten that she had run out of money. She told about her visit to the cemetery and tea at the hotel, at which point she wandered off into a long digression about how the town had appeared in bygone days, what buildings stood in place of those standing today, which businesses had been nationalized and which had been spared, who had to be bribed, how and with how much, and then launched into a nostalgic panegyric on the creampuffs at the former confectionery "Fogas"—a strange name for a confectionery, denoting as it did a fish, namely the zander—next door to the wine bar, how she had enjoyed watching the pastry chef apprentices squeezing the whipped cream from a pastry bag. She went on to mention the butcher's at market that sold normal meat from the shop entrance facing the main square and kosher meat from the one facing the little street, the photographer in one of the street stalls where her parents had one of the most important events in their life immortalized, of which in the carefully preserved archive of her inheritance perhaps the negative still existed, in which, with curly hair and a dimple on her chin, she clutched the teddy bear that she had received for her third birthday. Alas, she could no longer remember the name of the photographer. The one to whom she had brought her son, at exactly the same location, was called Gecsa. She mentioned summers past, when the grand middle class had come to the town, and writers, actors, and scientists had built villas here. Then she complained about the newly wealthy, social conditions, and the total soullessness of the profit-seekers, the pigheaded local rulers, and about the salary of teachers, which could be compared to an old woman's skirt in that it is seldom raised, and when it is, one doesn't have much to show for it.

That would have satisfied the doctor, but Anna Lévay continued and spoke about autumns perfumed with the scent of quince jelly, about winters redolent with the smell of wax candles and kerosene, Christmases with pepper cakes, blossoming spring meadows at the edge of town, festivals full of music, haystacks for lovers, gay and dissolute autumns.

As the scientific observer determined, the apartment was completely ordinary, even cheap. The most inexpensive furniture, yellowed wallpaper, a wall unit from the 1960s, no doubt paid for on the installment plan, a cracked ceiling fixture, a carpet of indeterminate color, cheap engravings on the wall, a single valuable picture, the gift of a former student who had become a painter. There was no one color that could have been said to predominate, even the various shades of green of the countless plants were randomly distributed. The entire setup was completely normal. Only the bookcase, which covered the longer wall of the room and was stuffed two deep with literature and reference books, distinguished this from the typical worker's dwelling. The doctor munched on the cottage cheese tarts, sipped his tea, and stole repeated glances at his watch, so as not to miss the moment when the cassette should be flipped over. In so doing, he failed to pay attention to the cup in his hand, which tipped, pouring hot, sugary, lemony tea all over his shoes.

"Don't move!" cried Anna Lévay to the apologetic man as she ran into the kitchen to fetch a dry cloth. The cloth, which she located under the sink, was one she had recently acquired at a sale in the department store in the market square and had not yet put into service. She kneeled at the doctor's feet and carefully wiped—so must Mary Magdalene have applied the ointment—the waterproof

leather shoes, which she herself would not have been able to purchase with a month's salary. Then she lay the cloth over the fresh
stain in the carpet.

The doctor experienced a peculiar tingling in his knees, which
Anna Lévay's head had approached within ten centimeters. Giving
the excuse that he wanted to tidy himself up, he went into the bathroom. He required noticeably less energy than usual to get up, and
since he hadn't anticipated this, he sprang up nimbly as he had not
done since the tempestuous days of his youth. He did not experience the painful grinding of cartilage that for years had been his
companion. To drown out the sound of the recorder's button, he
turned on the water. Then he turned over the cassette. After his amateur bugging device had again been set in operation, he returned to
Anna Lévay.

"In fact, Mrs. Lévay, I have come to tell you that I have been
thinking about your symptoms. It is possible that a sliver of bone
has broken off and been wandering around your system. Or perhaps there is a communication mixup among your nerve cells. Have
you perhaps recently bumped your head? Or have you had the feeling that colors have a taste or a sound, that you can see and hear
everything, or that you are being watched? Have you sensed that
you possess telepathic powers? Have you experienced feelings of
apprehension?"

Mrs. Lévay replied in the negative.

"Perhaps some blood vessels in your brain have become blocked.
We must x-ray your head and do an electroencephalogram. It is certainly nothing serious, but after all, when one has already paid for
one's health insurance, one should receive what is due. After so many
years, perhaps it is time for some repairs made under warranty, no?"
And he allowed himself a jovial laugh. "I called this morning because
a colleague of mine was present who is a specialist for such tests. He
is presently on duty. If you would like, I will take you there. We can
take the simpler recording now, and then make an appointment for
the more complicated one."

For the second time that day, Anna Lévay broke out in a cold sweat. She did not know the doctor so well that she should be entitled to special treatment, which was normally enjoyed only by the town's social elite. She suspected an ulterior motive. She was aware that her halo was not visible to most people with the naked eye, and that not everyone could detect its presence. In any case, her colleagues had not noticed it, and she assumed that such was the case with the doctor as well. She had been observing him during their conversation, and his gaze had never wandered above the level of her eyes. Although she had noticed nothing in particular about the behavior of her visitor, she had taken notice, for although she had no training in medicine, she had learned enough over the years from her colleague who directed the vocational programs at the high school to recognize that the doctor's transparent diagnostic hypotheses could easily be cause for further investigations, and perhaps her halo would be visible in an x-ray. Moreover, the doctor had a reputation for being privy to the dealings of the ambitious local politicians.

Therefore, she declined the invitation for an examination with thanks and with the excuse that she didn't want to bother the good doctor, he needed his night's rest, one should awaken him only in the most urgent situations, her symptoms were nowhere near so critical, the pills that she had been given on the previous evening had worked wonderfully, and she would undergo an examination only if it were absolutely necessary, and then preferably during working hours, for once *she* could play truant, why should it be only the students, with their faked medical excuses. In this way she excused herself.

The doctor drove his luxury automobile with the cracked bumper to the hospital. He made a beeline for the x-ray laboratory, explained that he had terrible pains, and asked his colleague to x-ray his arthritic knee. He even helped with developing the picture. But this couldn't be! He hunted up some earlier x-rays of his knee from the archive and locked himself into his office with them. If someone had told him, he would not have believed it. The most recent picture showed a completely healthy cartilaginous disk, while on the old pictures the deterioration was clearly visible, to such an extent that he had many times had a prosthesis recommended to him. Apart from his personal information, the picture could be identified only by a healed fracture, a vestige of a skiing accident years ago.

He was overcome with panic. He had never believed in the supernatural. Even now, he hesitated, except that it is not primarily a question of will. All great discoveries had been first considered supernatural until one had been able to explain them. Here, too, there must be a rational explanation, one merely had to find it. Like Pasteur, Koch, or Semmelweis one had to think logically, only logically, and with sober common sense, measure, examine, take notes, do a statistical analysis. He at once initiated such an undertaking. While the cassette in the recorder was rewinding, he drank a cup of coffee and switched on his computer. He closed the door and turned off the lights, so that the only source of light was the fluorescent shimmer of the computer monitor. Then he plugged a headset into the cassette recorder—the hospital walls were so thin that one could hear a sneeze three rooms down the hall—and began to type, a tedious affair. Normally, typing out interview transcripts was performed by his assistants. However, he had no desire to have them involved in this matter. All of them had been students at the high school or the vocational academy, and they would easily recognize the voice of Anna Lévay. He could not rely on their silence. He was not so afraid that they would repeat what they heard, but he knew that the teacher was greatly admired on account of her amiable severity and the good results achieved by her students in the university entrance examinations. If now one of her former students were to reveal to her, out of feelings of solidarity, that she had heard the teacher's voice on a tape, from certain fragments of overheard sentences Anna Lévay would be able to deduce the time that the recording had been made, and he would have lost her confidence at once, to say nothing of the possible scandal that might ensue. Needless to say, after he had transcribed the cassette, he would lock it up immediately in his private safe, so that Anna Lévay would have no proof—even if in the end she were to determine that truth was more important than hushing matters up—that she had ever called upon the neurologist for assistance. Then he could defend himself with the argument that everything had been done at the behest of the teacher, since he did not wish to burden her with a more public examination, but that could again be challenged from the perspective of professional standards and the laws of the protection of records; the devil never sleeps; those few uncompromising newspapermen could hear the grass growing, they had their people everywhere, perhaps even among the hospital staff; gossip travels quickly. If the affair should come to a head, the rabble would surely side with the poor teacher against the prosperous physician, even if he were in the right. This was a remnant of feudal society, which despised the wealthy out of simple envy, the poor will always be in the majority, and not even the vociferous contributors to the local press would turn this affair to his advantage, they already had too often attempted, on instruction from above, to hush up some dubious affair or other; they no longer had any credibility with the masses, and good lord, elections were coming up. Something like this is pointless, completely pointless, he thought, for he wished to mount the lofty political stage among his own constituency and not have to depend on the whims of political parties or circumstances beyond his control. Thus he set about to produce a transcript, even if it was a tiresome job, his fingers circling above the keyboard like birds of prey before swooping down on the keys, and he cursed the educational system in which a medical student was stuffed full of political economy and Marxist philosophy and other such nonsense, instead of preparing him for daily administrative tasks like typing.

After the first sentences a shiver ran down his spine. At the time, in his agitation he had noticed only that Anna Lévay had not given the usual responses to his questions. Now, having transcribed them, he began to form a concrete suspicion. He nervously waited for the antiquated dot-matrix printer to spew forth its paper. The apparatus was very noisy, and the shuttling back and forth of the print head along its track made him feel as if the bones of his skull were being gouged with a cookie cutter. He had finally obtained a computer of practically the latest model, but the printer would have to be cashiered at the next opportunity; he decided then and there that tomorrow he would inform the director that the noise of the machine was bothering the patients, some of whom had even suffered nervous attacks.

Finally, the paper was ejected. He saved the text, waited until the screensaver, which could be bypassed only with his password, had become activated, stood up, switched on the light, cautiously opened the door, and hurried into ward 7. That morning, the town's last rabbi, aged ninety, had been admitted on account of a mild spasm in the cerebral arteries. Because of all the excitement, the doctor had been able to spend only a little time with him. He had ordered an infusion and then hurried off to see the mayor.

It was ten o'clock. In spite of the late hour, visitors sat on both sides of the rabbi's bed. His wife and daughter were holding his hands; they would have preferred to have him transported that morning to the capital, where they knew a specialist. The family members were silent. They just looked at one another. The doctor politely sent the women home, they should get their sleep, the matter was not serious, the rabbi would be able to return home in two or three days, upon which the rabbi began to weep, the good doctor should not tell lies, he had dreamt of his parents, they were walking through a closed iron door and beckoning to him, they had gone in shortly before the Passover seder, and he had remained without, and now in his dream he said to them, "All right, then, we shall exchange places," but they answered that this was unnecessary, everything was arranged, they had opened the door wide and invited him to the evening meal, but within he had seen no table, only brightness. Then the two women began to weep, and the doctor went personally to fetch a tranquilizer, filled the syringe, squirted out the air, and pressed the contents into the infusion bag. Then he took precautions. He called the nurse to have the old man moved into the private room that had just become available, for it would certainly disturb a patient who his whole life long had been engaged in the most refined spiritual tasks to hear the other patients snoring by night and chattering by day about things that would bore him completely. He wouldn't even be able to read, since the letters in his books might provoke unpleasant comments. The nurse and the two women pushed him and his bed out of the six-patient room and into the private room. The doctor saw to it as well that the burnt-out fluorescent tube in the lamp on the night table was replaced at once, in case the patient wished to read. The women transferred the contents of the night table, and in thanks to the doctor for taking such trouble for the patient at so late an hour, they wanted to slip an envelope into his pocket, which the doctor refused: The family of a well-known local patriot shouldn't even think about such things, and in any case, all patients are equal, and this is the least that the town could do for its rabbi.

Ten minutes later, the patient was doing better. The doctor wished to be alone with him and would have liked to rid himself of the women as quickly as possible, but they did not leave until half past ten. Now the doctor sat down companionably at the rabbi's bedside, arranged the blankets, spoke about the nature of his illness, about the healing process, and mentioned, finally, as if he were merely revealing to the patient a professional secret and thus attempting to establish a relationship of equality as colleagues, that a patient of his was suffering from a religious delusion, one that could be treated only in the capital, since she could not be admitted to an institution as an inpatient, since she was, in fact, leading a normal life and was not a danger to the community, but in any case it would be good to know whether the sentences that she had been uttering in her delusional state were from the holy scriptures. "You will help me, won't you?" he said, and gently finished his speech with something of a conspiratorial smile.

The rabbi appealed to the weakness of his eyes and asked to have the texts read to him. He recognized at once Proverbs 8:20 and Psalms 118:23, and then Psalms 74:9; for the next few, he said, he was not the appropriate authority, but they were verses 22 and 23 from the sixth chapter of Matthew, an extract from the Sermon on the Mount, and then came Psalms 4:7, then from Bammidbar, better known as Numbers, respectively from the fourth book of Moses, verses 24 through 26 of the sixth chapter, Aaron's blessing, then again a psalm, the ninth verse of Psalm 116, then another extract from outside his area of expertise: Matthew 6:34. The rabbi did not ask why the doctor wished to know all of this. He asked only whether the patient considered herself a saint. He received an evasive reply. Then he asked whether the patient had a positive attitude toward life. To this as well the doctor responded evasively and added that she was more ready to criticize life than to enjoy it. The matter began to interest the rabbi, but the doctor said nothing further. The texts that had been identified so excited him that now, in possession of his annotated piece of paper, he wished to continue his work as quickly as possible.

Returning to his office, he immersed himself in the transcription of his secretly obtained texts. It now occurred to him that the teacher, although she had described the town center in detail, had failed utterly to mention the monument to industry in the market square that was pictured on all the postcards. This motif appeared even on the calendar in the doctor's office. Seen from afar, it might be considered a phallic symbol, and when one approached, the useless little cupola on top made it appear even more so. And the detailed description of how whipped cream was squeezed out? That was truly an apparently suppressed, thus socially accepted, cult of ejaculation. It's clear! Mrs. Lévay had been a widow for many years, and one has heard nothing about her in the way of sexual adventures. Obviously, he thought, what was being evidenced was sexual frustration. But then he withdrew some of the certainty from his "It's clear!" He still had no explanation for the unusual manner in which his knee had been healed and the behavior of the fishes.

Meanwhile, Anna Lévay slept the sleep of the just, a deep and dreamless sleep. The last time that Dr. János Lévay had appeared to her in her dreams was a year after his death, as he had every night before that; she had become almost sick from grief. She had brought her child into the world in a deep depression, and perhaps for that reason she had been incapable of being a good mother, perhaps for that reason her son had left her and gone to America. In those days she cursed her fate in her dreams, then sank into Dr. János Lévay's arms; they loved each other; she reviewed all the stages of their acquaintance, from meetings of the student association, to dirty cinemas, to courtyards, to the Pálvölgy Cave in the Buda hills, where with a bad conscience, which ruined everything, and filled with fear of an unwanted pregnancy, they had belonged to each other for the first time. After the marriage, when they were still living in separate dormitory rooms, they had finally been able to spend a couple of hours together in the apartment of a Budapest acquaintance while its inhabitant discreetly went for a walk. Usually, in her dreams they slept together, even after the birth of their child. Dr. Lévay had kissed her stretch marks, thought up pet names for his wife's hips, in the most perverse of scenes helped himself to a few drops of leftover milk, with the result that she felt a stirring in her loins followed by an orgasm, about which she was unashamed, since after all, the imagined delight came from her lawful husband. She made such an effort to dream about Dr. János Lévay that she once went so far as to knit him a warm sweater, so that he wouldn't freeze in the world of shades. János flitted in and out of her life like a character in a novel with two plot lines, or, better—a rather morbid idea—as if he were coming home from work. Just as Anna Lévay was about to present him with the sweater she had knitted, the child cried out from his bed, but the mother did not reach out to him to pick him up; in her dream both her hands were otherwise occupied in holding out the sweater to Dr. János Lévay, who stood with his back to her. He was just putting his arms into the sleeves when, as Mrs. Lévay conjectured, her late husband heard the crying child; he turned around and said, "You know, my love, we should separate." And he melted into the fog. From this she understood that Dr. Lévay considered her a bad mother and wanted her to focus her attentions on the child. From that hour he never again appeared in her dreams.

Until this night, in which the teacher awoke because János was calling to her. She did not see him, as in bygone days, but she heard his voice, and that quite close, as though he were standing by her bed stroking her forehead, as one would someone running a fever. She seemed to sense a fresh breath, smelling of toothpaste, escaped from lungs long since crumbled to dust, with which he said, "How are things with you, Annushka?" using the diminutive form by which only her mother and János had called her. For the teacher things were going badly. She sat up in bed, and again broke out in a cold sweat.

4

It was twelve-thirty at night. Anna Lévay slipped into her bathrobe, rummaged in the kitchen cupboard for the rum that she used
for baking, took a big gulp, and went back to bed. It was Saturday,
the first of November, and she did not have to get up early. On Sat-
urdays, she generally straightened up her apartment, doing the
washing, ironing, cooking—she took pride in keeping an orderly
household—and so the day passed. Usually, she went to bed early
and read or watched television, in order to be in shape for Sunday's
social obligations.

She spent this weekend in bed. She had no appetite, and so she
had no need to cook. She awoke at noon, drank the rest of the rum,
and prepared to return to sleep. She was curious as to whether he
would reappear; she desired it, she wished to conjure him up as
she had forty years ago, with almost tangible corporeality. Before
she closed her eyes again, she concentrated hard on her goal, but her
dream horizon remained unpopulated. In the afternoon she looked
through the photo album. Altogether, there were five photographs
of the two of them together. In one of them they appeared at a picnic near Budapest, in the second they were working side by side in
the university's obligatory volunteer summer work camp. The third

was a press photo; some fellow students had told them that their picture had appeared in the newspaper. At the May Day parade the then student János Lévay had put his arms around the shoulders of the student Anna Kuncz and kissed her on the neck, the right side, on the most sensitive spot, directly beneath her jawbone. At that, Anna Kuncz had blushed, but that could not be seen in the black-and-white photograph. They had not even noticed the photographer, who had presumably been in the grandstand, but they did not hold the matter against him (one protested against officialdom at the risk of ruining one's career); on the contrary, they searched him out at the newspaper office and asked for a print. The fourth and fifth photographs were wedding pictures, stiffly posed shots, as was then the custom: one in front of the registry, the other taken in a studio. There were also some pictures of János Lévay alone, both before and after he had become Dr. János Lévay, but those she no longer looked at, for the memory troubled her. She let the relics fall from her hand, and in her leaden weariness fell asleep.

And so Sunday passed as well, in a bedwarmed, perspiring haze. She was feeling a bit better, but that was mostly because—dutiful teacher that she was—she was concentrating on her lesson plan for the following day, and this intellectual activity distracted her.

The halo was still there. She touched it again and again, feeling its resistance, its warmth whenever her hand came within its force field. She felt nothing on her head. The halo appeared not to transmit her touch. It simply absorbed all physical effects. One should try it out in the rain, she thought; perhaps it would do instead of an umbrella, and then it suddenly dawned on her that since she had discovered the halo she had not repeated the procedure of washing her hair in the bathtub. The devil take it! Perhaps that would make it disappear whence it came; perhaps the cause of the apparition was nothing more than an inexplicably large soap bubble.

She jumped out of bed and hurried into the bathroom, plugged the drain in the tub, and turned on the hot water tap, with the result that the room was soon full of steam. She waited, looked at herself in the befogged mirror, then dumped bath salts and the usual capful of bubble bath into the steaming water, precisely on the spot where she calculated the broad stream of cold water would hit, then turned on that tap, and the water in the tub again began to surge. Anna Lévay convinced herself with a rapid hand motion that the water had reached the proper temperature, then threw off her nightgown and entered the torrent. She poured some shampoo into her hand and lathered her head decisively. She did not rinse her hair immediately, to allow the cleansing agent time to take effect. She placed a washcloth behind her head and stared at the ceiling, her head against the edge of the tub. This time, she had no desire to watch television. She had closed the door behind herself.

She glanced at the small crack in the corner above the tub, which had appeared during the time that a family from East Germany had lived in her apartment for a month each summer. Here they could meet their relatives from West Germany, for they were not permitted to travel outside of the Eastern bloc. West Germans were permitted to stay only in hotels or other official quarters, and they also paid for their East German relations. Every day, they came here to visit their relatives, who cooked for them, so that they would not have to go so often to restaurants, since when they departed they received whatever money those from the West had left over from their vacation budgets. She had never been able to determine how the crack had appeared. Her guests had maintained that it was the result of a wayward champagne cork. However, at the same time, the globe of a lamp had been destroyed as well. Anna Lévay had not understood why it had been necessary to be drinking champagne in the bathroom, nor why a second bottle should be opened when there had already been damage done by the first. If indeed it was caused by the first bottle. Had the first bang or the second hit the lamp? If it was the first, then the second hurt was caused willfully. But why? She had worried over this question for months.

For ten long years there had been no problems at all with the summer guests. There were two families of the intelligentsia, the women were a teacher and a lawyer, the men, a physician and an engineer, with two cute children altogether, of kindergarten age the first year they arrived. The West German girl grumbled about the poor quality and limited availability of food, and in a shop in the market square, and after a loud expression of disgust, had swept the cans of Russian sprats off the shelf. She did not know that such an action might be construed politically, and her parents suffered no adverse consequences only because they had Western passports. From time to time the son of the East German family would position himself strategically on the balcony and urinate on the passersby below, but the populace were used to such tricks, and since at the time nearly everyone depended on tourism for survival, such behavior was readily forgiven, particularly of a child; a mixed society vacationed here, and one could never tell whether one was dealing with Eastern or Western urination.

Aside from such minor difficulties, Anna Lévay had no problems with her summer guests. Others had much worse experiences. Many had new carpets ruined by vomit; other guests, drunk on absinthe, bled, upon being freed from the curse of maidenhead, all over their mattresses, burned cigarette holes in the sofas, tore off the wallpaper, and left the bathrooms in the condition of the Augean stables. But those who rented out their apartments in the summer complained about such atrocities, if at all, only after the end of the season, at the hairdresser, in the bars, or at work.

Since the affair of the champagne cork Anna Lévay had suspected that the now adolescent boy and girl of the family would take to fornicating in her apartment, but she had no proof. She could neither see nor hear anything, for she had turned over all of her rooms to her guests. Had she remained in the apartment, she would have received less rent, and so she moved into the garage, for she had no automobile. In those years she had spent the summer school vacation working in a hotel restaurant. There she baked cakes, strudel, and sweet crêpes, washed up, and generally helped out in the kitchen, all for twice her teacher's salary, a monthly bus pass, and three meals a day.

When there were pastries left over, as there always were, she brought them home to her guests. With satisfaction she looked on to see how they liked her art of Hungarian baking. The praise did her good. Occasionally, one or another well-to-do tourist tipped her for her delicious sweets. They sometimes wanted to deliver the tip into her hands, but she never left the kitchen. Manifesting oneself in person is not befitting a widow, she thought. Since the guests were not allowed in the kitchen, according to the rule set by the sanitation authority, it was usually the headwaiter who gave her the tip. God knows, if she had come out of the kitchen and talked to guests, she might have been seduced into marriage by a tourist who needed a good cook rather than a wife. Then she wouldn't have been able to lead the life of an intellectual, which is the life she had wanted, despite all the difficulties.

These Germans recommended her to their friends, who in turn chose this spot to reunite with their loved ones from the other half of their country, so that over the years her apartment saw many faces. However, none of her guests were as loyal as the first group. At the changeover between guests she often had only a single afternoon to get the place clean. It would even happen that one family left in the morning, and the next one came an hour later. She then asked them to leave their baggage, and she sent them out for a walk while she cleared out the mess, tidied up, and changed the sheets. To accomplish this she had to take the day off from work. Her boss understood the situation, or rather, allowance for such time off was among the terms of employment. The other kitchen workers supported her by taking over her tasks for the couple of hours, just as she did for them when it was necessary for their private business. Just as long as the work was done, that was the only thing that mattered.

The town's populace could be divided into two groups: those who obtained no income from tourism, and those who did. The latter were better off, were considered good customers in the department store, the shops, and the travel bureau, which even booked trips abroad. They received special treatment from the hairdresser, the beautician, the teachers, the officials, the police, in short, everywhere and from everyone. They were first-class citizens.

September first was the day on which Anna Lévay did her annual budget. After she had paid the last installment on her apartment, she deposited one-third of her summer income in her savings account, as reserve against an unexpected shortfall. The remaining two-thirds she spent. Since 1986 she had set aside one of the two thirds for her son, who was attending university, lived in the dormitory during the year, and in the summer worked as a waiter in a good restaurant in Budapest, where he was also provided with housing. He would not return home for a visit until the end of August, for he could not bear the summer tourist crowd. Out of the remaining third Anna Lévay bought herself one year a television set, in others, a video recorder, household appliances, books, and records; she also paid for short trips abroad, the last of which was to Italy, and she had had dresses sewn.

After German reunification, the flow of income dried up, and Anna Lévay descended from the stratum of preferred citizen to that of a lowly public employee who had seen better days. There were no longer small presents from her guests: magazines that they had finished reading; department store catalogues, which she thumbed through as though they were fashion magazines; plastic clothespins; good chocolate; cosmetics of a quality far superior to that of the home-grown variety; and other treasures of the Western world.

The crack for which the champagne cork had been responsible remained. It had happened in the last year of the family visits. Since then, they had never returned. For the first few years they sent cards at Christmas, but then these ceased, and Anna Lévay had neither the desire nor the money to have the apartment painted to get rid of the crack. Again, she speculated as to the circumstances under which the crack might have appeared; judging by the angle of incidence, whoever had opened the bottle must have been standing outside the bathroom, and then again, one did not drink champagne alone, and although since that time many years had passed and many liters of disinfecting agents had flowed down the bathtub drain, she still emerged from the foam feeling somehow unclean.

But first she dived beneath the foam to rinse off the greater part of the shampoo, and then she stood under the shower. She aimed at a point on her hairline exactly between the temples. She felt how the water enveloped her head, and waited until she figured that all the shampoo must have been washed off. Then she dried herself systematically, and with the damp washcloth wiped the mirror clean. The halo was there. It was held within a rainbow-hued soap bubble, which, however, soon dissolved in the warm flow of air from the hairdryer.

Anna Lévay did not fall into a panic. She humbly submitted to what appeared to be her fate.

She had forgotten to lay out a clean nightgown. She did not want to touch the sweat-stained one that she had worn for two days in bed. She walked naked to the wardrobe in the large room, and as she did so, the telephone rang. It was the doctor. He informed her that his personal assistant, to be precise, his secretary, who had nothing to do other than manage the files and admit the next patient, had unfortunately taken ill, and he needed someone who could replace her part time, for good pay, for a month. He had thought of her, Anna Lévay, because she knew some Latin, she would not have to ask what was written how, which was so embarrassing in front of patients, she would simply sign a nondisclosure agreement and that would be that.

At first, Anna Lévay was speechless. She could not decide whether to say yes or no. It was a great honor, she finally stammered, that the revered doctor had thought of her, but she did not believe herself suited for the job, and then there were her private students, whose sessions she would have to postpone if the times conflicted, and in any case, she was at present in no shape to make such a big decision. She quickly sidestepped the doctor's question as to her health. No, no, she said, nothing was wrong, she was just tired and was about to go to sleep, for tomorrow she had to get up early. She ended the conversation with a promise to think the matter over; the doctor could call the next day.

She felt faint. She lay down, but she could not fall asleep. She longed for darkness, even that of death or the underworld would have been welcome, if only to be released from this eternal light. She had darkened the windows completely, turned out all the lights, even closed the kitchen door so that the street lights would not shine into the room. She sat up, took a pair of battered old sunglasses from the drawer of the night table, put them on, lay down again with the hope of not having to get up until morning, and closed her eyes tightly. Yet the light from the halo penetrated her eyelids. She swept off the sunglasses and pressed the fleshiest part of her hand, the ball of her thumb, against her eyes.

She felt pain, and a dull pulsation. For a while it was completely dark, and she had just about calmed down when the pain became stronger, and a bright spot appeared between her eyes, in front, a bit above, where the third eye is depicted in mythological illustrations, a yellow-green point of a warm hue, which grew and grew, and began to pulsate, until it encompassed her entire field of vision; then came yellow circles with a green center, then green circles with a yellow center; they spread out from the location of the third eye along a curved surface, faster and faster, until she could no longer follow the individual accelerating, streaming figures; the whole had become a single heaving surface, in the middle of which within a few moments a black hole appeared, which grew and grew; then the stabilized image tipped gently downward, began to hover uncertainly, with the hole in the center, then again moved away, and then came ever closer, until millions of tiny halos hovered in her field of vision. At first she failed to understand. As a child she had played something similar with her little friends. She thought back to the time when she had pitied one of her playmates, who rubbing his eyes saw nothing within. When she finally identified the image, she immediately ceased to press; she turned herself on her stomach and crumpled up the edge of the blanket against her eyes in such a way as to keep her nose free. She was too tired to think. She slipped over the edge of unconsciousness, and fell asleep.

5

She awoke to find herself lying on her side. Her naked body was touching a cool, damp, expansive something with defined contours, whose movement followed the rhythm of her breathing. She kept still while she attempted to order her thoughts. On the previous evening she had bathed, but she had not succeeded in washing away the halo; as she nervously had gone to fetch a nightgown, the phone had rung; the doctor had offered her a position, and that was perhaps the reason that in her excited state she had gone to bed without a nightgown; she had neglected to turn down the heat, which on weekends she set during the day to the luxuriant temperature of twenty degrees; it had been warm at night, and she had thrown off the covers. Now she was lying naked, she must see how late it was. She could not make out the alarm clock on the night table. The total darkness for which she had longed the night before seemed now, finally, to have arrived. Panic gripped her. She tested her limbs one by one: wiggled her toes, bent her knees, slightly raised her hips, clenched her fists, shrugged her shoulders, nodded her head. With every movement she felt a cool, damp touch against her skin.

I am losing my mind, she thought, and made a decisive motion to sit up. Her movement was checked at the halfway point by whatever was touching her. She fell back, and the ensuing draft of air wafted the scent of fabric softener from the pillow into her nose, the cloying odor of nervous perspiration from her armpits, the oppressive stench of the bed sheets. She knew that she was in her room, but she could come up with no explanation for her condition. She ripped the two pieces of black imitation leather that during the night she had plastered to her eyes when it had become clear to her that she would not be able to sleep with the sunglasses, and opened her eyes. The light from the street lamps helped her to orient herself, but now wherever she looked, she saw greenish-black spots. With a practiced motion, this time accompanied by something cool and misty touching her, she reached for the switch to the lamp on her night table.

It took a few minutes for Anna Lévay to process the sight that presented itself. She was in a jungle. Like that of the progenitress Eve after the Fall, a hand-sized leaf covered her vulva. Delicate tendrils entwined her limbs. Near a nipple drooped a large red flower; a tangle of twigs had enveloped the halo, giving her the appearance of a fertility goddess as a naive folk artist might have painted her. The flowerpots in the room had shattered, and earth lay strewn on the carpet following the path of the plants as they had moved in putting forth their tendrils.

It had never before happened that the heat had been left at twenty degrees overnight, nor had she ever bathed so long in warm clouds of steam, but these occurrences could not explain the massive growth spurt exhibited by the houseplants.

She carefully turned onto her side and drew the clock from under the hairy, fleshy leaves of the African violet. Four o'clock. With her free arm she released her body from the buds of the Christmas cactus, pulled away the ivy tendrils that surrounded her ankle, pushed aside the palmate leaves of the exotic philodendron, which covered her entire pelvis and tickled her deep pink loins. She had not yet become aware of her position.

She became anxious when she felt the fleshy chill around her waist and back, which contrasted so with the atmosphere of her dream. She turned on the lamp and looked about her.

She jumped out of bed, ran into the kitchen, snatched up a pair of scissors, grabbed a pail from the bathroom, and began systematically to hack and prune the luxuriant vegetation. When the pail was full, she brought it into the kitchen, found a large glass bowl, filled it with the plant clippings, and put it into the microwave, which she ran on the highest setting for five minutes. Through the little window she observed with satisfaction as the bowl turned in circles, the mass of vegetation shrunk, and a brownish brew emerged. She watched as the deadly microwaves destroyed all the shoots, until the entire regime of plant extermination had drawn to a close. The neighbors could hear nothing, for the apparatus did not beep, for she had had the beeping mechanism removed, never mind that the warranty had been voided; she hated that sound, and she cringed each time she heard the dreadful screeching of her neighbors' machine through the wall. That the oven was through with its regime could be seen in that it no longer glowed. She removed the bowl, poured the liquid into the sink, the solid mass into another pail, placed the next portion in the microwave, turned it on, and waited. Then she went into the bedroom, filled the pail again, and continued the process until the very last stem had vanished. Finally, she placed the remaining solid mass, now shrunk to a bowlful, once again into the microwave, this time for ten minutes.

She carefully washed the scissors and the microwave oven. After she had poured off the last of the liquid, she poured an entire bottle of hydrochloric acid down the drain; then she shook the contents of the bowl into the toilet and pulled the chain. Finally, she placed the earth from the broken flowerpots into the empty pail and thinned it out in the bathroom with water until it turned into mud, which she then poured into the toilet together with the hot water she had used to rinse out the broken flowerpots. She effaced the last crumbs of dirt with the vacuum cleaner. The content of the vacuum cleaner bag was also thinned into mud and poured down the drain. The bag itself she burned in the bathtub and ran a stream of water over the ashes until they had all flowed away. Since she had no more hydrochloric acid, she poured a pound of salt into the toilet, so that the building's sewer, like the earth of Carthage in bygone years, would become unfruitful.

Anna Lévay felt certain that salt would do instead of hydrochloric acid, but for safety's sake, as an extra measure, she also poured down a half bottle of disinfectant. With the other half she washed out the bathtub drain, then washed her hands three times with antiseptic soap.

The philodendron, at the time a tiny shoot, had been stolen by Dr. Lévay from the palm house at the Budapest zoological park and gardens, where the couple had gone for a stroll shortly after the awarding of his diploma, since in the early afternoon on a weekday one could find numerous private corners for an embrace. The noisy groups of kindergarten children from the forenoon were already in their beds, and the pensioners were taking their afternoon naps, too. Dr. Lévay had noticed the shoot, and in an unobserved moment had cut it off with a scalpel that he had taken from the clinic for the purpose of cutting a piece of linoleum to cover the cold tile floor of his dormitory room. The operation having been successfully performed, he wrapped the booty in his handkerchief, quickly loosened his belt, hid the handkerchief in his underwear, and thereby spirited the cutting away. In the streetcar he sat so carefully, on account of the contents and location of the handkerchief, that they both laughed. In the dormitory, Anna Kuncz at once wrapped the purloined cutting in damp rags and placed it on the radiator until suitable potting soil could be obtained, and when it was transplanted, it put forth roots, and since then she had lovingly cared for it.

When she moved into her current apartment she had personally carried the prized flowerpot up the stairs. Even at that time it was already taking up a fourth of her bedroom; her guests were amazed, and Anna Lévay told everyone its story. Now she had destroyed it in a sudden rage and with particular ferociousness, and only because it had innocently touched her private parts. And it had been a gift from her husband. The soul does not vanish, it only changes form, perhaps he whose voice she had so recently heard in her dream could appear to her in no other way, which is why she had hesitated before beginning her rampage. But her fright at the supernatural had triumphed.

By six-thirty she had finished with her cleaning.

She was eating her accustomed bread with rosehip jam when the telephone rang. It rang a long time. She was unused to receiving telephone calls at such an early hour, and therefore, she decided not to answer. The caller finally gave up, but two minutes later the phone rang again. It had been ringing for about fifteen minutes when Anna Lévay, reasoning, "It must be very important if the caller is so insistent," lifted the receiver.

It was the doctor. He apologized for the early disturbance, asked whether the teacher had already been awake, and after a number of formulaic politenesses and questions about her precious health arrived at his earlier request: Would she be interested in helping out in his practice, for his secretary was ill? He knew very well that Mrs. Lévay would be one hundred percent capable of doing the work, she knew some Latin, one would not have to spell out each diagnosis, she wrote quickly, and was a careful reader, for two months she would be the ideal medical assistant, one did not really need a specialized education, even high school graduates did it as a stopgap before they began at university; of course, she would not be working without compensation, in two four-hour shifts per week she would earn as much as a full-time teacher. She could start this very afternoon, she would have to work Mondays and Thursdays, in the afternoon from four until eight, a uniform would be provided, as well as laundry and door-to-door transportation, and should she have any problems with her health, as a quasi-medical employee she would have the right to receive priority for all medical treatment, and special treatment as well, that is how it was. Anna Lévay made no mention of their previous conversation; this time, too, she said neither yes nor no; she merely stammered and asked for time to

think about it. "You are an angel, Mrs. Lévay! I will telephone you
later this morning at school." The doctor, certain of a positive reply,
quickly said goodbye and rang off.

Had the doctor's offer come by chance, or was it a challenge?
Anna Lévay chewed it over for a long time. If the doctor suspected or
knew something, he was trying to tell her that he could blackmail her
if he so chose. He could let it be known, for example, that she was in
treatment with him, though not for neurological problems. One or
two malicious remarks spread among the local elite, and as a result of
base suspicions, she would experience, despite her professional com-
petence, a reduction in the number of her private pupils, and she
would be treated badly by the authorities. From this point of view
the situation was particularly acute, since she would soon be living
on her pension. That is just what I need, she thought. One should
not get into an argument with the doctor and the town worthies,
even if their popularity in the polls was tending to zero. Recently,
while shopping, she had run into some pollsters, commissioned by
the town—well paid, of course—who were inquiring into public
opinion, and although the questioners were students from elsewhere,
she declined to answer, since she trusted neither the claim that she
was part of a random sample nor the promise of anonymity. The
practices of the previous political system remained deeply ingrained.
Who knew whether there was a hidden camera nearby by which one
would be identified. Other citizens, however, cleansed by the new
political waters, bared their anonymous souls, and soon the result appeared in the newspaper that the doctor's popularity was at an all-
time low. Nonetheless, he had great influence in the town, and he
constantly thirsted for more. Perhaps he really needed someone to
work for him, but it was equally likely that he was running an experiment. To accept the offer is dangerous, she thought, but even more
dangerous to turn it down, but on the other hand, I am currently so
financially strapped that the increased income would come in quite
handy. As she continued to think over the matter, it occurred to her
that the doctor could actually prove nothing. It was almost certain

that he could not see the halo, and he could not make a further examination of her without her consent. Partly from anxiety, resulting from being to some extent at the doctor's mercy, partly on account of the financial advantage, she decided to accept the offer.

She lay down again. At around seven-thirty she telephoned the school and reported that she was ill. Marika, the secretary, asked with sincere concern whether it was something serious, but Anna Lévay mollified her, she was just feeling weak, could hardly stand up, such were the fruits of old age, but in the afternoon she would assuredly go to the doctor, who would prescribe something for her that would keep her going a while longer. Marika wished her a speedy recovery and promised that she would see to it at once that the appropriate vice principal arranged for a replacement. Anna Lévay then opened a jar of stewed pears and ate them in bed. She waited for the doctor's call. Presumably, he would try to reach her at school. That afternoon she planned to ask him to stop calling her at school, the people there would think heaven knows what if she was constantly being called by neurologists and psychiatrists, even if the calls were of a personal nature. She could have called the hospital to apprise the doctor of the changed circumstances, but she decided against such a course. First of all, it would give him something to think about when he was told that she had called in sick, and furthermore, she wanted to know how important this entire business was to him. The call came at ten-thirty. The doctor expressed his concern over the state of Anna Lévay's health, but to his question she replied that there was no cause for concern, she had simply wished to loaf a bit, even she was entitled to a bit of laziness, so many of her colleagues were absent on the flimsiest of pretexts. After she had accepted the job, they agreed that on the first day she would start about twenty minutes earlier than otherwise, so that she could learn a bit about the filing system and get to know her way around. He would pick her up from her home at three-thirty.

After replacing the receiver, Anna Lévay called the school. Marika reported at once that only five minutes ago the doctor had called, wanting to speak to her, it must be something quite important, his voice had sounded so nervous when he had been told that he would be unable to speak with her. Anna Lévay reassured her, the doctor was simply overly conscientious, on Friday she had felt positively unwell, she had felt faint, she had had a headache, and had called on him—they had known each other a long time, he and her husband had studied together—an x-ray had even been taken, he probably wanted to tell her that a brain tumor had been detected, but then again, he would be in no hurry to deliver such news: One never gains popularity as the bearer of ill tidings, and even if indeed the diagnosis turned out to be correct, she would never consent to an operation, she had lived long enough. One shouldn't paint the worst possible picture, replied Marika in an effort to parry this pessimistic view; she must enjoy the years of her retirement, take it easy, travel, pursue her hobbies, she could have a full and enjoyable life for a good thirty more years, if the heavenly powers willed it, she simply shouldn't convince herself of something that was most likely untrue to begin with, one has heard of people who convinced themselves that they had some disease and then actually contracted it. Anna Lévay replied that she had called to make sure that someone would make use of her prepaid lunch.

Shortly before he began his rounds, the doctor, who had spent the entire weekend with his family, was informed that on the previous evening the rabbi had died suddenly. Before his death, the cause of which could not have been his cerebral hypertension, he had spoken completely coherently, had called for the doctor, had continually spoken the word "patient" and mentioned the number thirty-six. The doctor scolded the nurse for not having called him. She apologized, one had not wanted to bother the doctor, one had not known that the patient was so important to the doctor. After making his rounds quickly and superficially and completing his administrative duties, the doctor hurried to the town hall to discuss matters with the mayor.

Meanwhile, the press continued to report on the strange occurrences in the harbor. The angler who had taken the large number of fish had been released, since the office of the public prosecutor was unable to prove that he had gained possession of his catch by illegal means. The fishermen's association also called off their proceedings, since nothing in their statutes forbade the gathering of fish that had thrown themselves onto the shore in suicidal frenzy. All that there was in the statutes on the subject of dead fish was that those found in the water were to be disposed of by the fishing industry, while those that had drifted to shore were under the purview of the town. From that point of view, the angler had actually done the municipality a favor by carrying out the task of disposal on its behalf. Of course, the dead fish should have been destroyed by the offices responsible for such matters, but there was no prohibition against taking home and eating what had not yet been classified as hazardous waste. The physician in charge of public health had, in fact, designated the fish to be suitable for human consumption, though they were not allowed to be sold, since the fishing industry possessed the exclusive right to the commercial catching and selling of fish. A person gathering such fish would have committed an infraction of the rules only through publicly selling the fish or providing them to a catering service. And there the matter ended.

Immediately after the affair had become known, the local reporters were informed that the moment that their reporting on the incident went against the interests of the town, they would have to do without their official weekly press briefing as well as any cooperation with the town's public information office, not to mention additional boycotts of an undisclosed nature. The journalists who seemed now unable to restrain themselves were not those who had been present at the press briefings. Their names had been carefully noted. There were also lists relating to who had made telephone inquiries into the matter. All the leading editors among the various media were once more informed that the municipal offices would readily provide information the moment anything that was truly newsworthy became available. Respected ladies and gentlemen of the news media, please just be patient and refrain from harming the town and the tourist industry with half-truths. And finally, it is a matter of regional, indeed national, interest that the approaching season not suffer from artificially created problems, one knows only well enough how much tax revenue would be lost to the treasury if things were to go badly. Matters would become worse for the populace, and then the newspapers would have to cut back on staff, which would serve no one's advantage, don't you agree? And then legal proceedings would be initiated against the offending news organ itself.

The majority of the papers did not take these warnings too seriously. They appealed to their right to freedom of information and strategically placed their informants, who provided news of an increasingly colorful and delicate nature. One tabloid did not hesitate, in its lead article with the headline "Let the cadavers speak!" to suggest that if one could find no better explanation, then one should take a cue from medieval superstition and make all the inhabitants of the town proceed to the harbor. As they filed by the dead fish, surely the truth would come out. The doctor shivered at this idea. The mayor, himself a member of a formerly liberal party that had miraculously—or rather from the will to power—transformed itself into one of the most conservative in the country, allowed an oath to escape his lips against the unfettered freedom of the press, called the author of the article a stupid pig, immediately instructed his secretary to strike the name of the troublesome journalist from the invitation lists for the three-day Pentecost banquet at the start of the season, the summer folk festival, and other official events. But first, she should contact the party chief so the two of them could discuss the matter; this was no longer simply a local news event, it had already become a political question. But the party chief was neither at home nor reachable on his cell phone.

The doctor took a small pill from his briefcase and offered it to the mayor with a glass of water. "Go on, take it, or you'll have a stroke!" Then he added that there was a way that the entire affair could perhaps be turned to the benefit of the town, and they would be able to profit greatly. But first they should take a deep breath or two, or as many as they needed to calm down.

Although it was scarcely five hundred meters away, the doctor and mayor drove to the hotel where after her visit to the cemetery Anna Lévay had eaten the fruit salad decorated with pineapple. Over lunch they developed a strategy and took a solemn vow of secrecy.

While they were eating their soup, the doctor's cell phone rang. It was the hospital pathologist, who said that he could determine no natural explanation for the rabbi's death. The blockage of the cerebral arteries had disappeared, and no traces of organic illness could be found. The lab results also showed no pathology. "Then report it as old age," suggested the doctor, and ended the conversation.

After lunch, they returned to the mayor's office, instructed the secretary not to put through any calls, and set to work. At three-fifteen they received from the notary at the county seat a facsimile copy of a license to register a corporation, which also served as a license to conduct a business. The newly founded limited liability corporation, hereinafter "the Company," the proprietors of which, for the purposes of obfuscation, were distant relatives of the mayor and doctor who were living abroad and which was managed by two local individuals beholden to the mayor, consisted of several companies and among other things was licensed to carry out environmental rehabilitation and harbor basin upkeep as well as physiotherapy for those with neurological disorders and physical disabilities. The seed capital for the establishment of the Company was provided by the municipal treasury, since the Company was in operation for the purpose of extending the tourist season to the benefit of the town; it would be tax-exempt until it was entered in the registry of businesses, at which time the loan was to be repaid to the town, so that the bloodhounds in the press wouldn't get too much wind of what was going on.

The draft contract had been completed by three o'clock that afternoon, according to which the water-management firm responsible for the harbor, at the request of the mayor and due to the unusual situation, granted the Company the exclusive right to make use of everything that came out of the harbor in accord with the relevant environmental laws and to have it analyzed by a laboratory, and they took upon themselves the obligation to grant the Company the right to remove without replacement, at its own cost, everything coming out of the harbor or its surroundings, that is, within a radius of three kilometers. It was not clear why this provision was needed, but since the water-management firm could see no disadvantage, they went along with it. The contract was ready for the director of the harbor basin maintenance company's signature, and he signed it.

Five minutes before three-thirty the doctor looked nervously at the clock and hurried off with a promise that he would be available tomorrow at the usual time for further discussions. As arranged, he showed up in front of Anna Lévay's building. Everything went like clockwork. The teacher carefully washed her hands, then calmly took her place at the desk across from the doctor, as if she had been doing such work all her life, with her back to the screen behind which the patients undressed, checking one after the other whether the pens were working and whether the ink pads were properly damp.

Eighteen patients appeared that day. The doctor was satisfied with Anna Lévay's work. He had her total the fees that the patients had paid for "extra" services beyond what was provided by the national health insurance, and out of this he paid her, giving her more than the sum on which they had agreed. He placed the money in an envelope, and while Anna Lévay was washing her hands, wrote out for her, as one would for a truant, a medical excuse for her absence from school. He then drove his new assistant home, accompanied her to the staircase, complained about the lack of public security, waited until she had turned on the light, wished her a good evening, and drove home.

That evening, he was unusually rude to his family. He rebuked the cook because he found his dinner too rich. He observed how his wife carefully transported each bit of food from one side of her mouth to the other, tasted it, and then chewed it. The word *ruminate* came into his mind. Then in a sudden fit of temper he called his wife a fat cow, a domestic animal that can neither be enjoyed in cheerfulness nor long endured, a foul ape that did nothing but eat, drink, and defecate. She threw down her silverware, left her chop untouched on her plate, and withdrew to the bedroom to cry her heart out and to wait until the stormy quarrel turned into even stormier sex. But it did not happen.

The doctor spent the night on the sofa. He did not undress, nor did he bathe; a leaden weariness oppressed him, yet he could not sleep. He thought over the events of the day and about the death of the rabbi. He knew that the rabbi's words had been meant for him, but he could not find the connection between his patient and the number thirty-six.

At eight-thirty, as Anna Lévay was eating her supper of spaghetti with cheese and sour cream, the doorbell rang. The reasons for hesitation that would be appropriate in a city were not sufficient in her case—the electricity, cable television, and gas bills had been paid, so there was nothing to fear—and so she went at once to the door and opened it wide. On the doorstep stood members of a sect who were going from door to door selling religious pamphlets. She could not explain why it was always she who was thus accosted, whether on the street, in the metro, in the train, or in the pedestrian passage. The suspicion that it lay in her simple appearance allowed her to dismiss promptly every attempt at conversion by such modern missionaries.

This time it was the same story: She opened the door and saw the visitors, and the moment one of them opened his mouth to say something, she trumped him at once: "I know thy works, that thou art neither cold nor hot: I would thou wert cold or hot." Then the

other one was about to speak, but the teacher preempted him as
well: "Wisdom is before him that hath understanding; but the eyes
of a fool are in the ends of the earth." Then the first one took a
chance and opened the book that he had brought and began to read
from it with upraised voice. But she replied triumphantly, "The legs
of the lame are not equal: so is a parable in the mouth of fools," and
slammed the door. Her blood pressure soared, her limbs shook,
weakness overcame her. In the bathroom she let cold water run over
her wrists, then drank several glasses of tap water in the kitchen,
stumbled into the living room, and searched, trusting to luck, for
the verses that she had quoted, but in vain. She knew not that they
were the sixteenth verse in the third chapter of Revelation, the
twenty-fourth verse in the seventeenth chapter of Proverbs, and
the seventh verse from the twenty-sixth chapter of that same book.
She was quite certain that the visitors had not seen the halo. As she
thought further about the matter, she came to the conclusion that
either her halo did not exist, or those religious men were frauds. She
recalled their untrimmed fingernails, the clothes reeking of cigarette
smoke, their awkward attempts at speech, and based on these observations, she favored the latter hypothesis, and therefore decided
to put an ordained priest to the test in the nearest future. With this
thought, she lay down in her room, now almost entirely freed of
plant life, read until ten-thirty, and then fell asleep.

    The next morning she awoke refreshed. She stretched and
thought over a strategy for maintaining her dignity. What she came
up with seemed to her so brilliant that for sheer joy she allowed herself a double portion of tea and bread with rosehip jam. She did not
even curse when she got some of it on her sweater, but simply pulled
on a new one: Bordeaux red with almost provocatively translucent
crochet work. She then set out for school, singing softly as she went.

6

It was in a rumpled state that the doctor left for work. His wife had locked herself in the bedroom, and he saw no point in hammering against the door or shouting through it, nor had he any desire to prepare himself breakfast. He had not even the energy to drive his car, so he ordered a taxi.

The gatekeeper at the hospital recognized him only when the taxi had drawn very close. The doctor had himself driven inside the gates, right up to the entrance to the neurological unit. He instructed the head nurse on duty to bring him coffee, "a bucketful, and so strong that the spoon stands up in it." He showered in the employees' washroom, put on a clean lab coat, and on returning to his office, drank his coffee as he read over the report of the night-duty staff, busied himself with this and that, and prepared for grand rounds. Later—he still had plenty of time, and in any case, they all accommodated themselves to his wishes—he ordered in a ham and cheese sandwich, which he ate as he looked through the mail.

It was not the regional but the national newspaper in which he found the death notice. There was also a lengthy obituary. With astonishment the doctor read what an important man the rabbi had been. At the end of the article the following was written: "He was truly a *Lamed-Vav,* one of the thirty-six hidden righteous men." That brought to his mind one of his girlfriends from student days, who, conscious of her heritage, to spite the political system, and to annoy her parents or perhaps because one was not allowed to study religious subjects, had learned Hebrew. He had frequently visited the young woman, for she lived alone, with only an elderly aunt to look in on her twice a week at appointed times. Her parents were government officials who served the regime with lengthy foreign assignments somewhere at the other end of the Socialist empire. The girl and the medical student would always sit together in the then fashionable deep puffy chair, Éva on his lap, snuggling together along the lines of the Hebrew letter *he,* the book opened in front of them on the coffee table. The moment he entered he was consumed by the desire to satisfy his lust, but first he would have to spend hours testing her on her letters and vocabulary, until he, too, knew it all by heart. Of course! The Hebrew letters have numerical values. He sat down at once at his computer, logged onto the Internet, and using his favorite search engine found within a matter of minutes the Hebrew alphabet. The letter *lamed* has the value thirty, and *vav,* the value six. So there was thirty-six, and the letters L V for lamed vav.

János Lévay had always been an outsider. A great future had been predicted for him. It was thought that he would become a brilliant surgeon, having gained quite a reputation in his first year of residency for his skill, honesty, and, most important, the capacity to empathize. L V, Lévay, Levi, Levite. So that was what was afoot. He had never mentioned the name to the rabbi. The synagogue was open on a regular basis only in summers, and even then there was not always the minyan of ten men, for there were only seven Jews who lived in the town. And Anna Lévay was known as a confirmed atheist. Curiouser and curiouser!

After school, the teacher again went walking in town. She looked in the shop windows in the first floor of the office block that had been built behind the former bank building. She was curious to see what was on display in the book store located there. There could be no question of her buying anything. Not only because she couldn't afford it, but because the tastes of the readers who frequented the shop were anathema to her. They bought nothing but trashy novels and the basest self-help books; she had often overheard outrageously pretentious conversations displaying vast ignorance from behind the bookshelves. She much preferred the little smoke-filled antiquarian bookseller off to one side of the "House of Lords," and she enjoyed conversations with the proprietor of that establishment.

When she had seen enough, she walked with resolute steps in the direction of the church. She had never been inside this church and was uncertain how one should behave. Of course, she had some experience from her cultural–historical investigations, but now she was seeking something more. She did not even know, for example, which was the men's side, and which the women's. Oh, well, if she simply strolled about as if she were at an art gallery, nothing could be taken amiss.

The sky was overcast, and so the light that came through the stained-glass windows was meager, and the lamps had not been turned on for reasons of economy. For a few moments, Anna Lévay's optic nerves recorded nothing as she advanced from the light into the interior dimness. She noticed as she took her first steps in the direction of the nave that water droplets were falling on her face, hands, and clothes, but it appeared to be only some dampness, of little significance, and so she decided to ignore it.

She sat on the very last bench, almost under the gallery. She was alone. She sat quietly for about half an hour and thought about the winter a year from now, when she would already have retired and would have no one to talk to. Would she then take up passing the time in church with the other old women? Or would she spend her days in the library, in the warm room where one could read the papers, and turn off the heat in her apartment to save on her heating bill? She finally stood up, for she had become cold with sitting, threw some change in the poor box, and left the sanctuary. At the exit was a spot where the feet of the faithful treading over the centuries had worn a depression in the stone floor. Here the rainwater had collected into a puddle, into the center of which Anna Lévay now stepped. The water entered her not quite waterproof shoes, and was warmed as it seeped into the material, being finally absorbed by the insole, with the effect that she felt as though she were walking on a damp cloud.

She did not dare to walk to the harbor. She walked by the former café Balaton, now owned by Italians and renamed Bella Italia, and by the old Kö store, with its large venerable showrooms where in her first years as a teacher she had bought her dresses, gloves, and umbrellas, and which had now been transformed into tiny shops, each no larger than a mousehole. She stumbled over one of the aluminum structures designed to keep the automobile traffic off the pedestrian walkway. She was kept from falling by a former student, who had himself become a teacher, but was now selling popcorn, newspapers, and chocolate on the street corner. Alas, for what he has come to, thought Anna Lévay, and after thanking him, she asked why he was not working in his chosen profession. He tersely replied that he had no talent as a hunger artist. With a forced smile she proceeded on her way, passing the former café Hangulat, now reborn and redecorated as the Shanghai teahouse, and proceeding between the children's library, rebuilt after an earthquake, and the once life-threatening, but finally after much wrangling rebuilt, bright blue railroad overpass that connected the harbor and the park.

She turned left again at the next corner, hurried past the café that had been built on the site of the former market stalls, past the restaurant and the travel bureau with its clock tower, and then over the bridge as fast as she could go. To her right was an enclosed market encased in red steel beams and glass walls. She entered through the side door with the intention of purchasing some quince paste with walnuts from the old man whose stand was at the other end of the long hall, near the front entrance. She had walked halfway to her goal when she suddenly slipped on the unwisely chosen ceramic tiles. Her leg slipped to the side as though she were attempting to perform a difficult balletic maneuver. There was a loud thud as her more than one hundred kilogram body hit the floor. Immediately, purple bruises appeared as burst veins poured their contents into her tissues. But Anna Lévay felt only a light weakness, a gentle tingling. An inattentive shopper tripped over the outstretched leg, which was unnaturally extended and lay immobile with its foot bent backwards, the ankle twisted. At once, Anna Lévay was surrounded by stand owners and marketwomen, some former students of hers among them. The accident, the like of which had now happened frequently, had attracted the attention of half the personnel of a nearby meat stand. A well-built butcher's apprentice, who liked to compare his craft with that of a surgeon, risked the observation, "I can see that she has dislocated the joint in her leg." Those present were vying for volume in a discussion of whether to call an ambulance, and a vegetable dealer—a former policeman—offered, with a completely uncharacteristic selflessness, to call the ambulance on his cell phone, which did not exactly qualify as a saintly deed, since calls to the ambulance service are free. Helping hands extended themselves, and Anna Lévay arose.

Mind had triumphed over matter.

She grasped the edge of a table on which apples lay piled; in her zeal, she almost pierced the skin of an apple with her fingernails, but she pulled her hand away in time. She felt no pain as she carefully tried out her limbs, swinging gently the leg that had gone awry, which resulted in a faint but audible cracking sound, like the joint of a chicken leg breaking. Then she took two hesitant steps, accepted someone's offer to brush off her coat, and left the circle of unbelievers with many protestations of thanks. One of the marketwomen followed her crying, "Are you really all right, Mrs. Lévay?" For she believed that the teacher was shamming and that she really was in great pain. Many offered to give her a lift home. But during this inquiry, Anna Lévay simply spread out her coattails, smoothed her dress, and indicated with a wave that everything about her body was in good working order. Then she gave thanks for the offer of transportation, but declined it. To demonstrate that she was all right, on her way to the table with the quince paste she bought a pound of medlars, the same quantity of lentils, and a horseradish.

When she had packed everything away, she opened the heavy glass door and walked to the corner of Vilma Street, past the shops. She could have turned to the left and proceeded along the four-lane highway, past the gas station and the hospital, her usual way home, but she preferred to stroll along the small, quiet parallel streets. Something was different today. She long pondered what it might be, and only when she was at home, unpacking the lentils, horse-radish, medlars, and quince from her shopping bag, did it occur to her: The barking of dogs that usually issued from behind almost every fence had been absent.

At exactly the moment that Anna Lévay was closing the door to her dwelling behind her, the parish priest was entering his church, and he noticed that the font for holy water was empty.

Until he saw that it was a sign to be taken as a wonder, he had assumed that as usual, a tramp had been there to let his dog drink from the font. The first tramp that he thought of had once been a forester and had accidentally—or so they said—shot a timber thief, for which he had been put in prison, where he had gone mad. Since then, he had roamed about the area and was known for pinching the nuns who served the food in the soup kitchen where he always took his lunch. But then it occurred to the priest that "Old Poacher" had died the previous year; indeed, he had buried him himself, and moreover, the man had not owned a dog.

His suspicion then turned to the other well-known tramp about town. Ah, yes, he thought, it would have been nothing new for him, for this homeless man had frequently been asked not to dese-crate the sanctuary. The tramp, however, always countered that the municipal fountain was turned off in autumn, and there was no other water available for his dog. He could not allow his canine companion to drink from the lake, which would probably make him sick, and furthermore, he knew of nothing in Scripture that forbade the use of holy water for the succor of innocent creatures.

In the end, he was asked to ring at the parish house when his dog again was taken by thirst within the confines of the city center, and the housekeeper would be happy to give the animal to drink. The priest thought about all this as he poured new water into the font. But when he cast his eyes down, he noticed the footprints.

These were no usual footprints. Someone must have been walking barefoot on the pavement. Water, puffed up like quicksilver, stood in the tracks that led into the church garden and then to the street. The last imprint—that of a right foot—pointed in the direction of the monument to industry in the market square. At a loss, the priest returned to the church and stood, absorbed in thought, at the entrance, like a detective attempting to reconstruct the scene of a crime. The crown of light, soldered together from brass plate and wire, on the statue of the Virgin in the side altar across from the door shone with an unusual glow. At once, the priest hurried closer. He knew that the cleaning woman could not have polished it, for today was not her day. The flowers in the vase below the altar, which had been on the point of decay, were standing erect and glowing as if illumined by a strange and vivid light from a hidden source within a few of the brass stars at the front of the crown. The priest managed to touch one of the stars by standing on an old prie-dieu. Suddenly, a note emanated from the highest register of the organ. There being no access from the sanctuary to the organ loft, he hurried out and fetched the key to the loft from the parish house, and as he attempted to turn the key in the outside wooden door next to the main entrance, he did not even notice the loud, "Good morning, Father," of a passing parishioner, even when it was repeated. When he finally succeeded in opening the lock, he hurled himself up the winding stairs, but then paused halfway, for though driven by curiosity, he feared he might be about to become the victim of a prank. In summer, in the concert season, the absent-minded organist had once been locked in while he was practicing by a well-meaning passersby who saw that someone had accidentally left the key in the lock; and so they had conscientiously left the key with the housekeeper, who had spent the entire morning in the kitchen. The priest himself had been officiating at a funeral, and the unfortunate musician had called and called in vain, pulling out all the stops and pressing all the keys and pedals to call attention to his plight, but all his noise was swallowed up by the outside traffic; he played the *Miserere* fortissimo to no effect. Those who did hear, laypersons all, did not recognize the melody and thereby unravel its implicit cry for help. Since the organist was not so fortunate as to have had a cell phone with him, he sat in the choir the whole day with neither food nor drink, until the worshipers arriving for vespers discovered him and released him from his bonds.

To avoid the risk of being locked in, the priest returned to the bottom of the staircase, removed the key, closed the door behind him, and slowly, carefully, made his way aloft. Not that he feared that someone was hiding in the organ loft with evil intent. His faith enabled him to accept supernatural manifestations, but he was a rational being, and a man—even a priest—meets such events only occasionally, and so he sought a logical explanation, and wished to see whether his ear had deceived him when he had believed to have detected in the sound of the organ something not of this world. The organ had been fitted out with an electric bellows, and therefore should have emitted an even tone, not such a soft, hollow sound that ebbed away, like that of a singer who squeezes the last bit of air through flagging vocal cords.

The organ loft was empty. The organ was closed, and the bench was covered in a thin layer of dust. The reverend father walked to the balustrade and cast his eye over the nave. The glow on the statue of the Virgin could still be seen. From above, one could also see that the wet footprints at the entrance shimmered with all the colors of the rainbow. Shining water droplets lay like pearls on the long wine-dark carpet and plunged the last seat in the furthest row, the bookrest, the prie-dieu, and the arm of the bench into an iridescent mysterium.

The priest rushed down the staircase as quickly as he could, closed the door behind him, ran to his study, and delved into such books as he possessed that dealt with such matters. He had no desire to inform his ecclesiastical superiors before he had put his own thoughts in order. Alas, he could not inquire of every resident of the town as to who had seen someone, someone with a size thirty-seven foot, walk barefoot through the church on the afternoon of November the fourth between two and three in the afternoon.

The doorbell rang. A parishioner asked him to officiate at a relative's funeral. As they discussed the details, a tour group of Western pensioners entered the church, for here, in contrast to a museum, one could enter without paying an entry fee. Here, one could rest, after the exertions of sightseeing in the town, where it was not so cold, and one could sit without having to order something, a cup of tea at least, as would be necessary in a café. The blades of grass and grains of sand that fell from their shoes testified to the fact that they had come directly from the park in front of the railway station. Thirty-six pairs of muddy shoes walked over the shining quicksilver rainbow of footprints. The profane beams of eighteen flashbulbs snuffed out the light of the crown of stars.

After the bereaved man had left, the priest went once again into the church. He was certain of what he had seen, and he wished to secure the footprints and lock the side door, which had been his intention, though he had forgotten to do so. He found nothing remaining of the apparition; only one small droplet still shimmered on the arm of the bench, until he, doubting Thomas, touched it, and the drop evaporated. Then he hurried to the telephone and made an appointment with his good friend the neurologist to be examined for hallucinations brought on by overwork. He described what had transpired in considerable detail and remarked that in such cases it was better to treat the symptoms as soon as they appeared, before matters took a sharp turn for the worse.

Having just returned home, Anna Lévay turned up the heat to twenty degrees, placed her shopping bag on the kitchen table, took off her shoes, and removed the felt inserts, which she had cut with her own hands for each pair of shoes that she possessed, incredible, what thin soles the shoe industry produced, just so that they would wear out the sooner; such is our consumer society, but just on account of that one shouldn't be required to have one's feet freeze, she liked to say. She laid the inserts on the radiator to dry, rinsed the lentils thoroughly, and put them on the stove to simmer. Then she scrubbed the horseradish, grated it, rinsed the grater, and prepared the pastry dough. When it was done, she placed the buttery mass in the refrigerator for half an hour while she took out the pastry board she had inherited from her mother, floured it, stirred the lentils, made a roux, stirred it into the soup, waited until the pot had boiled, and then turned off the gas. She rolled the chilled pastry out thin, cut out circles with a biscuit cutter for want of the proper implement, cut out circles with a smaller biscuit cutter from half of the pieces of dough, and then put the circles and rings on a baking sheet lined with parchment paper, which she shoved into the preheated oven. Linzer cookies had been the late Dr. Lévay's favorite. She had begun to hunger for them while she was at the cemetery. She recalled a date with him in the university cafeteria, where they had drunk cocoa with whipped cream and blown the powdered sugar from the cookies into each other's faces.

While the cookies were baking, she ate a bowl of lentil soup with plenty of bread and horseradish, which brought tears to her eyes. She turned on the radio. After precisely twenty minutes she removed the baking sheet from the oven, spread a thin layer of pear jam on the group of rounds without holes, put a thin slice of quince paste in the middle and topped each cookie with one of the disks of pastry with a hole. When she was done, she stacked the cookies on a plate, scattered powdered sugar with ground walnuts over them, and cleaned up the kitchen.

Her student, the daughter of a bank director, a girl who wanted to study law, had an appointment for six o'clock. Mrs. Lévay was to explain symbolism to her and help with certain practice questions for the university entrance exam. She offered the girl some of her cookies. While she was explaining the material of the lesson and the girl, in turn, listened, Anna Lévay's glance repeatedly returned to the kitchen—had she missed anything in the cleaning up?—and then her eye fell on the cookies. They looked like little halos.

Her stomach tightened. She interrupted her student, and since the hour was up anyhow, she gave her a new assignment and dismissed her. She wanted to be alone. She took a sleeping pill, set the alarm clock, closed all the blinds, put on her nightgown, and got into bed.

She was awakened by the ringing of the telephone. It was the doctor. He asked whether she would like to stop by his house. A lively eclectic group had gathered on the spur of the moment to pass the time, just as in the old days. He expressed his regret that Anna Lévay had no desire to leave the house, noted that her voice sounded tired, and asked what she had done that day to have so worn her out. Only the usual, she answered. She had taught, strolled through the town, sat a moment in the church to think about what the following winter would be like when she had retired and would be sitting at home all day wrapped in blankets against the cold with no one to talk to. Then she went to the market hall, luckily survived a fall, her greatest fear having been that when she got up she would knock over a pile of apples; she had already once accidentally tipped over a pyramid of jars of preserves and been terribly embarrassed. Then she had gone shopping, brought everything home, and eaten all alone; then her private student had come and gone, and now she wanted to sleep. The doctor then reiterated his regret that she was unable to join the party, she should hear what the reverend father had just finished telling, he was a most superstitious individual, his mental state no doubt completely intact, yet he feared that he was suffering from hallucinations, he had seen a miracle, incredible the things that occurred. Should he pass the receiver to his reverence for Mrs. Lévay to ask him to relate the story to her directly? But Anna Lévay politely declined, she had no desire to burden the priest, and furthermore, she was completely immune to miracles; she was not even a believer.

The doctor was noticeably relieved by this reply. He could, though, still count on Mrs. Lévay on Thursday at his office? he asked, and they agreed to meet at ten minutes to four in front of her building.

Then Anna Lévay unplugged the telephone, lay down again, and slept with a tranquil heart; she knew not that a dream was being granted her that would suggest to her that she should resign herself to her fate. She dreamt of honey, more precisely, of a river of honey, which according to our dear Professor C. G. Jung represents the goal of spiritual completion. She swam in it, naked, for she had left her blue skirt and white blouse on the low bank. In the dream, she was young, no longer a teenager, but already at that ideal age at which goddesses, actresses, and fashion models are represented. The stream carried her, she did not resist, only sometimes she looked at the shore, at times her eye fell on her clothes, from which she concluded that she was swimming in circles. She should have seen an island, but she saw none; she stretched her neck upward, while the thick, sticky, warm stream played over her limbs; she felt contentment, until the stream became stronger and stronger. A deathly dread now gripped her as she imagined that the whirlpool would swallow her up. Her surroundings, which had hitherto been bright, became dark; she swam about awhile, until her fear passed, and then she found herself on the shore, next to her clothes; her limbs were completely dry, and her skin had the scent of honey. She dressed, lay on the grass, and fell asleep.

In the morning, she decided to pay no further attention to her halo, but to act as though nothing had happened. This was to be her strategy for maintaining her dignity. She stuck to it for over a month.

7

On Sunday, the seventh of December, Anna Lévay went with one of her colleagues to a forested hill just outside the town to gather rose-hips. In times past, a wooden three-story watchtower had stood on the hilltop, and from there one had a commanding view across the lake and to the mountains beyond, and young couples who could find no other shelter went there to make love. Some of her students had revealed to her once how the system worked. The couples waited below in line, while from a nail at the highest point of the tower an undergarment was hung as a signal that the tower was oc-cupied. The tower, having become unsafe, had been torn down over ten years ago. Old wives with sharp tongues maintained that the wooden structure had been unable to withstand the continual rock-ing to which it had been subjected, and now the thick, black stumps of the supporting columns rose up like phalluses—a fitting and stylish end—from the concrete foundation.

The weather was calm. Enormous white clumps of clouds hung lazily from the sky, casting shadows on the windswept trees in the forest below, dulling the colorful roofs of the houses beneath the hill, and scattering dark flecks upon the water of the lake.

Here above, there were wild roses aplenty, yet they were of little interest to those who dwelt here, and even less to the proprietors of vacation houses and weekend cottages. Anna Lévay had actually planned this trip for the middle of November, but she had kept putting it off for reasons that seemed beyond her control. She had not dared to travel by public conveyance, and even if she had, she had been afraid to be alone in the hills, not on account of the gangs of criminals and rapists, but for fear of visions. Since she had become aware, on the third morning after her discovery of the halo, of the religious and cultural significance of the wild rose, she had expected something bad to come of this trip. But now she could wait no longer. The jar of rosehip jam that she had bought at the natural foods store had long been polished off, and since that purchase about a month ago the price had doubled, and was now beyond what her circumstances would permit.

To be sure, her income was being regularly supplemented by payments from the doctor, but she had decided to deposit that money in her bank account, down to the last fillér, to be used for unforeseen expenses.

On this day, her colleague, the same woman who had accompanied her to the cemetery, picked her up at ten o'clock in the morning. They did not converse during the ride in her car. The woman was listening to a recording by her—as she called him—"best beloved ex-lover." She was visibly lost in the music, and Anna Lévay did not wish to disturb her.

The ride took about fifteen minutes. The colleague suggested that they look at the lake from the steep promontory above before beginning their gathering expedition, but Anna Lévay replied that she was afraid of heights. So when they reached the end of the town they turned not to the right, toward the lake, but to the left, in the direction of the hill, parking the car at a roadside snack bar that was closed in the off-season. From there they traveled on foot. After a walk of a kilometer and a half they encountered the first suitable rosebush, far enough from the roads with their automobile exhaust gases, to the right, on a slope, between a hunter's platform and a rustic picnic table fashioned from a tree trunk. There they gathered the fruit, which had already seen the first frost and thus fell easily from the stalks, placing them in the rucksacks they had brought along. They worked without speaking, completely under the spell of an atavistic gatherer instinct. Within an hour they had picked ten kilos, enough to fill all the containers they had brought. Anna Lévay's colleague, who lived free as a bird, from day to day, like a lily of the field, had no use for rosehips; she was helping Anna Lévay only because she had nothing better to do and loved taking trips to the countryside, though not alone, and not with men; she had one disappointment behind her and was harboring no current candidate for her affections. The colleague therefore suggested that Anna Lévay could continue picking while she returned to the car with their spoils and then drove into town to get some plastic bags. Anna Lévay agreed to this.

She figured that she would be alone for about half an hour. While she was waiting, she climbed onto the hunter's platform, which the hunting club had erected on this less densely forested area of the hill. From here there spread before her a magnificent view of the western part of the lake, where the doctor had recently invited her to go sailing in the unusually warm autumn weather. During the conversation in which this invitation had been given, Anna Lévay had become suspicious of the doctor's motives. She had been sitting in the doctor's living room, where the television set stood. The whole time, the doctor's daughter had been watching documentary films, one of which was about the Sea of Galilee; it was not five minutes after this film that the invitation had been given. The doctor, too, had stolen an occasional glance at the television, and Anna Lévay had noticed that once he had begun looking in that direction, his reaction time to her remarks had lengthened; he made longer pauses, as if there were arising in the gray database of his cerebral cortex an image of that first adventure at the harbor and the ensuing supernatural phenomenon, as if he wished—like a systematic researcher—to perform an experiment to validate his theory. For this reason the teacher graciously declined the invitation with the excuse that she easily became seasick, and would be nothing but a burden to the company. She produced this excuse so convincingly that the doctor had to put his experimental plans on ice.

On the platform, the air was clear, and the entire farther shore could be seen. The north wind bore the fresh scent of the still waters aloft. Less than five minutes had elapsed when she heard a rustling in the nearby bushes. Her glance sought the source of the noise, whose volume suggested a massive being in motion. At that moment, she heard a rustling from the opposite direction as well. She turned in the direction from whence it came.

She was surrounded by deer. There were six of them. Then two rabbits appeared, several stray dogs, and a pair of foxes, two wild boars, and right below her, several hedgehogs. The animals sat peacefully together, apparently having completely forgotten that they served one another as nourishment in the hierarchy of the food chain.

Field mice came streaming in her direction; worms stretched their little heads from clods of earth; insects covered the branches of the surrounding shrubs, though they remained invisible to Anna Lévay, who had left her eyeglasses at home. In any case, there was no time for leisurely observation, for she was suddenly surprised by a flock of seagulls. These birds circled about her head, so thick that they darkened the sky as in the fairy tale. Several swans joined the throng, and a pair of wild ducks put in an appearance. The swans were so close that at times their wingtips became caught in Anna Lévay's hair. In sudden horror at their sharp beaks she shrank into a corner of the platform, crouched down, and covered herself with her arms. Then the birds alighted on the railing. A swan, which away from the water can maintain its balance only with difficulty, landed on the platform, searched for her glance, and attempted to bore with its head between Anna Lévay's legs.

From afar, Anna Lévay heard her colleague approaching. And soon, she was calling to her. In addition to the bags, she had brought warm knackwurst, rolls, and a small tube of mustard. She had acquired hunger, she explained, and a little snack would do them good. So they sat down at the table, overgrown with ten years' accumulation of shrubbery and now giving a view only to the west, and ate their lunch. They squeezed out little mounds of mustard onto the revolting wax paper, into which they dipped the sausages, the colleague dabbing systematically from the edges, Anna Lévay plunging her sausage directly into the middle. The meat made a crackling sound at each bite, and Anna Lévay became self-conscious, for she had never yet partaken of such a repast with her hands, having always honored propriety with a knife and fork. This mode of dining seemed to her rather erotic, the taking of a bulging sausage directly into her mouth. They were almost done, when she nearly choked on a piece of sausage, for in the center of the hill of mustard the paper had become translucent, the yellow colloid forming a thin surrounding border, and she saw that it looked like a halo.

During the rest of the day, they picked another twenty kilos of rosehips. Anna Lévay was so lost in her work that she took no notice of the dried leaves and twigs that stuck to her. Her colleague, who had been scratched by thorns all over her face, looked long and hard at Anna Lévay with envy. "Tell me, then, haven't you gotten a single scratch?" she finally asked, upon which Anna Lévay turned around and looked at her colleague for a few seconds uncomprehendingly. The colleague continued. "My God, you look like . . . but really . . . you could be a model for an icon of an early Christian martyr!" Prickly twigs abounded in her hair, sticking out like rays, forming the outline of a halo. The colleague wanted to help her to free herself from the twigs, but Anna Lévay nervously put her off. She would attend to that when they were done; now, they had two beautiful bushes in front of them, the effort would be wasted. She was sure that her colleague's interjection had been merely chance, she of all people would see nothing and sense nothing, she was much too earthbound to have noticed anything, perhaps later, when her monthly periods had been replaced by religious enthusiasm, then, perhaps, she would understand something; but the observation nonetheless had made her uneasy.

At two-thirty they began the journey home. The colleague helped to carry their treasure into Anna Lévay's apartment. She stayed awhile, drank the cup of coffee that was offered while Anna Lévay washed the first batch five times in the wash basin and then set it on the stove in the largest of her kettles filled with cold water. They discussed the ancient recipe, by which one had to put the cooked mash through a sieve to separate out the seeds and furry skins and then cook the pulp—which in bygone days one could buy at the market—with sugar to taste. As Anna Lévay accompanied her guest to the door, she promised to give her a jar of the finished product.

Until eleven o'clock that evening, Anna Lévay was busy preparing the rosehip pulp in numerous batches. From time to time, she worked on grading papers, but arose after every second notebook, stirred the thick bubbling brew, and when she saw that it was done, poured it into the clean stainless steel washbasin to cool. At eleven, she began to push the mass through a sieve; then she cleaned up the kitchen. At one in the morning she was done. She planned on finishing the jam the next day, after her work at the hospital. She tidied up and went to bed.

She awoke early the next morning in pain. She was suffering from abdominal cramps. At first, she thought they were muscular, and so she arose, took a painkiller, and slept peacefully awhile longer. When she awoke the second time she felt something moist on the bed sheet, but she attached no importance to it. She went into the kitchen, drank a cup of tea, ate a piece of bread with butter, listened to the radio. Only when she went to dress and tossed her nightgown under the bedspread with the usual flick of the wrist did she observe the scarlet stains. As had happened with Sarah, so with her, too, had a woman's nature been restored.

She became nervous. It occurred to her that yesterday she had made a connection between religious feeling and menopause. She quickly rinsed out her underclothes and lay them on the radiator in the kitchen. She was so worked up that she walked right into the containers full of rosehip pulp standing on the stone floor. She suddenly thought of the symbolism of the thorn bush and its fruits.

She hurried back into the bathroom and stood before the mirror. The halo was sitting in its usual place. She decided, in keeping with her strategy of maintaining her dignity, not to fall into a panic. She had no feminine articles in the house, for it had been years since she had needed them, so she shoved a handful of toilet paper into her underdrawers before going downstairs to the store to lay in the necessary supplies. Of course, she made other purchases as well so as not to call unnecessary attention to herself; and so into the shopping basket came three lemons, a tin of sardines, a bottle of mineral water, and a container of sour cream. As she was paying, in walked her young neighbor holding her child, who again began shouting shrilly and reaching out to touch the halo. "I'm sorry, Mrs. Lévay," apologized the mother once more. "It's nothing," replied Anna Lévay, again turning red, the more so, since the woman was looking with surprise at the sanitary napkins in the shopping basket.

In the kitchen she unpacked her purchases. First, she changed her underwear and then called the school to say that she was unwell.

Exhausted, she went back to bed and stared for a long time at the ceiling. At about ten o'clock, she finally got up, checked the state of her sanitary napkin, washed her hands, and began to cook the rosehip pulp with sugar to turn it into jam. She watched the bubbles as they rose from the pot, and as she mechanically stirred the mass with a wooden spoon, enveloped in a sweet cloud of steam, she decided that she would put up the lot of it, about twenty liters, in small jars and give it to her friends and acquaintances. While she went over in her mind the list of recipients, a quiet resignation overtook her, which was not to leave her during the entire time that she bore the halo on Earth.

From this day forward every action of hers was informed by the presence of the halo, and therefore she was careful in her contacts with others, as though she had been a leper.

Indeed, what happened was in this wise: The apple that she had touched the previous Tuesday in the market hall was purchased by the wife of a well-known businessman who was also a member of the municipal council. This woman did not really have to do her own shopping, but out of conjugal affection for her husband, who on that day had been in the hospital undergoing an operation, she had insisted on selecting herself some fruit for the "invalid." She had no way of knowing that upon opening the man's abdomen the chief surgeon had discovered a metastasized carcinoma in an advanced stage, and although he completed the operation, had not felt the need to take any particular care with it. He had determined that the patient was incurable, which he wrote in his chart, and then pondered over how he was going to inform the man's family, a task that was always difficult, but in this case would prove particularly awkward, since the terminally ill man was a member of the council. He would not die so quickly that he would not be able to attend at least the next three council meetings, but he would be experiencing symptoms, and God in Heaven, to top it all off, it occurred to the surgeon that the council could end up considering legislation that would negatively affect the hospital. When the patient's wife came to visit, he therefore decided to approach her discreetly, but thought better of it when he saw the man, awake now for several minutes, eating—slices of apple, if he saw correctly—from the hand of his better half, and so he asked a nurse to inform the wife that he awaited her in his office. The nurse then came to the surgeon's office and told him that the patient had gotten out of bed, was walking about, and wished to be discharged.

The head surgeon did not believe his ears and immediately went to see his patient, who loudly thanked him. The surgeon ordered him to return to bed, gave him a sedative injection with his own hands, and at once ordered an exploratory operation. But first, he asked whether the patient had perhaps taken a strong stimulant of some sort, perhaps some invigorating beverage. He was sorry to be putting such questions to the patient, but he must ask, since it was not customary for a patient to be walking about so soon after the completion of abdominal surgery. Upon receipt of a decisive reply in the negative, he then checked whether the incision in the patient's abdomen was intact. To his great amazement he saw the stitches hanging loosely from the patient's skin. Where the incision had been made could now be seen only a faint pearly scar, resembling nothing more serious than the stretch marks of pregnancy, a scar as might be expected an entire month after surgery. The surgeon did not wish for his patient to notice that a miracle had occurred, for the latter was too educated not to become suspicious. Therefore, the doctor applied a thick coating of antiseptic spray, wrapped the area thoroughly with a waterproof bandage, and made the patient promise not for anything to remove the bandage; he was trying out a new and experimental clinical technique on him that would, it was hoped, prevent the proliferation of scar tissue and thus spare the patient the lifelong presence of a thick red bulging scar on his abdomen.

The following day, all the lab tests, tissue cultures, and computer-aided tomography confirmed that the cancer was in complete remission. There was no explanation for the phenomenon.

The chief surgeon invited the wife into his office and asked whether she had noticed anything unusual during her visit with her husband. The woman could report only that he had eaten nine apple quarters, that is, two entire apples and again one-fourth of an apple, and that he had felt an unusual appetite for this commonplace fruit, which she had bought on the day of the operation from the fruit and vegetable dealer that she usually patronized in the market hall.

The chief surgeon arranged for the entire stock of that dealer's apples to be purchased on his behalf, but the laboratory that he commissioned to study the fruit was able to find nothing out of the ordinary, despite the employment of the latest investigative methods. The patient was kept in the hospital an additional eight days; every second day the surgeon inspected the healed wound, behind closed doors, with his own hands, an inspection of which the patient, lying on his back, saw nothing, for even should he chance to look down, the incision would have been hidden by the enormous mass of his chest. He was frightened of pain, and continually requested a double allotment of his placebo medication, which was granted him. On the eighth day, when the stitches were removed, he could marvel, aided by a mirror, at his restored flesh, which the healed businessman wished to honor with an additional payment, which the surgeon attempted to refuse, for please, it was an honor to be permitted to treat the distinguished councilman. It was only after repeated urging that the doctor finally allowed the envelope to slide into his pocket. He murmured apologetically that he was only performing his duty, he treated all his patients equally, but if the gentleman, having been cured, insisted that he accept, he would use it for the purchase of professional books, for education is a lifelong process. And with this he placed the check, which represented three times his monthly salary, in the drawer of his desk. In preparing the patient's discharge papers, the operating room report would have to be "doctored."

After the patient had been discharged, the chief surgeon hurried to the south wing of the hospital to his friend the neurologist and told him of the unusual recovery. The neurologist did not appear particularly astonished. He assured his colleague that the will to be healed could at times work wonders, for according to modern magical thinking, bodily illness is merely a symptom of the soul's desire for health. Perhaps the patient, in considering the advancement of his various entrepreneurial enterprises, had simply concluded that he could work more and harder if he did not have to pay attention to recurring pains in the left side of his abdomen. They chatted another half hour over a cup of coffee; the surgeon said thank you, no, he did not require a mild sedative, which, taken in modest quantities, freed one of the nerve-wracking effects of stress and all types of anxieties; he preferred to get a proper rest during the night shift.

On that same evening the neurologist inquired of Anna Lévay what delicacies might be available in the market hall, it was so long since he had gone shopping, his wife took care of everything, he had not been to the market at all since it had been remodeled, certainly, one could buy strawflowers and pumpkins and red beets? Anna Lévay, who saw through the doctor at once, replied evasively. Teachers' salaries are so low, she said, that over time she had trained her reflexes to see only what she could afford, and thus she did not see everything that was to be seen. And besides, she did not like to go to the market hall, because the floor was so slippery, and so many had fallen there.

She also showed no sign of agitation when on Monday, the fifteenth of December, the doctor sat down right behind her at a concert given by the popular local jazz band in the coffeehouse run by the cultural center. He sat behind her and observed her every movement. The concert was very long, and at some point Anna Lévay had to leave the room. It was cold in the washroom, in the lobby as well, where she waited until the number being played came to an end. At the first sign of applause she slipped into the room, but the musicians did not stop for the applause, and they began the next piece at once. There was no exit; she did not want to remain standing by the door, for this was right next to the band, in the most conspicuous place. So she proceeded without hesitation directly to the table at which she had been sitting with her colleagues. The singer was crooning "Oh, when the Saints go marching in" with a studied African-American accent. On her way to the table, Anna Lévay's glance caught that of the doctor. From his piercing gaze she concluded that he was observing to see whether she would react to the marching in of the saints. She did not react. Nor did her step become uncertain; she did not even blink.

When later, in the company that had gathered after the concert, the doctor asked whether she had enjoyed the show, she replied that she had been incapable of not enjoying it, and so she had enjoyed it, indeed, she had cramps in her legs from involuntarily tapping her feet along with the music, but unfortunately, she understood no English, she really should learn it, but at the time she had been actively studying foreign languages, English had been out of fashion, so she had been unable to understand what was being said at the places where some in the audience had laughed.

The concert had begun at seven, and so they had finished up at the doctor's office at six-thirty. Even so, they had almost arrived late. Anna Lévay had already removed her white lab coat and was waiting in her overcoat at the entrance, when a former patient rushed in demanding a private interview with the doctor. He informed the latter that he had been requested to undergo a psychiatric evaluation at the university clinic in the capital because he had stated that his advanced Parkinson's disease had disappeared without a trace after several visits to the neurologist. He had no idea why this request had been made, he had thought that they wanted to praise the doctor for his accomplishment, but they had wanted only to find out the doctor's name. He wanted simply to warn the neurologist that perhaps some investigative commission would be dispatched, or that some inspector general would send patients who were only pretending to be sick; who knew what might transpire? He did not care how the good doctor had accomplished the cure, the point was that he was well, over the past five years he had undergone one treatment after another, and all in vain; if necessary, he would testify in the doctor's favor, even if the doctor had made a pact with the devil.

The doctor had recently noted several such cases. These unusual cures occurred only among the patients who had come to his private office hours, and then only with those who had come into some degree of physical contact with Anna Lévay.

Anna Lévay knew all about this, but she said nothing to anybody, for she feared that she would be subjected to unbearable examinations, and the strategy for self-preservation that she had adopted required her to act as if nothing had happened, to continue playing the social role of respected educator and stick to her previous views about everything.

At the end of the convivial social hour, when the doctor's wife rose to leave, Anna Lévay noticed that the woman's high-heeled shoe had gotten caught in the long leather strap of her handbag, which had been standing on the floor. The bag, in turn, had gotten itself caught in the leg of the chair as it was pushed back. In short, if Anna Lévay had not caught her, the woman would have fallen.

That evening the doctor reexperienced normal married life: a candlelit dinner, no boredom during the dinner conversation, and—in contrast to the experience of years past—lively and joyful sex. And so it remained from that day forth. His spouse, cured of her house-wife's depression and her eternal migraines in bed, now blossomed and developed into an animated and gregarious individual. The doctor called to mind images of that previous meeting and concluded the following: The teacher had visited them two times altogether, but his wife had not greeted her with a kiss on the cheek, as women usually do among themselves, but had excused herself on the grounds of having a cold, which may well have been a fabrication on account of the difference in social standing between the two women. Moreover, she had brought snacks and drinks in dishes and bottles, and one had served oneself. She had given her nothing directly into her hand.

After the doctor had convinced himself, as a result of his own experience and the extensive study of a number of case histories, that it was indeed Anna Lévay who had elicited the unaccountable physical and mental amelioration, he dropped in, loaded down with documentation, on his friend the mayor. Behind closed doors they went over the matter, calculating all the angles and ramifications. On Thursday, the eighteenth of December, the municipal council met and voted a large sum of money for remodeling the former va-cation home of a now defunct Socialist enterprise located near the harbor into a resort sanatorium.

The city fathers did not ask what sort of cures would be carried out at the now dilapidated structure. The entire matter seemed to have been settled in advance; no one said anything specific, but the usual signals and channels of information seemed to indicate that one was expected to vote in the affirmative on the resolution. The mayor read the significant points of the proposal as well as those of the supplementary proposal and recommended that they be approved. No one wished to comment. Present were the editor-in-chief of the local newspaper, four physicians from the hospital, two high school principals, two other councilmen who had bought up valuable municipal land, and then two lawyers who had previous experience with handling municipal affairs, as well as the bank director, after whose election the council had directed all civic institutions to transfer their accounts to this new councilor's bank, nor had they wavered when news was leaked about bankruptcy proceedings against the bank and for several days all transactions had been frozen. That made twelve of the eighteen council members: an absolute majority. There was in addition a pensioner, the former director of a government enterprise; and the rest were businessmen. One of these, who owned a hotel and restaurant, had made it onto the council through the party list, since on his own account he had obtained only eight votes. And even by that route he had become a councilor only because his employee the hotel manager, who as local party leader was first on the list, had for some reason accruing to his own advantage, or, more likely, under pressure from his employer, elected not to sit on the council, and was now no longer the hotel manager. None of these worthies posed any questions about the proposed allocation of funds. Each pressed the appropriate button and thereby discharged the duty that loyalty demanded. The measure passed with fifteen ayes, two nays, and one abstention.

All of the council members considered at once how they could profit from the sale of the building to the town. Since they had nothing to do with the more lofty purposes of the venture, the hotel owner and the baker, although belonging to different factions, landed the catering contracts. The doctors were promised access to a private practice, the lawyers were granted a contract for managing an associated insurance and travel agency. The pensioned economist demanded a place on the board of directors of the new corporation. The school directors wanted the free use of a ballroom for school events. Only the editor-in-chief of the newspaper hung his head, for he had no idea, no idea at all, how he might make a profit out of the building.

They planned provisionally for the new institution to open its doors as early as the beginning of March. According to their business model, even in the first month there was a projection of enormous revenues. The surprisingly large amount did not appear to strike anyone as odd, not even the economist. Only a salesperson, who against all expectation had managed to obtain a seat on the council despite his hopeless position on the original party list, queried the doctor, though a bit anxiously, because he had to recognize this man of great intellect as his consular equal, and therefore, by the unwritten law of etiquette, had to address him with the informal "thou." He posed his question during the break, when the doctor was drinking coffee with the mayor in the anteroom to the latter's office. He walked right up to them and gently breathed his question: "Tell me, where are we going to find so many patients, and how are they going to be cured here?" The doctor pummeled him on the shoulder in a comradely manner and answered that these questions should be entrusted to those who had worked out the plan, for they had thought of everything. If they said that there would be so-and-so many, then there would be. End of discussion.

In the past, the town had invested enormous sums in the search for mineral springs, but all such searches to date had shown that within the town limits there were no thermal waters worth exploiting. It was with great envy that the town looked at the little village about ten kilometers to the south, where on the territory of a former collective farm a spring had been discovered, around which an entrepreneur had set up a thriving guest house, open the whole year round, to which foreigners flocked to soak their limbs; for the most part it was German pensioners seeking to avoid the overcrowded watering places frequented by the multitudes.

That hot spring must certainly be profitable, remarked one of the town fathers bitterly. Two well-upholstered women get into the pool with their even better upholstered husbands, and immediately one needs six hectoliters less water.

Another worthy quickly replied that where money was concerned, there were no aesthetic criteria at all; it made no difference who provided their income; beauty was no criterion in the tourist industry, at least not in the selection of guests.

A third councilor eagerly suggested the following scheme: There was a company in town that built oil pipelines. They hadn't much business, so why not build a pipeline to carry the overflow of thermal water from the village to the town; such a venture would even provide jobs, for which one could probably obtain a government subvention; a pipeline didn't care what flowed through it, and the tourists would flock to the town in droves.

A fourth, whom the third had prevented from getting a word in edgewise, replied that the second of the four, so one had heard, had been seen traveling about on his bicycle during the tourist season, noting, surely for the benefit of the tax inspectors, in whose lot which car with foreign registration plates was parked and had himself—if one were to believe the rumor, and one certainly believed it more than one believed the local press—rented garages to hide the automobiles of the foreigners staying with him, in case it should occur to someone to do unto him what he was doing unto others; and moreover, he had forbidden the tax inspectors from the tourism board access to his house.

They had practically come to blows when the mayor's friend, the doctor, separated them. He informed them that they perhaps had not thoroughly read the supplementary material that had been distributed afterward, since it had not been in the bundle of documents, according to which the planned reconstruction of the complex, to be carried out at public expense, would not be run by the town, but by a newly established joint venture; they could apply to this firm with their plans; in lieu of rent the firm would pay the town fifteen percent of the audited profit, and in fact, would do so until December 31 of each year; for this, too, they had voted; he and the mayor had been against such outsourcing, and if they didn't know this yet, he was happy to tell them.

Only one councilman and his business associates were less than pleased over the investment, since they had used their certificate of restitution, which they had obtained in compensation for alleged or actual damages suffered under the previous political system, to buy up the land under which, according to their spokesman, thermal springs were certain to be found. They had hoped that the spa would be built there and that the town would buy their land as well as pay them compensation for taking their land out of agricultural production.

On this land the town had paid for experimental drilling, which, though it brought no warm water to the landowners, would at least, according to their calculations, provide compensation for damages due to the drilling and the loss of agricultural use. They would use this compensation to buy shares in the new corporation.

In the week that followed there appeared hints in the pages of the newspaper devoted to local news that a certain newly registered corporation, substantially foreign owned, in fact, the one that was to run the "cure center," had obtained exclusive rights to the use of all the sludge dredged from the harbor. Was there perhaps something crooked going on, and was there some secret connection between the sludge and the cure center? And what did this all have to do with the still unexplained fish kill at the end of October? Was this yet another case of valuable public property being privatized? The article was not the product of a reporter; rather, it appeared in the section in which, in an apparent show of democratic access, questions submitted by readers were answered. Before the reply there generally appeared the name and telephone number of the reader who had submitted the question. But this time there was no name, and the telephone number given was that of a public pay phone across from the railroad station. Those numbers could be found in the telephone directory, though most readers of the newspaper did not know this. The question had been addressed to the mayor, who answered that this was a free country with a market economy, and anyone with capital and an idea worth the risk of that capital could launch an enterprise. None of the accusations touched on political issues, and so he was not the appropriate person to be replying to the question. If the reader meant that there was some dirty work afoot, then as a citizen of the country he had the right to report the matter to the competent authorities; however, in such a case he was under the obligation to show concrete evidence to support his suspicion and provide precise details, to make known his name, and to take full responsibility for his statements. The question of whether there was a connection between the mysterious events of October and the corporation was one that he could not answer; the situation was still under investigation, and the press would certainly report on it in case a reasonable explanation could be found. Until then, it was all in the realm of speculation. Whoever could not contain his curiosity would have to turn for assistance to the numerous fortune-tellers and UFO enthusiasts in the town.

To the naive, this downplaying reply made the entire matter seem worthy of scorn, the question by the unidentified reader appear laughable, and the mayor come across as an ambitious politician. However, those who could read between the lines noted behind the arrogance a ridicule of the public at large, and the single caller who rang the number given in the paper for just this purpose asked why the mayor found it necessary to answer phony questions accompanied by phony phone numbers. The caller, disguising his voice, gave the number he had called as his own number. The matter was, of course, not taken seriously, or at most to the extent that the local correspondent for the newspaper ran in a panic to the mayor to report that someone had discovered the trick.

8

For a long time before the holiday she had found herself in a highly
emotional state, but Christmas passed pleasantly for Anna Lévay.

At the beginning of December the reconstructed and renovated
school building had been dedicated. Previously, it had been necessary to take the smaller classes, particularly the small language
classes, through the pedestrian tunnel under the four-lane highway
into the former Party Committee building, which offered endless
opportunities for unexcused tardiness and absences, opportunities
of which the students had taken full advantage. They were caught
more than once smoking in the passage between the buildings or
even drinking beer in the nearby pub. With the completion of the
renovations there was now a new auditorium, and it was here that
the Christmas program had been given, an adaptation of Oscar
Wilde's story *The Happy Prince,* which had moved Anna Lévay to
tears. She had not particularly liked the original story; she had
found it too saccharine, which could be attributed to the universally
acknowledged tendencies of the author, but the performance had
shown how much of themselves the young people had put into it.
But it was not for that reason that the tears were streaming down
Anna Lévay's face, but because she knew that in a few years the

seriousness of life would turn these sincere youngsters into burned-out, cynical adults.

On the evening of the same day she had attended a concert with several of her colleagues in the Lutheran church. Anna Lévay sat in the last row, way over to the side. While she was looking at the sunken heads, the downy hair on the tensed skin of the napes of necks, she had quite given herself over to the magic of the human voice.

During the *Ave Maria* the audience felt a strange shiver. The listeners felt as if they were rising from their seats. They lost their perception of three-dimensional space. Darkness reigned before their open eyes, and they listened to the music not with their ears, but with the inmost cells of their brains. The women's bodies softly pulsated, and as for the men, all the pores of their skin contracted. Anna Lévay felt unwell. A wave of heat had overtaken her, her skin had reddened, and she looked at the listeners with their sunken heads and understood the connection. Therefore, before the universal law of gravitation could be violated, she rose without a word and quit the church. Those who remained offered resounding applause for the unusually uplifting musical experience.

Anna Lévay walked home alone. In her mailbox she found a postcard depicting an American Santa Claus; it was from her son. He wished her a happy holiday, and informed her fully, to the extent that the real estate of a postcard allowed, of his successes of the past year and, more superficially, of his love life, and promised that a longer letter would soon follow. It was the same every Christmas. Hanging from her door was a plastic bag of Christmas cookies from the English teacher, the woman with whom she had picked rosehips in the late autumn. On the accompanying card was a greeting and a "user's manual": She was to place the cookies on the window sill as food for the Christ child, or, as the case may be, Santa Claus. She spent the entire Christmas holiday at home, the greater portion in bed, reading. Her sisters telephoned, as did her brother László. The telephone was cheaper at Christmas, and they took advantage of this to talk for more than half an hour. Getting together was out of the question. Her sisters had families, and Anna Lévay did not wish to be a burden to them on the holy evening. Her brother lived in a distant town, and she did not wish to travel so far. They always invited her, but she knew that the invitation was out of courtesy. She had grown accustomed to being alone, nor did she wish to be among happy families that would just remind her of her late husband and emigrated son and make her sorrowful at the happy event.

By the first day of Christmas vacation she had accomplished all of her shopping, and on the second had cleaned her dwelling; on the third she had completed her cooking for the week and baked cookies in case of unexpected visitors. Now, she was taking it easy. She did not put up a Christmas tree. The extent of her holiday decorating consisted of a fir branch and a lovely red apple, whose stem had been replaced by a thin wax candle. On the evening of December 24 she ate her supper by the light of that candle while she listened to the sounds of the house. She held to the traditional meal of fish. Fresh fish was too expensive, and required too much preparation, and so she fried some frozen fish sticks together with some leftover rice and tartar sauce. For dessert, she ate a slice of a pastry filled with poppy seeds, also in deference to tradition. Then she lay down to sleep, to recover from the exhaustion of the previous weeks.

New Year's Eve brought lentil soup. She wiped her mouth on the soft, red napkin with the English greeting "Merry Christmas!" which she had purchased before Christmas in the paper-goods department on the first floor of the department store on the market square. She had actually gone to buy shoes: simple, sturdy, and black, which would go with everything. But then she had decided to make do with the old ones, or at any rate to wait for the winter sales; the ten thousand forints being asked for the pair that she liked most of all was more than she could afford. Embarrassed at having been caught in the act of being poor, she wandered through the other departments, as if in search of a Christmas present for someone, as though she had the means and the recipient. The napkins, which she would spread in her lap according to the English custom, were unusually large, and the package would not fit in her handbag; therefore, she carried it in her left hand. Even though she was not carrying the package aloft, it nonetheless stood out sufficiently. She had borne it through the town like a trophy, for this purchase of napkins would suggest to anyone who might have taken note that she would be having visitors on Christmas Eve, that she would be cooking, that she would be eating in company and ipso facto would not be alone, for solitary women did not set a fancy table, or at least they did not shell out three hundred fifty forints for Christmas napkins.

She took a sleeping pill so as not to be disturbed by the partying in the house and the fireworks. She soon fell asleep, long before midnight, and was sleeping soundly when the New Year arrived.

On January 5 she picked up her monthly salary. She was annoyed that the central office had not yet deigned to transfer the thirteenth monthly payment directly into her bank account. Furthermore, there were some municipal employees who had already received their payment in mid-December. Her salary had been increased: Her take-home pay was now 39,000 forints. Of this she needed 6,000 for the payment on her home improvement loan, 4,000 for her lunches at school (the price had gone up), 7,000 for gas (fifteen degrees, and gas for cooking on the weekends), 2,500 for electricity, about the same for water, 2,300 for condominium fees, 1,000 for the basic television charge, 1,200 for cable television (one must have a bit of luxury in life, and since there was no money for foreign travel, one may as well see the world from the comfort of one's living room), 1,000 for a subscription to a weekly literary magazine that was too lengthy for her to read at school, 1,000 for charity, for she considered it her duty to help those even poorer than she was. That came to 26,000, which left 13,000 for food, clothing, and cultural enrichment. With that she would have to make do; her supplementary income from the doctor went directly into the bank, so that she would not have to rely on the municipality to pay her burial expenses. And there should also be something left so that the lovely daughter of her sister Éva, who against her parents' advice and that of all her acquaintances had become a schoolteacher, would be able to pay the inheritance tax, for Anna Lévay had bequeathed the girl her apartment, the will had already been written, it had been already a year at the notary. She should have a better life, she shouldn't have to beg to be allocated an apartment or have to make love in the park or in someone's apartment that might be free for an hour, as she as a student had had to do. The girl should be able to lead a normal life, one worthy of a high school teacher and intellectual. Thus did Anna Lévay spin her plans as she climbed the stairs to the teachers' room on the first instructional day of the new year in possession of her salary in crisp banknotes.

In the course of renovations, the offices, computer room, and library had been moved to the top floor. In addition, a video room and a studio for the school radio station had been created. Many of Anna Lévay's colleagues complained about the number of steps they now had to climb, first upward, and then down to the teachers' room to fetch their class registers, and then after class the whole thing in reverse. There were also steps leading to the snack bar, to the cafeteria, and the classrooms above. By the second period one already had cramps in one's legs. Anna Lévay experienced nothing of the sort, although one could hardly have said that she was a paragon of physical fitness.

That evening at the hospital she met the newly appointed massage practitioner. There had been many patients that day, and the consulting hours had been extended. It was ten-thirty before she finally got to bed.

On January 6 she awoke late, contrary to her habit of decades. She had only fifteen minutes to dress before hurrying off to school. As she arrived, the bell was already ringing. The school principal, a cross between Narcissus and a hyena, watched with Argus eyes to observe the late arrivals, as if the quality of instruction depended on those two minutes. Anna Lévay noted that it is not difficult to be punctual when one has to teach only two class periods per week, as in the case of the principal.

In the first break Anna Lévay went to the office to make a telephone call. Marika was sitting with her head down on her desk and with a groan asked for a painkiller. These were kept in the first aid box in the cupboard, and the key to the cupboard in Marika's desk drawer. In order to reach the drawer handle, Anna Lévay had to push the secretary gently out of the way, and thus she was able to open the drawer. She fetched a tablet, popped the pill through the foil backing of its plastic package, walked to the sink, where she filled a glass to the very top, went back over to Marika, and gave the pill to her to take. Marika smelled a sour odor; she felt sick, and to combat the urge to vomit, she began to swallow rapidly and breathe deeply; she again laid her head on the desktop. The clock struck two, and Anna Lévay had to leave. In the second break she heard that Marika had been sent home in a taxi to avoid a scandal: She had been thoroughly intoxicated.

During the long break, Anna Lévay had to go to the toilet. She took advantage of the facility to the left of the teachers' room, the place where on the first morning of her haloed era she had spent such unpleasant moments. As she was washing her hands, she sensed the same sour odor that Marika had detected in the office. She quickly turned off the faucet and returned to her place. At exactly that time, on the ground floor, one of the custodians, who, as everyone knew, was no enemy of alcohol, was placing a pail under the faucet. His colleague, who was hammering in stakes near the concrete entrance road, was accusing the first custodian, him of the faucet and pail, of being crazy for having dared to suggest that wine was flowing from the taps. To prove his point he emptied the pail and placed it under the faucet, to demonstrate that what came out was nothing but chlorinated water. And in fact, it was nothing but water. The second custodian accused his colleague of having brought the wine from his own cellar at home in order to play a practical joke on this holy day of Epiphany. The two got into such a heated argument that neither of them did any work for the rest of the day.

That evening, Anna Lévay decided to take a bath. She allowed a sufficient quantity of water into the tub, systematically: six minutes of hot, two minutes of cold; only a little, not for an hour-long bath. She quickly removed her clothes and slid into the water. It was only when she was sitting in the tub that she became aware that her skin was burning. She was sitting in heavy, aromatic, golden wine. Anna Lévay made no attempt to wash herself. She heaved herself out of the tub, dried herself off, put on her nightgown over her sticky skin, and went into the kitchen to calm herself with a cup of rosehip tea. The water for her tea had also turned into wine. She had no choice but to drink mulled wine, and with a great feeling of pity she thought of Marika.

The next morning all had returned to normal.

The number of patients was growing rapidly, for although all the cured patients had been strongly urged to keep quiet about improvements in their conditions, the matter could not long remain secret. By the middle of the month, patients were beginning to arrive from abroad. The hotels and private rooms were soon full, and the patients, whom the locals took to be tourists, accepted whatever was available, even putting up with rooms in the poorer quarters of the town, in dwellings in which a respectable middle-class citizen would never set foot. Those who were more particular took up residence in the neighboring towns and villages and set out from there for treatment. The shop owners who lived in larger cities during the off-season soon got wind of the new influx of tourists. Many reopened their shops, as though it were the high season, while others rented a supply of bunk beds and oil radiators from towns farther afield and turned their stores into provisional hotels.

The flow of tourists saw no ebb. In accordance with the law of supply and demand, prices rose, and the cost of a modest room was the same as that of a five-star hotel in Budapest. Even the grocers sought to profit from the additional season; they doubled their prices, which were already by no means low, and now only foreigners patronized their stores, while the local population had to traipse to the neighboring towns.

The market square teemed with crowds as in summer, for during their free time the visitors to the town were out in search of supplies. They went riding and swimming, they went shopping, and they went walking in the harbor, and there was such demand that only one thousand pedestrians were permitted at any one time in the harbor and the rose garden, and they had to pay to enter.

The tourism professionals had no idea what was causing the sudden influx. They sent public opinion pollsters into town, who attempted to discover from the visitors the reasons for their journey, but they could discover nothing. In almost every case the person being polled replied mechanically: One had heard what a pretty town this was, had it not won the prize this year for the most flower-filled town on the continent? The people are friendly, the food good, and there is no lack of entertainment opportunities. Some of the pollsters posed as employees of the bureau of tourism and stood in the parking lot of the cultural center; perhaps a tourist, in a hurry to see a performance of the hastily reconstituted summer operetta, would ask for directions, which might give them some information. But without success. So they went to work as taxi drivers. But even that yielded them nothing.

There were two explanations for their lack of success. One was that those who told others about the miraculous cures always impressed upon the newly initiated individual that he was not to reveal the reason for his presence in the town, for then the magician doctor would notice this at once and refuse to cure him, and moreover, his condition would get worse. The other reason was that the doctor feared that he would have crowds storming his office, and so he engaged a masseur, whose nameplate outside the office was significantly larger than his own. He sent this masseur as his assistant, in the company of Anna Lévay, into town to the patients who had made ap-

pointments with him. This masseur had been recommended to him
by a tourism professional who had long involvement in the network
of local power. The doctor had chosen this man on the basis of his
physical appearance. In point of fact, he was an unemployed shepherd from a remote farm, with large and sinewy hands, and a wispy
gray catfish beard, like those that could be seen by tourists in the pictures of highwaymen painted by those purveyors of kitsch who lined
both sides of the street, except that the traditional white trousers had
been replaced. It was Anna Lévay's job to communicate with the patients and to help the nearsighted oldsters among them to mark, with
a skin-friendly felt marker, the places on their bodies that were to be
massaged. The old shepherd, who had never in his life been con-
fronted with such work, had, however, in the course of an afternoon,
learned the fundamentals from the doctor, and began work that very
day. In the pub he proudly told of the fresh young women who
passed beneath his fingers, and moreover, that he was even paid for
this. Later, they would take a small marble vessel filled with a cream
made from ninety-five percent Vaseline and five percent sterilized
sludge from the harbor, which Anna Lévay, as the masseur's assistant,
would pass to him, and he, in turn, would work a tiny amount into
the patient's skin, as though it were a rare life-saving elixir.

The doctor received calls for new appointments only on his
new, unlisted telephone number. During his working hours patients
could leave their addresses and telephone numbers on the answering machine, so that the doctor could call back or seek them out.
The patients did as they were told, and waited day and night for the
doctor to make an appearance, as though he were the Messiah.
Business flourished. Anna Lévay was earning more than ever, although she continued to pursue her moonlighting only on Mondays and Thursdays. The doctor paid well. Not because his soul was
generous by nature, but because he wished to keep Anna Lévay in
good spirits, bind her to him, and motivate her with money. For he
was not quite certain whether the teacher was aware of her supernatural abilities.

One afternoon in the middle of January, Anna Lévay was walking through the pedestrian underpass near the high school when she was stopped by a foreigner, who asked the way to the house where he had rented a room. To be sure, the tourist information office, located in the water tower in the market square, built in 1912 and now protected as a monument to the water management industry, was now open day and night due to the unexpected invasion, but it had run out of tourist brochures. Their reserve supply had all been distributed, and they had ordered a second printing of next season's brochures, but at the moment there was apparently nothing to be had, for all that the man in the underpass possessed by way of guidance was an indecipherable copy of a section of a town map. Anna Lévay explained to the visitor how to proceed, and then he asked additionally for the nearest restaurant that she might be able to name. The stranger stood a long while and stared at her uncomprehendingly, which prompted Anna Lévay to repeat her sentence two times over, for she guessed that he had not understood. Then the man, over whose face an indescribable joy had spread at her initial reply, asked her to accompany him to the restaurant, for he wished to invite her to lunch, for he had never in his life thought that in this far-flung corner of the world he would find someone who understood the Basque language. He begged her pardon for having forgotten himself by addressing her in his mother tongue instead of in one of the major international languages; he was so happy, he felt as if he had grown wings. He did not let go of Anna Lévay's hand, but stood there in the underpass, pressing and patting it. Then he bowed to Anna Lévay and asked her where she had learned this rare language spoken by a tiny population, which, according to legend, comes from an era before the Indo-European invasion and is so strange and complex that few not born to it ever manage to learn it.

Students were walking by; Anna Lévay removed her hand from that of the visitor, returned her students' greetings, and informed her interlocutor that she had absolutely no knowledge of Basque, that there must be some mistake. The foreigner began once more to praise her; the wise teacher should not be so modest, she is, of course, a teacher, one sees that from how her students greet her; forty years is a long time; in the West one has read that many responded to Communism's reign of terror by educating themselves extensively, to keep themselves busy; the newspaper had also written that they in fact particularly studied the most irrelevant and abstruse subjects, so as to pass the time not in dispiriting hopelessness but in doing something of purpose; she should not be ashamed of this, but proud. And he again invited her to the restaurant. Anna Lévay wished to say no in German, but instead, she stammered out a yes in Basque. Then she set off with the foreigner.

Slowly they climbed the steps of the underground passage to the air above, as if ascending from a sacrificial altar. The foreigner was a man of medium height, in his late thirties, with short dark-blond hair and a strong tendency to baldness. He wore an intellectual's glasses with gold frames; his warm brown eyes behind them looked as gentle as a calf's. He chatted as they walked. He pointed to the green building that housed the local government and the large block of the culture barn, covered with beige-colored ceramic slabs, and asked was it not true that one called this Socialist Baroque? He had prepared himself for his trip, he had read many books about the country before deciding to make the journey, and he asked where in town one could eat genuine horsemeat, ridden soft under the saddle.

Anna Lévay wanted to reply that the residents of the government building had wanted to name it, on account of its color, the White House, but at a later renovation it was painted a different color, and now it had been given the nickname "Green Hut," though this transfiguration had not signaled a change in the quality of work. But now they had become engulfed by the crowd, for the market square was teeming with humanity. The people streamed together like the whirling primeval Chaos. Dislocated ankles and spent hip joints, thin shoulders, and breasts housing tumors moved centimeter by centimeter, to avoid direct contact. The teacher did not move, and the reason was that she saw the square as if from above, as though she were standing on the roof of the water tower, whither, because of her considerable fear of heights, she had ascended but once, when she was newly married to Dr. János Lévay, on the day she introduced him to her parents.

The heterogeneous collection of human exemplars, clothed in a variety of fabrics and colors, slowly arranged itself into columns, of which there were four altogether. The first extended to the former supermarket, from there to the pedestrian overpass, and beyond to the cooperative department store. A second stretched to the newly constructed office block, or, more precisely, to the corner where there was a building housing a bank on the ground floor and whose second story, owned by the mayor, was rented out for unclear commercial purposes. The third wended its way from the head of the long street leading to the cemetery all the way to the four-lane road. The fourth led between the Italian bakery and the Chinese store to the building on the second floor of which the brothel, called by the euphemism Intimate Center, was located.

Anna Lévay at once grasped the situation; she let the Basque gentleman stand in mute amazement and without a word entered the information bureau in the monument to industry. The gateway of shoulders opened before her; a severely disabled man, Scandinavian by appearance, with a head the color of lilac due to his hypertension, politely moved aside his crutches, which he had placed at the entrance in the form of a cross as protection against the crowd. She had no need to ask in order to know what they wanted. With a firm voice she requested that all who were lame or unable to walk be brought forward; everyone would receive a personal information sheet, only please be patient, patience, please. Within seconds the lines had arranged themselves. The wheelchairs rolled to the front, then those walking on crutches, followed by those with but a single crutch, then those who managed with only a cane, after whom proceeded those with splints or with a leg in a cast, and finally, those who walked with a limp, all in decreasing order of severity of handicap. The remainder of the group consisted of individuals with a variety of bodily and mental ailments.

Anna Lévay walked resolutely to the copy machine, punched in the number three hundred twenty-four, and pushed the start button, without having placed anything to be copied on the glass plate. In a steady rhythm the stripes of light moved along under the cover. With a glassy stare the teacher distributed the blank papers as they were extruded: With her right hand she withdrew a page from the machine and with her left placed it in the hand of the next person in line, who in turn looked at the paper, expressed thanks, smiled, and then exited the tiny room.

Within half an hour the crowd had dispersed. Only the Basque gentleman remained. He asked when the next flight for Madrid would depart. He spoke confusedly; he kept saying that now everything was all right, he was very grateful, he had something that must be taken care of at once, it was witchcraft, but then so be it, he would never have thought, he had meant, the way was a fool's errand and everyone for himself and the devil take the hindmost; but no, quite the opposite. Then he begged pardon, he had not meant to bedevil her with questions, and asked where he could find a public toilet. No one understood him except for Anna Lévay, and she remained silent. She did not wish to speak with him, out of fear that the women in the tourist bureau would hear her; they were not unintelligent. She feared that one of them, even should she happen to have no knowledge of Basque, would understand that an unusual language was being spoken. The man continued to speak without pause to Anna Lévay, but she acted as though she did not hear him, and so he addressed his questions to the employees in the room, making his necessity known by an internationally recognized gesture. The employees, all of them women, pointed out to him, likewise with gestures, the way.

At last, they were gone; the place was empty. Anna Lévay thought over the events of the afternoon and pondered a summer career as an interpreter, but then discarded the idea, for when she considered the source of the miracle, she was seized with apprehension. Suddenly, and but for a moment, she was completely disgusted with human society.

All about lay discarded crutches and canes, but most of their owners had not even noticed that they had lost something; they had simply stared at the paper that Anna Lévay had given to them. Their consciousness was overcome as if by a narcotic, and they followed but a single compulsion: As salmon seek fresh water, they wanted only to return to their homes as quickly as possible. Those in wheel-chairs had not dared to stand, for although they felt their blood flow with unaccustomed vigor, they put it down to the feeling of shared suffering among so many fellow disabled persons. The particularly doubtful escort of one of these individuals peevishly asked what there was to read on a piece of blank, ordinary, low-quality seventy-gram paper, to which his wheelchair-bound charge replied, with a question of his own, whether his companion did not see the writing in white letters, why even a blind person could see it, and he did not note the logical contradiction in what he was saying, but continued his harangue without pause: The escort was being paid for pushing a chair, not for providing a running commentary; he should be glad of his job and behave appropriately if he wished to keep it.

The director of the tourist center, who up to now had been standing transfixed with amazement, would have turned off the copier with thanks, had not it already been shut off. The apparatus was cold, the supply of paper in the tray untouched. The director reached for some coffee, and she wanted to offer something to Anna Lévay, her former teacher, but the latter, by now exhausted, turned around and with effort made her way to the bus stop, along the way avoiding with a rapid slalom movement the lethargic neutered cat that crossed her path, and arrived just in time to catch the bus. The city buses were painted in the town colors, blue, green, and yellow, with a wavy pattern that made her seasick every time she looked at them. She was certain that it was not out of civic pride or an aesthetic sense that the town officials ordered such patterns to be painted on the buses, but as a cheap means of publicity. She disliked riding in these buses. But now she felt that she could not walk home.

An hour later the roads leading out of town were congested with traffic.

The situation began to become embarrassing when the members of an organization of disabled persons from a neighboring country bequeathed all of their orthopedic supplies to the cheap hotel where they had been staying, with instructions that they should be given to others in need. The fact of this gift could not be kept secret, for the custodian of the building, which had been converted from a sanatorium belonging to a factory, had a ten-year-old son, who, after the group had departed in their private omnibus, seated himself at once in a wheelchair upholstered in dark red leather and rode it about through the town. The lad told everyone who would listen where the wheelchair had come from. Every now and then, he would park the vehicle, climb down from his throne, and demonstrate the full functionality of his limbs, as proof that the tourists must be mad or wealthy; they were childless, to be sure, for otherwise, they would not have simply left behind such a fantastic toy.

The doctor had observed the tumult from the window of the mayor's residence that was not used as a residence. When he was still on his way home, he had heard the first reports from the groups of people that were gathering. The crowds on the street threatened to cause a traffic jam, and so he had notified the police that without interfering with the pedestrians, they were to block off the road and divert traffic. This was accomplished within five minutes, for the police headquarters was located but a few minutes away, just across the road from the brothel. The doctor saw Anna Lévay pushing through the crowd with the Basque gentleman; he saw the strange, gaping expressions on the faces of those returning with their blank papers, as though they had just emerged from a pool of honey, calm, their movements slow, synchronized, and balanced.

When the square was empty, the doctor hurried down to the street. He wished to summon Anna Lévay, but he called after her in vain. She did not turn around. She had quite a head start on him, and perhaps she indeed had not heard him; she proceeded straight ahead until the door of the bus had closed behind her. The doctor watched as she walked directly, without a side glance, to the very last seat. The bus had crossed the canal bridge before the doctor shifted his view from the moving vehicle to the street. He called the sanitation department on his mobile telephone and gave instructions that all the discarded medical supplies were to be collected. To remove this obstruction to traffic as quickly as possible he even assisted a bit himself. As he was placing the last piece of equipment on the truck, the son of the building custodian came rolling by and related his story.

The doctor then turned his steps to the office of the local newspaper and informed the editor that in the next day's edition the following was to appear, without attribution:

In the interest of speeding up the acceptance by Parliament of the law governing the rights of the handicapped, volunteers from a number of locations on the continent have been visiting our town. These individuals, who are actually not handicapped at all, wished to call attention to the problems of the handicapped by appearing with and employing various medical devices. Those providing accommodations were not informed about the true nature of this operation. Upon their departure these individuals took the unconventional step of donating their wheelchairs, crutches, and other aids to the surgical department of the municipal hospital.

Those offering private accommodations to apparently handicapped persons who have departed are hereby requested to report any medical supplies left behind at the following toll-free number, so that the donated equipment may be picked up and delivered to the hospital. All those involved are also requested to report their experiences with these individuals through the given telephone number or in writing. The contributors of the ten best stories will be awarded a week's preseason vacation in one of our sister cities.

In connection with their preparations for the coming season, those providing accommodations are further requested to make a special effort in upgrading their facilities to accommodate the disabled. Follow the good example set by the municipal authority, which, after a fatal accident at the most dangerous intersection in town, in which a young girl in a wheelchair was killed because her escort, on account of the high curbs, could not push her fast enough onto the sidewalk, installed ramps at all the pedestrian crossings in the municipality. A town that takes such measures can count on being visited by larger than usual numbers of handicapped visitors, who are just as capable of paying their way as their nondisabled countrymen. It would be helpful if the required alterations were completed by the end of March, when the annual procession of the handicapped will again take place in the town. Smaller investments in the public domain will be undertaken by the municipal authority, while renovations of private sites will be supported by interest-free loans, applications for which are available from the town office.

The statement made by the group that has just left provides evidence that there are recognizable signs that this is a town that takes the handicapped into account. But the most important point of orientation, the information center in the market square, is inaccessible to the disabled on account of its steep staircase. Therefore, the group decided to end their stay by staging a silent demonstration that consisted in all of them trying to access the information center at the same time. It took an entire hour for all of them to be assisted. The members of the group have offered their apologies and asked for our understanding for having created a certain degree of traffic blockage, and they wish everyone a good season.

The doctor then proceeded at once to the mayor's office in order to inform him about the recent developments. Together, they determined that the situation was serious and threatened to become even more complex, and that one could well do without the army of rumor-mongers who spoke about miraculous cures, but that on account of the commercial broadcast media's hunger for news and desire for sensation, one would have to deal with them. It was clear that Anna Lévay would have to be neutralized. Therefore, the high school should be required to turn over her file, though of course, not only hers, but those of all the teachers, so that no one will know what is going on, the reason given can be that their job classifications are being reviewed. The mayor's chauffeur picked up the fifty files in the mayor's white Volvo. An examination of Anna Lévay's file showed that in September of last year she had completed her sixty-second year, and thereby her forty-first as a schoolteacher. She had been one of the youngest teachers in the country, having begun as an instructor at age twenty-two, and so it was high time to award her a distinction and send her into retirement. In the end, she would simply cause trouble, indeed, damage the foreign tourism, and since she was not a member of the council, one could not call her to account or otherwise manipulate her; in short, she was not subject to blackmail, and therefore a difficult sort of citizen to deal with. She would have to be put under some obligation.

This type of teacher required a lovely, tearful celebration with soft music, champagne, bunches of flowers, a bit of money—say, three months' salary—a silver plaque, a school choir, a speech of gratitude by a former student who had accomplished something in life, television coverage, and an article in the newspaper, which she could hang over the sideboard. She would be nourished by the memory of this event for the rest of her life; she could tell the other old ladies at the hairdresser's and in the market, while waiting at the butcher's for a stewing chicken, and at the cemetery while weeding her husband's grave, what a wonderful celebration it had been and how much honor had been accorded her.

9

On Monday, the nineteenth of January, Anna Lévay was called to the principal's office during the long break. The principal informed her that he had been shocked, shocked, to discover—he knew that women found the question a touchy one, but in fact, if truth be told, a man is only as old as he looks, while a woman is only as old as she feels. In any case, the powers that be are not asking Mrs. Lévay how old she feels, but instead have noted that according to official documents she should have retired already last September, and therefore, and furthermore, because the school is under a legal obligation to do so, the situation must be regularized at the start of the new semester, that is, as of February 1. Please, Mrs. Lévay should shed no tears, one is grateful for the job she has done, there will be a lovely farewell ceremony, and she will certainly be permitted to continue working with a study group or some such arrangement, there is no cause for anxiety, in any case, she is not working with a graduating class, her classes will be taken over by her colleagues, she should have faith in them, yes, of course, everyone considers that he or she alone knows best how to teach the material, especially teachers who are approaching retirement, but that is nothing more than a transitional condition. You will soon find your sea legs, so to speak, Mrs. Lévay. You must understand, we cannot offer you any continuation of your contract; the school simply cannot undertake this, it would contravene a direct order from the mayor, who has personally intervened in this affair; I did not intend to go so deeply into an explanation; I did so only in consideration of good collegial relations; surely, an intelligent person like you can understand this and can read the handwriting on the wall; and the rest will do you good, one should not have to spell it out any more clearly.

In a fatherly tone, he offered to leave the room and close the door behind him; Anna Lévay could remain there until she had collected herself; it would not be good for the students to see such a popular and respected teacher in such a condition.

In her next three classes, as in her remaining nine days on the job, Anna Lévay abandoned her instructional regime and read to her students and talked with them. They did not understand the sudden change in her manner; they had become accustomed to their strict teacher.

That day, Anna Lévay informed her colleagues that she was soon to retire, and also that her pension would not even suffice to cover her fixed expenses. Therefore, she asked the other teachers to recommend to her any student who might request a tutor in literature or grammar. Anna Lévay brushed aside the general expressions of sympathy, and in the fifth, her free, period, she calmly ate her midday meal in the cafeteria, sharing politically incorrect jokes with the retired but still teaching physics instructor, making fun of the employees from the town hall, among whom was a woman so concerned about the beauty of her artificial fingernails that she would not touch the underside of her lunch tray with her fingers, with the result that the tray, upon gently bumping against the leg of a chair, slipped out of her hand, spilling its entire contents on the cafeteria floor with a loud crash; and now the fashionable woman stood shamefaced like a vampire exposed, while a thin stream of tomato soup ran gently over her hand, dripping from the long, red, polished fingernails.

The physics teacher called the tomato soup the blood of martyrs, since it was always served with little sprocket-shaped noodles with a hole in the middle that somehow were reminiscent of the Spanish Inquisition. Anna Lévay did not think of the other possible interpretation of the iconography of the noodles, that of the representation of a halo giving forth rays of light, and she continued spooning up her soup. She also devoured her meat and rice, drank two glasses of tap water, returned her tray as she always did, tossed the silverware into the plastic receptacle, and distributed the remaining items each to its assigned place. In leaving, she looked at the menu for the following day, and then ascended the stairs, through the new auditorium, and then up another staircase to the teachers' room, where she sat awhile. After the optional sixth and seventh periods she put on her worn-out overcoat and walked home.

Her mailbox was full. She began reading her mail while climbing the stairs: The telephone bill, an advertisement for a private pension plan, the program from the house of culture for the next month, in which she found the announcement that yet two more promising young writers would be reading from their work.

Even a free copy of the national newspaper, sent to all who did not subscribe, had come with the post. Anna Lévay, who upstairs in her kitchen was assailed by symptoms of anxiety, wanted to give no more than a passing glance at the newspaper—she had her own negative judgment about direct advertising—but her curiosity was stronger than her revulsion. In relation to the sudden increase in tourism, the mayor was quoted to the effect that it could have to do with nothing other than the expertise of the tourism professionals and their ability to promote their product, it was all just as he had promised in his election speech four years ago, and until the end of his term in office, this coming autumn, he would actively promote the participation of these experts at international trade fairs and would encourage them in their enticement of foreign tourists to visit this country. He also mentioned contacts with sister cities, the town's own web page, even the highly effective, even though incurring no

cost to the town, awarding of a prize of "most loyal visitor" to those
tourists who returned every year. All this showed, he explained, the
error of those who argued against the public funds that had been allocated to the promotion of tourism. Those who provided accommodations were now raking money into their own pockets that the
town had expended on promotion.

At the same time, he denigrated the journalists and other citizens who had decried the trips taken by town delegations to German, French, Slovenian, Transylvanian, Finnish, Israeli, American,
and Mexican sister cities as so much self-serving extravagance that
did nothing to help the tourism industry. Those watchdogs of the
public purse would have driven them out of the five-star hotels in
which they stayed, even as they envied their clothing allowance. After all, one could not expect the town's representative to live in a
camping bus and dine on hamburgers; he had to represent the
town, and in any case, the town had to pay only the transportation
costs; room and board were covered by the foreign host. To be sure,
when the invitation went the other way the situation was reversed,
but one hand washes the other. That it was always the same individuals who traveled was not a form of cronyism, but was determined exclusively by professional considerations—against which
nothing could be uttered—that it should always be the most competent individuals and most deserving employees who traveled. He
promised that should he be reelected in the fall, he would continue
to promote tourism by similar methods, and of course, one must
continue to hope that the search for thermal springs within the
town's borders would be continued.

Anna Lévay overcame her intellectual nausea. The mephitic
cloven hoofprint of the Satan of manipulation hung so obviously,
thick and hairy, from the article that Anna Lévay, were she not herself involved, would have liked to telephone the responsible parties
with the demand that the lies be withdrawn. Perhaps she would
even have written a letter to the editor, of course without any hope
that it would be published, but simply to let off steam; if what one

had here in this country was an illusory democracy, then at least one should preserve the illusion; anyway, one couldn't hurt her now. If they wished to suspend her from teaching, they could stand at the lectern in her place for her last few days at school. But Anna Lévay knew that she would write no such letter: If she revealed the real reason for the surge in tourism, no one would believe her, and moreover, those leeches—those who rented out rooms, who owned hotels, who plied a trade—would be anxious about their profits and would suspect that she was just trying to get a share of the take. At once, they would all converge upon her, demand proof, or simply declare her mad. She would have to be silent about the true reason, incomprehensible to normal human understanding, in order to maintain her dignity.

The worst thing about the whole matter was that the doctor, the mayor's confidant, most probably knew this. The text oozed a sort of unshakeable self-confidence that can be produced only by one who is absolutely determined and will stop at nothing. In reading the article, Anna Lévay had not even gotten past the part about the crutches in the market square when her temper came to a boil, and under normal circumstances, her blood pressure would have risen so high so rapidly that she might have suffered a stroke, had her body been subject to normal physical influences.

She felt only that from her scalp, from where the halo came closest to her skin, a strong stream of energy flowed forth. She had sensed something similar long ago, before the appearance of the halo; during a conversation in the teachers' room she had remarked that the matter under discussion made her hair stand on end, whereupon the physics teacher took the ebonite rod that she happened to have with her, quickly rubbed it behind her back on her nylon smock, and then held the electrostatically charged object above Anna Lévay's head, causing the teacher's thin, soft, undyed hair to rise straight up into the air.

When the doctor arrived that afternoon at four o'clock to take her to work, Anna Lévay was not standing in front of her building.

From outside, she could hear vigorous, aggressive honking. That day, they took care of seventy-two patients. The doctor then asked her not to come any longer to his practice, for things had become too conspicuous after the most recent events. The landlords had already figured out too much. It had occurred to some of them that in the places where Anna Lévay and the masseur had appeared, the guests had rapidly disappeared. These people had begun to suspect that Anna Lévay was working as a tax inspector for the tourist board, a job that was warmly recommended in official circles for reducing joblessness among qualified teachers. As a consequence, the doctor had rented a large house in a village located in a nature preserve not far from town and had the patients transported there in buses, under the pretense that they were going on an excursion. To avoid arousing suspicion, the bus left every day from a different location, which was revealed to the riders only a half hour before the bus was set to depart. The discretion of the bus driver could be relied upon. He was a former patient who had been cured, and the doctor had convinced him that his cure would last only so long as he continued to take a particular medication, in the form of pills that the doctor concocted on weekend nights out of wheat bran and pharmaceutically approved binders with a machine that he had purchased especially for this purpose. The bus driver's wife assumed that her husband was out drinking with his friends. Once, she had even quarreled with him when he came home not reeking of beer. Surely, he had been with a woman, and she searched his clothing so meticulously for alien hairs that since then he always made sure to imbibe a sufficient quantity of alcoholic refreshment before returning home from work.

After his consultation hours, instead of taking her home, the doctor took Anna Lévay to the building where the future "cure center" was to be located. By day, work on the renovations was still underway. One could see where walls had been torn out and tiles replaced; otherwise, the building was shrouded in darkness. The electricians had not yet completed their work. The pair were admitted by the security guard. The doctor said to her that he only wanted to see how far the work had progressed; the next day there would be a meeting of the commission, and during the day he had had no time, but he did not want to leave Anna Lévay waiting alone in the automobile. The teacher was so tired that she offered no resistance. She trudged after the doctor, up the echoing staircase and into the ballroom, at one end of which were floor-to-ceiling windows that offered a magnificent view of the lake, which was separated from the building by only a narrow promenade. It was not until they were standing at the very last window that Anna Lévay sensed a trap. The doctor opened the window and began with a request that she reveal to him how she had accomplished the trick with the fish. But at this the teacher pressed her legs together, begged his pardon, and hurried in the direction of the toilets.

She oriented herself by the moon and the light from the street lamps. When she had reached the opposite end of the ballroom, she did not go toward the bathrooms that were being tiled, but simply stepped into a pile of rubbish, so that the doctor would think that she had gone in that direction. She saw clearly in the dim light that he was peering in her direction, but she knew that he could not see her. Carefully, she crept down the stairs, into the courtyard, and around the building, so that she could not be seen from the street; then she squatted down, for she really did have to go. She was now almost directly under the window that the doctor had opened and then closed again on account of the cold, and while she was freeing her bladder from the pressure that had tormented her, she uttered in her thoughts the wish that she might find a solution to her dilemma before the last drops left her; but no solution occurred to her.

She returned to the building to beg of the doctor that he drive her home; indeed, it had grown quite late, and after all, on the morrow she did have to teach. As she passed by the toilet and trod, for the sake of her alibi, in the rubbish heap, she heard from outside in the garden a dull thud. In amazement she watched the doctor open wide the window, lean out, and then return, close the window with great difficulty, and come toward her, holding his dripping arm far from his body, a perfect imitation of Dracula in a bad horror comedy. "Damn it, who left the damn faucet open again," he cried, and ran down the stairs.

Anna Lévay followed. Below, they met the security guard, who reported that the workers always closed the main valve at the end of the day. The three of them darted around the building like dark shadows.

Anna Lévay held back a bit, not only on account of her age and her girth, but more because she was full of foreboding. The doctor, who had seen nothing before the water had hit him full in the face, assumed that he would again see a fish-covered shore, as on the previous October 30.

At the corner of the building they breathed deeply: There was no odor of fish. They stood blinking and peered into the night while the moisture in the ground penetrated their shoes. Then the security guard ran forward and fitted the lever for the rear lights into its slot, and in the light that now streamed down, Anna Lévay and the doctor could see the marvel that had occurred. Exactly in front of the window where the doctor had stood but a few minutes before, in front of a laburnum bush, there shot forth from the ground, with ceaseless turmoil seething, propelled to the height of the windowsill, as thick as a man's leg, a shaft of pure water, yellow from its iron or sulfur content. From its high point, the column of water fell, as if something were sitting at the top of it, into little sprays, in which the reflected light broke up as if refracted through many small prisms, resulting in an array of colors, an almost tangible rainbow.

The doctor approached the shaft of water with outstretched arms, allowing his elegant winter coat and suit, indeed, right through to his underwear, to become completely soaked. He stood in his expensive leather shoes up to his ankles in water. He danced, oblivious to all around him, for a full five minutes, in the shower that came forth from the earth. The security guard, who had mean-

while returned, looked quizzically at Anna Lévay, whereupon the
doctor, pointing to the stream of water and continuing his dance,
called to the guard as if in explanation of his strange behavior, "It is
warm, my good fellow, warm water! Don't you believe me? It is at
least thirty-six degrees! Come in, come in at once!"

The watchman had no choice. This was no time for refusing to
obey a command, even though couched as a suggestion, made by
one with power in town affairs, one on whom depended whether
work on the building would be expedited or brought to a halt; if the
doctor wished it, a decision could be taken against continuation of
work, and the watchman would return to the rolls of the unemployed; no, anything but that, better he should get a bit wet. Before
the watchman stepped into the water, he sought Anna Lévay's
glance, but he found it not, for in the interval the teacher, not wish-
ing to have to lie about her activities, for she had no desire to admit
to her squatting on the ground in the place whence the water had
gushed forth, had left the scene and with rapid steps walked home.

The doctor did not notice her absence until the arrival of the
fire brigade, together with a commando unit from the oil refinery,
who installed a pressure-control valve and then wished to hear from
those who had witnessed the event. After Anna Lévay's disappearance, and before the fire brigade's arrival, the doctor had frolicked
for a long time in the warm water. He attempted to touch the main
column of water, but despite many attempts, was unable to do so.
Each time, as he approached within a cubit of his goal, a mysterious
force pushed him back, and so he could not partake of the actual
source of the water, but only from the falling streams that branched
off from the central column. He spent perhaps a quarter of an hour
in his shamanic dance and cogitation over how the income from the
future hot springs might be spent.

Then he reached for his mobile telephone and called the fire department, to whom he had to explain several times just what it was
that he required, while the person on duty, who knew the doctor,
suspected that the worthy physician was drunk. His suspicion was

particularly aroused by the description of a rainbow and the assertion that the water did not mix with the harbor sludge; and therefore, the duty officer did no more than send out a car to the scene
to ascertain the facts in the case. After the doctor had ended the call,
he received a call from the fire department, which wanted to know
whether the call had in fact come from him, upon which the doctor
became filled with wrath and stated forcefully that the fire department was a municipal institution, and if they wished to be considered next year when budgetary allocations were made, then they
should kindly send out a fully equipped company at once.

When they were done with their work, the troop commander
from the fire department wanted to consider the incident in greater
detail, particularly on account of the unidentifiable and strange
quality of the water, which shimmered with all the colors of the
rainbow, and as it fell was reclaimed by the earth without a trace of
dampness.

It occurred to the doctor that perhaps Anna Lévay could offer
an explanation, even though at the moment the spring had appeared she had not been present, having gone to the toilet. Even so,
if anyone had an explanation, it would certainly be she.

The warm spring proved to be pure and abundant. As a result
of this happy turn of events, the firm entrusted with the renovation
of the building was instructed to reconfigure the plumbing. They
must build a system independent of the municipal water supply
that would conduct the water from the spring directly into specially
constructed pools in the treatment rooms.

The authorities entrusted the drawing up of the necessary permits and the entry into the official register of mineral springs to six
lawyers, all of whom accepted the assignment in the hope—as was
usual in this town—of rapid and unethical self-enrichment. There
was only one who was opposed, the councilman on whose property
there had been test boring for thermal waters, but he was without
veto power.

Now the number of tourism professionals had to be increased.
To avoid future chaotic scenes like the recent tumult in the market

square, room rentals were now offered over the Internet. An additional column on the town's home page was devoted to health tourism for the promotion of mud cures and thermal waters. The page was divided into three columns and constructed so that to the left appeared the names of those who had been cured of their ailments. This new method of communication made it possible to keep track of everything that was going on in the tourism sector. The travel agencies were promised individual web pages at no cost for self-promotion, and a tax incentive was offered for bookings made over the Internet. Shortly thereafter began the surveillance of all e-mail that passed through the town's server.

The doctor had not at first noticed Anna Lévay's disappearance. In the time between the discovery of the spring and the installation of the pressure valve he had removed his winter coat, and in a transport of joy bordering on madness had planted himself, with legs akimbo and arms outstretched, as close as he could to the warm stream and embraced it to the extent that the water's repulsive force allowed. Viewed from above, the column of water stood in the center of the triangle formed by the doctor's head and arms, like the eye of the Lord in representations of the Trinity. Viewed from the ground, it looked as though the doctor were celebrating in the ramified stream the potency of an all-powerful creator, as though the drops of water falling from the liquid phallus were impregnating the womb of his most secret desires. The jet of goldgleaming water broke between his fingers and flowed as two small fountains back to Mother Earth. In the raked light from the watchman's lamp the droplets of water glittered on his cheeks in all the colors of the rainbow, his hair clung to his head like the dried skin of a nut in its shell, and from the strong light that broke into droplets between his upraised hands there arose a rainbow that arched from one hand to the other. He could not turn his eyes from the sight; he simply stood there, shifting his weight from one foot to the other, gazing aloft.

Thus, until the arrival of the firemen, he showered in the water that came forth from the earth. The leader of the group recoiled at the sight of him, but dared not make an observation on his appearance. He merely murmured, "So, that's who it is. Who would have thought?" and he at once called out so all could hear, "A good evening to everyone! All right now, who set this water loose? Whoever it was might have done it a bit farther away so that the building doesn't get washed away." It was only then that the doctor noticed that Anna Lévay was no longer standing where she had recently stood.

Long after midnight, after everything had been settled, he walked, drenched to the skin, to the place where he had been standing when Anna Lévay had left to go to the toilet. He opened the large window, looked below onto the lawn, and attempted to find a logical explanation for the events that had transpired.

A gentle breeze caressed his face.

The following morning, he was discovered by the workmen, who knew nothing of the nocturnal goings-on. He was asleep on two tables that had been pushed together and was covered with his wet winter coat, whose folds closely followed the contours of his body. An ambulance was summoned, and the medical orderlies could determine only that he was asleep. Yet they could find no explanation for his being at the construction site covered with a soaking wet winter coat, his damp hair giving forth warmth. To be on the safe side, they transported him to the hospital. Since they could find nothing physically wrong with him and since he had not awakened in the ambulance while he was being examined, he was taken to the neurological unit. A hospital worker who could think of no other explanation for his condition voiced the suspicion that perhaps the doctor was drunk. However, the physician on duty wanted to choke off the dubious rumor at once to avoid putting his career in jeopardy, and so he stated that there was no possibility that the doctor was intoxicated, the doctor assuredly suffered from a serious and chronic disease that was associated with a disturbance of consciousness; how wonderful that he nevertheless summoned so much energy to assist in the town's affairs!

The doctor's clothing had become completely rigid and had to be cut from his body before he could be dressed in hospital pajamas. The stiff clothes showed the wrinkles on his skin, even the hair on his body and the coins in his inner pocket. His hands rested on his abdomen, but his wrists were bent in such a way that they formed a triangle with his forearms. His bodily functions seemed in order, though this was contradicted by an unusual rigidity.

His colleagues were unable to make a diagnosis. The lab results were singularly unhelpful: All were negative. A consulting specialist was summoned. This gentleman from the capital, a man at the pinnacle of his profession, determined that one was dealing here with a rare case of nervous exhaustion, which until now had been diagnosed only among those in the arts and military commanders.

The doctor slept soundly for three days, during which time friends, relations, and acquaintances came to the sickbed to pay their respects. He was in the same room that the rabbi had occupied.

Upon awakening, he went into the physicians' common room, observed that the calendar indicated that today was Thursday, the twenty-second of January, determined that he must have been lying unconscious for three days, and then measured his blood pressure and checked his reflexes. Then he bound his left arm with an elastic, sprayed the skin with disinfectant and anesthetic, found a suitable syringe, located the vein at the crook of his elbow, and stuck in the needle. At that moment the nurse on duty entered the room.

He had wanted only to draw some blood, he said in his defense; he was fine now, it was necessary to undertake a complete routine physical examination to arrive at a proper diagnosis. The nurse finished drawing the blood, and then asked the doctor to lie down on the small sofa. She covered him with a blanket, sat on the edge of the sofa, and began to stroke his forehead as though checking for fever; she spoke soothingly, he needed rest, his condition forbade him to get up, he would work himself to death. The doctor interrupted this sentence in a fury; he felt it necessary to convince the nurse of his physical capacity in no uncertain terms, which she duly noted. Then the doctor stood up, studied his chart carefully, wrote down a conclusive diagnosis of nervous exhaustion without waiting for the laboratory results, declared himself cured, canceled the order for a substitute to be on duty the next day, said good-bye all around, and went home.

His wife, who arrived at the hospital half an hour later, found in the hospital room nothing but a disordered empty bed and the nurse on duty, who was preparing the bed for a new patient. She told the doctor's wife that her husband had left the hospital, at which the woman burst into tears, uttered, although she was an atheist, a prayer, and scolded her irresponsible husband for not looking after himself, surely he would work himself to death.

That same morning, Anna Lévay calmly walked to work. She had not prepared for her classes. She no longer considered that necessary, since in the days remaining she wanted only to give her students a last literary experience to take with them. She arrived early at the teachers' room; no one else was present. She walked around the four long tables. Usually, there lay on the table to the left by the door the "special offers." This was an activity in which they shared out of nostalgia for a bygone era, a leftover from the time when certain things could be obtained only under the table and by knowing someone who knew someone. For most of the items— such as chicken, eggs, vegetables, pasta, and baked goods—were now readily obtainable, and the bulk discount was small. Today's event was a delivery of chocolate wafers and chocolate-covered brandied cherries.

During the long break Anna Lévay visited Marika in the main office and paid for the items she had ordered, which she placed in her drawer in the large communal table. Before going to lunch, she spoke to a colleague who moonlighted as the representative of a cosmetics company and who had invited her to look through a catalog that offered creams to remove the wrinkles around the eyes, tone the skin, and redden the cheeks.

Anna Lévay explained to her that at her age she was no longer interested in pleasing a man, and particularly not a man who would require of an old lady that she possess a face made youthful by creams. It would ruin her financially, for she would have to spend her entire pension on such stuff. At this, the colleague interrupted with the hope of changing her mind: One need not make oneself beautiful just to please others, no, one did it for oneself, indeed, a beauty appropriate to one's age gave one self-confidence, which, after all, is the basis of success. Anna Lévay thought to herself that now her colleague was delivering a slick marketing spiel on the fundamentals of self-beautification, as though she were addressing a neophyte tart fresh from the village. Anna Lévay turned without a word and walked in the direction of the cafeteria.

Her younger colleague observed behind her back that old age had affected Mrs. Lévay's mental processes, a remark that was related to Anna Lévay by a witness immediately upon her return from lunch. Then Anna Lévay took her package of chocolate-covered brandied cherries, carried it to the teachers' room, closed the door behind her, placed a worn-out copy of the *Divine Comedy* in front of her, and began to read the *Purgatorio,* apathetically, more for the rhythm than for the meaning. The syllables resounded in her brain. While reading she unwrapped one chocolate-covered brandied cherry after another with the relish of a chain smoker going through a pack of cigarettes. Earlier, she had eaten such things more cautiously, biting off the chocolate base first, then drinking the liquor out of the little chocolate chalice, then biting into the fruit, licking the delicious pink syrup out of it, and then gulping down the rest at once. But now she devoured the candies with abandon. This time it was but a single bite that crushed the candy, followed by a quick chew, a rapid swallow, and that was that.

She twisted the gold foil wrappers into tiny balls and placed them on the table, under whose glass top lay a large map of the European Union. And thus to the five-pointed stars marking the European capitals was added a collection of over fifty golden balls.

At three o'clock in the afternoon the cleaning woman found Anna Lévay with her head on the table, surrounded by the little gold balls. "Saints alive, what is wrong with you? Are you asleep? Are you unwell?" The cleaning woman may have suspected that Anna Lévay was drunk on the brandy, but she revived the instant the woman touched her shoulder, and she immediately grasped the situation. It is nothing, she answered with aristocratic hauteur, she had stayed up late correcting homework and not had enough sleep, and then the change in the weather, and the poplar outside her window had rustled its branches all night in the wind; when she finally got to bed, she had been unable to sleep. This reassured the cleaning woman, who returned to her work.

The teacher collected her things. She put on her overcoat, but before setting out for home she went to the women's toilet and ran cold water over her wrists, washed her face, and because she had to throw up, repeated the process several times. She did not care for alcohol and did not tolerate it well. She had been drunk only three times in her life.

The first was with the student János Lévay, when they were offered and occasionally made use of a fellow student's room in Józsefváros for a few hours, so that they could be together in civilized circumstances after returning from expeditions to the neighboring hills west of Budapest. There they had first enjoyed an entire bottle of sweet wine and then the delights of love.

The second time, after Dr. János Lévay had been killed, the neighbors of his relatives had gotten her drunk to prevent her from acting on a rash impulse to run out into the street and provoke fate with maledictions against the regime while bent over the corpse of her husband, so that she, too, might die; but the janitor of the building, who had seen from the gate below what the student Anna Lévay had seen from above, restrained her, brought her down to the first floor, and entrusted her to a family who kept her under control by giving her tea laced with strong kosher wine; on the following day, they took her to her parents.

The third time was when Dr. Péter Lévay, who had obtained entrance to university only with great difficulty on account of his father's past and after slaving away for four years as a laborer, a stevedore at the train station in Köbánya, who after receiving his diploma with honors set off on a trip to East Germany, and in August 1986 sent her a postcard that he had arrived in the free world, then, then, all on her own, she had drunk four half-liter bottles of apricot brandy and not left her garage for a week. She called in sick to the restaurant where she was working. She wished to see no one. There were East Germans staying in her apartment at the time, but she did not wish to speak with them either.

She left the school and walked home. There she found the doctor already waiting for her, even though they had agreed that Anna Lévay would either get to his office on her own or be picked up by the masseur. But the doctor had come to her this day because his secretary, who knew nothing of the strange goings-on, had decided that he would be unable to work for a while and had canceled all his appointments. Now he had come to tell her that she would have no work today, and that for tactical reasons and to increase demand, he would not see any private patients for another week, and to continue thereafter at another location. Let the patients wait, and in any case, there was no one whom he had promised to see immediately. During this hiatus in his practice Anna Lévay would, of course, continue to receive her salary. But could he not, now that he was here, perhaps come up for a brief conversation?

Anna Lévay had no desire for an interview. It was clear to her that the doctor's success depended on her collaboration and that the doctor knew this just as well as she. Therefore, she brushed him off so curtly that it bordered on insult. She was tired, she said, and would rather lie down than converse with him.

And so Anna Lévay went alone up to her apartment, drank a cup of tea, and then read the newspaper in bed. On the local page she learned that work on the so-called cure center had been accelerated and that it would open on February 1, primarily because, as had been reported in the two previous issues of the paper, the long-sought mineral spring had finally been found, the spring in whose existence only fanatics and local religious zealots had believed.

Announcements followed thick and fast: beautiful, optimistic, demagogic. Work on the building was proceeding day and night, said the mayor in answer to a reporter's question; international interest was intense, and this was to the credit of the municipal authorities and the tourism industry, for this interest was due solely to well-targeted publicity. The water had already been tested, and it was determined that it had a remarkable effect on certain illnesses affecting movement of the extremities; the board of directors was doing everything in its power to ensure that the required permits and licenses would be obtained as quickly as possible.

The news drove Anna Lévay's blood pressure to new heights, at least that is how it seemed to her; she stood up, stuck her head, together with the halo, under the taps in the bathtub and let cold water run over her neck, as she often had done. While the halo and the stream of water were in contact, a period of about five minutes, the holy healing power of the halo moved through the water pipes in the entire building, out through one of the main lines of the municipal water system, and thence into the main waterworks, whence it passed into other main lines and spread throughout the town. Of all this, Anna Lévay observed only that she had become unbelievably tired; therefore, she lay down again and at once fell asleep. Reports, about which she heard the following day, suggested a mysterious—and, according to a private formulation of the doctor, one causing unauthorized and immeasurable economic damage—escape of water from the mineral spring. In the market square, tourists who had just arrived for treatment celebrated their departure by holding a spontaneous street party. In the hospital, a patient who was scheduled to undergo an operation for kidney stones and had just taken his evening medication with a glass of tap water found himself suddenly free of pain and left the hospital without

symptoms. At the same time, down in the emergency room, the application of a cast, the plaster for which had been mixed in water, resulted in a child's shin bone, broken in three places in a bicycle
accident, being knitted together perfectly. The wife of a town councilman who had just made soda water in a siphon experienced that
evening a potency in her husband that she had never known before;
the councilman wondered about it, too, for his energies in that direction had long come to rather a standstill, despite a variety of
treatments. To conceal this he had repeatedly declared that he had
no interest in young girls, but preferred mature and experienced
women, to which his colleagues generally were wont to remark
malevolently that those were precisely the ones who did not demand
so much. There were many other cases that could be mentioned:
Decades-old migraines disappeared, rheumatism vanished, skin tormented by acne became smooth, eczema went into remission, ocu-
lar refractive indices adjusted themselves, complex inflammations
subsided, cancer cells perished.

The next day the talk in the town was of nothing but this miracle, the cause of which remained hidden from the populace; they
simply could not imagine how these cures could have happened.
What was clear, though, was that many illnesses had been cured, and
many put it down to the unusually fine weather. The mayor had instructed his spokesman to arrange a press conference for that afternoon, in which the mayor was to admonish the populace not to
spread unfounded rumors of miraculous cures. Finally, the mayor
thought it advisable not to speak himself, and so he ordered his
spokesman to read the text of the communiqué written by a loyal
journalist and the doctor, and not to add anything of his own. And
so the spokesman stood and read to the effect that whoever believed
himself to have experienced such a cure should consult his physician,
assuming that he had available suitable documentation of his prior
condition, for otherwise, the claim would be simply beyond belief
and would do damage to the town's tourism industry. He quickly
sketched the consequences of such false propaganda. One of the first

would be a drastic decline in the number of visitors to the town; indeed, the town would likely be boycotted by foreign travel agencies, and that would be good for no one. He promised to make a public announcement the moment that a single believable case of a cure had been established. Until then, one would do well not to fall into the kind of mass hysteria that one encountered in descriptions of Biblical miracles. He stated that at the behest of the populace an investigative committee had been set up under the chairmanship of the doctor, adding that the doctor was a neurologist and psychiatrist. Thus he read from his prepared text, and that haltingly. Any questions? No questions? Thank you.

That evening he sent an expanded version of the speech to the local television station. The reporters belonging to the media supported by the council received instructions not to get involved in these matters, not even to report on the phenomenon with irony or to deny its existence. The journalists from out of town were put off the scent in the usual way. It was announced that the council was in no way attempting to close the door on an investigation. In fact, a special commission had been set up, and so there was nothing for them to investigate. And in the end, what does not exist cannot be reported on.

Friday, the thirtieth of January, was Anna Lévay's last day at school. She spoke to her students about Bulgakov, Solzhenitsyn, and the psychology of creativity. In her last two weeks she had become particularly loved by her students. It was as though in this short period of time they had forgotten all about the taxing homework assignments, their bad grades, the stress of examinations. Perhaps the students had learned that Mrs. Lévay had been precipitously forced out by the school principal, a man they detested, and wished to make known their sympathy by seeking her company outside of class and asking her advice about their schoolwork or their personal affairs. One could have called these last hours "The Master and His Disciples," except that they were not seated in a beautiful place in a half circle on the floor, but on uncomfortable benches in a stuffy classroom. Five minutes before the end of the lesson, the warning bell sounded. Anna Lévay was consumed by anxiety, her stomach gently quaking in her agitation. In five minutes her career as a teacher would be over.

After the final class, Anna Lévay was ceremoniously received in the teachers' room. Her colleagues surrounded her, offered her drinks, cakes, and cookies; one of them gave a speech, to which she did not listen. A collection had been taken and a gift had been purchased, as is usual on such occasions. The principal slipped an envelope into Anna Lévay's hand, which contained her January salary and a cash bonus, but before she could thank him, the receipt for it was placed under her nose for her signature. The principal could not say loudly enough how sorry he was over Anna Lévay's retirement, though behind his sour smile the teachers suspected a thinly disguised sense of satisfaction and relief, since he was finally rid of an adversary. Everyone knew that Anna Lévay had sat on the commission that had evaluated the applications for the principalship and that she was one of those who had spoken strongly against the appointment of this man.

After the usual polite formulas had been exchanged, Anna Lévay squeezed herself through the crowd of colleagues, went to her place, took the books that were lying on her shelf, calmly put on her winter coat, and waved goodbye to those remaining with a gesture copied from that of the wife of the former president of a neighboring country whom she had once observed. It was meant to be taken ironically. She left without a word, for she feared that if she opened her mouth, it would give forth a bitter tirade. She might even begin to weep and be unable to leave with her dignity intact.

When she arrived at home she unwrapped her gift. It was a silver candleholder and an engraving that depicted St. Francis of Assisi preaching to the animals. She had admired the picture when visiting her colleague, the drawing teacher. It had been hanging in her dining room. Viewed from afar, it appeared that the animals, gathered in a circle about the saint, who was leaning against a tree, were attending to the words of the preacher, each with its mate. But when the fine lines of the engraving were viewed up close, one saw that the rabbits were rutting, the dogs copulating, the snakes entwined in coition, the bears sniffing each other, the deer mating; in short, they were paying no attention to the sermon, being otherwise occupied. God forbid they should understand human speech and be able to speak themselves, her colleague had said, then they would probably tell the saint to fuck off, which had annoyed Anna Lévay. The artist was surely a genius. Her colleagues must have contacted him and purchased another copy for her. Anna Lévay burst out in laughter as she recalled the moment when a colleague handed the gift with the comment, "Put it out of your mind!" He had meant her being forced into retirement. She kept on smiling as she hung the gold-framed picture on the wall above the telephone. So much for perspective, she thought. As she walked in front of the picture and glanced several times at the scene of mass excitement, she imagined some of her colleagues and acquaintances in place of some of the animals, each according to his or her character. She then fell asleep over her evening reading with the pleasant feeling of mild spite.

Throughout the following week, she worked in the cure center, which had been constructed of the finest materials, without regard to cost, and finished in record time. And it was full to bursting with paying guests, although one could not simply walk in off the street. The number of patients treated each day was strictly limited. One could register for the sanatorium only over the Internet, and even then one could obtain a place only by outbidding others. To be sure, prices for treatment and accommodations were set according to a fixed schedule, but the firm had complete latitude as to whom they accepted, and they always offered a place to those who offered the most money.

Anna Lévay had the task of querying the patients, in the role of interpreter, in the presence of the doctor, and after a diagnosis had been established, to place the worn remnant of a fossilized mollusk, a *Congeria ungula capra* from the Tertiary geological period, known as a goat's claw, with the open side turned downward to touch the affected part of the patient's body, which was then covered with warm mud, and the patient wrapped in blankets. The wealthier patients were then treated by a sturdy masseur. Then the patients sat in a row on the floor clothed in the prescribed uniforms for the bath, hand-woven white linen nightshirts that reached to their ankles, which had been washed in seawater—they were said to emit positive emanations—under which the patients were as naked as angels. There they awaited the doctor.

This was not the same doctor who had discovered Anna Lévay's supernatural abilities, for which reason we shall hereinafter refer to him as the spa master. The doctor about whom we have had much to say to this point had withdrawn from active participation in the sanatorium's affairs in order to preserve his professional reputation, for the enterprise was raking in enormous profits, and he did not want to attract the attention of envious parties or officials of the internal revenue office. And so he had engaged an internist as spa master, a man thirty-five years old, with black hair, blue eyes, well trained, by far not at the top of his profession and completely impervious to nonrational phenomena. But the doctor was certain that the fat old foreign women would gush over him. The spa master had learned his role well and held a celebration for each of the miraculous cures, at the expense of the cured foreigners. He had devised a particular ritual for these celebrations. The meal consisted of a thin fish broth and steamed fish with vegetables, followed by a dessert of chocolate-and-nut-filled crêpes twisted into the shape of a snail and served with an intense golden Tokay wine poured into crystal goblets whose feet had been dipped in the healing mud. The spa master enjoyed these parties most of all. He continually experienced medical success and enjoyed an active social life, with plenty of opportunity to meet young women. Anna Lévay did not appear at these parties, for she was not invited. The patients departed the next day completely cured. In their bags they took away the goat's claw, the linen nightshirt, and a book with pictures of the town, and it was impressed upon them that they were to say nothing of the details of their cures. This cult of secrecy served as the best advertisement. Within a month, there were over one hundred applications a day from around the world.

In mid-February an international commission arrived at the center to investigate the inexplicable cures. They were put up in a hotel belonging to one of the members of the municipal council. During their stay, Anna Lévay was granted a vacation from her work. For quite a while she had been complaining of exhaustion, but the doctor had until now been able to convince her to continue working. The investigative commission arrived unannounced, just at lunchtime. The reception desk immediately notified the mayor, who at once called the doctor. Five minutes later both of these gentlemen hurried over to the scene of action. The doctor reported that he had to leave at once for the city where Anna Lévay's brother László lived, and he asked her whether she would like to come along. She could take an afternoon off. The patients could wait, it would be a welcome change for her. If she were in agreement with the plan, she could pack a few things, and could even remain there a few days, she looked exhausted and certainly could use some rest.

The commission checked all the documents regarding the curative waters and mud, examined the results of tests as set down in the authorization papers, and looked into the entire treatment process. During their stay, not a single miraculous cure took place, though in the previously documented cases no physical explanation for the cures could be found. The results of the investigation were duly recorded, the commission concluding that the first such cases could all be regarded as having a psychosomatic origin. The commissioners had no wish to involve themselves in phenomena that could not be scientifically explained, and so the later cases were put down to the placebo effect of the earlier, now legendary, miracle cures.

Anna Lévay spent ten days at her brother's house, and during that time she only once went into the town. She did not wish to see anyone; she feared open spaces. She spent the greater part of her visit sleeping and cleaning the apartment of her elderly bachelor brother. She cleaned in corners where dust had collected for years, applied hydrochloric acid to the remains of long-forgotten meals that had burnt into the side of the gas range, beat the carpet, scoured the floors. The physical labor did her good, and as a reward to herself she invited her brother to accompany her to the theater. *The Master and Margarita* was playing, which she had long wanted to see. She was curious to see how Bulgakov's novel had been dramatized.

They walked to the theater, almost two kilometers. Cats followed them: tiger cats, spotted cats, calico cats. Behind the gates, through the culverts, and along the walls of houses they followed the pair and withdrew only when they reached the lighted edge of the city center. In front of the city archives, near the statue of the founder of the city, the cats established themselves in a tulip tree, and as a vulture waits for carrion so they patiently waited until the retired schoolteacher Anna Lévay and her brother László Kuncz should pass by after their evening at the theater. The teacher had noticed them. Her shoelace had come loose, and she had halted in front of the Benedictine monastery. As she looked between her arm and her leg, she saw a row of green cats' eyes gleaming along a broad tree branch. The eyes shone in pairs from the tree, like green, unripe, magical fruit that needed to be protected by a wakeful king's son.

They made the return trip by taxi, since Anna Lévay's leg had suddenly begun to ache. They had almost arrived at her brother's house when the left front wheel of the taxi began to rattle, and the car went into a skid. The cab driver swore. Another rutting cat killed, he said; they begin early, the winter was mild, they run across the streets unaware of the danger. He always used to swerve to avoid them, not because he was a lover of animals, but because he didn't want blood on the underbody of the car and in the wheel wells.

Recently, a colleague, in an attempt to avoid hitting a cat, had turned the steering wheel sharply and run into an oncoming car, two dead, extensive damage, and since then he swore that he preferred scraping off a few bloody cat remains to such an alternative.

The taxi driver stopped his chatter only when it finally occurred to him that his passengers had become unusually quiet. As he glanced back through the rear-view mirror he looked into the painfully rigid visage of Anna Lévay. Upon receiving his fare, he drove quickly away.

10

Anna Lévay's days passed in monotonous labor. In the cure center two pools filled with the curative water had been put into service. In one of them men soaked themselves, in the other, women. There were now various categories of services offered: In addition to the mud packs one could take a thermal-water sauna, a mineral water bath, a steam wrap, or a special treatment in which the mineral water was drunk. The least expensive treatment was a simple soaking in the pool.

Which category of treatment was offered to a particular patient did not depend simply on what the patient could afford. Each new guest's regime was determined by a commission, and any deviation required additional payment. And before treatment began, the patient had to sign a number of forms.

In one of these, the patient had to affirm that the methods and results of treatment, whether positive or negative, would be kept secret. All were informed, orally, that any violation of this agreement would result in the cure, which even the best scientists were still unable to explain, disappearing as quickly as it had come, and that the patient's disease would reappear in a more severe form than before the treatment. Indeed, there was an example of this phenomenon, namely, that of a patient suffering from a pulmonary mycosis, who had been one of the first patients cured. He had revealed the secret to his confessor, and within a few minutes he had died. When the priest, puzzled at the sudden silence on the other side of the aperture, opened the door of the confessional, the body was already showing signs of advanced decomposition. The corpse was in the state that it would have been in at that time had no treatment been given. To increase the effect of this warning it was added that it had later been learned that this patient's disease was that known as the "pharaoh's curse," and alas, a short time after the occurrence of these events the priest and the men who had carried away the corpse also passed away.

On another form each patient had to declare that he, respectively she, had duly noted that in his, respectively her, room there was medication that "affected normal perception," which was to be taken during treatment on the patient's own responsibility; this was untrue, but should anyone break the vow of silence, one could show this paper to anyone making inquiries. The vague formulation could allow one to draw the inference that the patient had been hallucinating.

A third form obligated the patient, in the case of successful outcome, to transfer ten percent of his next five years' income to a specified foreign bank account as well as to make an annual donation to a registered charitable organization in the patient's country of residence as specified by the cure center.

The fourth document served to cover the actual costs of the treatment. It was a credit contract between a certain foreign corporation and the patient, according to which the firm granted the patient instant credit should he find himself short of cash while abroad; the term of repayment was sixty months, the interest rate was ten percent of the patient's current net income, but no less than _____ , and in the case of nonpayment the patient was under obligation to pay triple the interest to the bank of issue in his home country.

Cash was required only for room and board, though a bank managed by one of the mayor's associates that had opened a branch in the cure center accepted credit cards.

Until these administrative matters had been attended to, the patient was not permitted to enter the parts of the cure center where the actual treatment was carried out. But on the floors where the guest rooms were located, they met patients who had been cured, from whom they could learn about—but about this only—the results of their treatment. The treatment itself was considered a *magnum mysterium,* for which even the indecisive soon longed. If at the moment no spectacular cures of the lame or of those with dramatic dermatological conditions were available to put on display, a man specifically engaged for the purpose would appear in the hallway, with its plush red carpet, and before as many witnesses as possible throw his crutches into the trash bin.

The large number of tasks that had to be accomplished before treatment could begin convinced even those who had at first hesitated of the urgency of reaching a decision. Previously, it had happened only once that someone had withdrawn from the program after having arrived, and this for the sole reason that his credit could not be guaranteed. According to the conditions in the application form, this individual was not entitled to reimbursement of his deposit.

For the cost of a single night in the cure center one could have spent a week in one of the best hotels in the capital. In the restaurant, the cost of a steak, à la carte, without a single side dish, was equivalent to the wholesale price of half a steer. Therefore, citizens of poorer nations contented themselves with the prix fixe, which was delivered, by order of the mayor, from the high school cafeteria's kitchen. The cost of this simple meal was what one would have paid at one of the finest restaurants in town. On account of the unexpected income that the high school contributed to the enterprise, the mayor graciously decided not to raise the price of a school lunch that year. The patients were permitted neither to seek quarters outside of the cure center nor to dine out, for at the time they registered they had to sign an agreement that to preserve the secrecy of the center's operations, they would not leave the building except in organized groups. Any breach of this agreement would result in an immediate termination of treatment and the forfeit of all monies paid.

When all agreements had been signed and treatment could begin, the patient had to sign yet one more agreement, agreeing to accept all responsibility for the results of treatment, including any adverse consequences, releasing the cure center from all obligations with regard to the outcome of the thermal treatment and the degree of amelioration of the patient's condition, and consenting not to seek reimbursement of payment through said patient's health insurance. This paper, together with a formal notification form on which appeared the account numbers of a foundation for the care of the sick with a religious-sounding name that was registered in a number of countries, was given to the patient with the admission forms.

All the other documents were locked in the cure center's safe. This procedure had been formulated by an attorney who led the international group of lawyers that had drawn up these transactions. Earlier, this lawyer had been engaged in much smaller matters such as finding investors for various enterprises to whom he promised enormous returns as well as certain pieces of real estate as security should the investment fail; but then it turned out that the real estate was not owned by the enterprise and that by the time the agreement had run its course, the enterprise had already initiated a declaration of bankruptcy. The lawyer, thanks to his connections in the legal world and various delaying tactics, got off scot-free, and had since been appointed the head of the town council's ethics commission.

Anna Lévay knew nothing of all this and did not want to know anything. She calmly went about her work. She wore a loose smock on her oversized figure, and on her feet she wore high antiskid shoes, which gave her the appearance of a cleaning woman; every half hour she went into the bathing hall, let her right hand rest in the water a moment, and then declared that the guests might now exit the water. This declaration was not made verbally, for the incident of the Basque tourist had been a warning; it had been a long time since she had spoken with the foreign visitors. Sometimes, she would hold her wet hand in front of her eyes and look at her watch, and then touch the middle of her right hand with the fingertips of the left, so that the fingers of the left hand together with the palm of the right hand formed a "T," the internationally recognized symbol in athletic competition that made it clear to the assembled bathers that their time had expired.

The patients stood up like herrings in the hundred-forty-centimeter-deep opaque water, dressed like Adam and Eve before the apple, for the mineral content of the water would have dissolved their bathing suits. Standing around naked had such an effect that one of the guests suggested to the others that they all close their eyes, fold their hands in prayer, and be silent. He began to declaim from the Holy Scriptures, and with all sensing as they climbed out of the pool that their ills were about to be cured, the feeling spread that water and prayer complemented each other. For a time, readings were held in various languages. When later, patients began arriving from all parts of the world, the directorate put an end to the multilingual readings and had all texts read in Latin, until someone came up with the idea that all readings should be in their original languages, with the result that no one understood anything, and from the scriptural readings was to be taken only their unctuous intonations.

The reader was granted a special place. He sat at the base of the thick marble-clad wall that separated the men's and women's pools, on a marble plinth decked with a woolen carpet, his back to the separating wall, so that his voice was carried by the walls above the waters.

Bathing sessions for atheists were also available, for which one had to register specially. Instead of scriptural readings there was a choice of four soothing instrumental selections. The directorate did not increase the selection, because they did not wish to segregate the population of patients on the basis of their musical taste. Therefore, these four musical offerings were presented as though it had been established by independent authorities that they had a stimulating effect on the healing.

The patients were led to the baths at half-hour intervals. From time to time, the pools were cleaned. First the women entered, into the farther pool, naked, and then the men into the nearer pool. When the waves had subsided and the bodies had come to rest, the reader took his place. Then all was still; the patients closed their eyes, listened to the words attentively, piously, for from piety they hoped for healing. Legendary statistics made the rounds as to which language was the most effective for the cure, and that rekindled the age-old and long-forgotten debate as to which language was the first to appear on Earth.

A group of Anabaptists rented the baths during the night hours for their rituals. In the semidarkness secret rites were performed, in which the women stood in a circle around the edge of the pool while the head of the order lay on his back in the water and floated midway on the waves generated by the faithful by beating on the surface of the water. Whither and how rapidly he was borne on the surface of the water determined the basis for his prophecies. Later, the place occupied by the leader could be assumed by others, for a fee, and the curative powers of the water and the unusually erotic nature of the situation encouraged many patients to apply who wished to combine the utilitarian with the congenial, even though not a single nocturnal cure was ever verified. In any case, the visitors to the cure center partook of all the cures offered by day, including Bible readings and the presence of Anna Lévay. The nighttime service was so beloved that arrangements for women were also made, whereby women floated in the pool and men beat the water. Out of politeness, the mayor was invited to one of these evening events; he had a reputation for vanity, and he happily took up the invitation anonymously. A shriek from his wife, also present anonymously, put an end to his calm flotation, for she recognized the masculine ornamentation of her lawfully wedded husband. A week later, these nocturnal services were canceled by the municipal authorities on the basis of ordinances relating to hygiene and sanitation.

Those with the greatest infirmities were given special treatment. They were made to wait meditatively in their rooms until the masseur, now promoted to pool attendant, came to fetch them. They were required to have their wheelchairs positioned at all times with the handles pointing toward the door. The pool attendant came during the half-hourly breaks when the shifts in the pool changed. Like Orpheus, the patients were not allowed to look back. The pool attendant rolled them down the corridor, transported them in the elevator to the ground floor, and then pushed them, together with their nightshirts and wheelchairs, into a specially shaped sloping basin. Three times the patients were pushed in up to the level of their noses; they were not permitted to make a sound; then the attendant pulled them out, and brought them into a cell clad in black granite, where ethereal lights glowed, and where from hidden speakers church choirs punctuated by soprano and tenor soloists sang, while the patient, trembling in fear, received instructions to pray for a cure. Then a strong light illuminated a goblet in a niche on the opposite wall, allegedly containing holy water, which the patient was instructed to drink, after which he would remember nothing and awake in his room completely cured. When the patient was unconscious, the pool attendant, who waited for the appropriate moment aided by a hidden surveillance camera, brought the patient out of the cell into the changing room, where Anna Lévay, wrapped in a heavy blanket, dried his face, blow-dried his hair, and then returned him to the care of the pool attendant. He, in turn, returned the patient to his room, dressed him in a clean night shirt, just like the one that had been recently removed, closed the curtains, hung an inscription for the patient to read upon awakening on the rusty hook located on the upper third of the wall opposite the bed, placed a New Testament in the patient's native language on the night table, opened it to the Book of Revelation, and marked with a sponge dipped in thermal water the last sentence of the first verse of the third chapter as well as the second and third verses: "I know thy works, that thou hast a name that thou livest, and art dead. Be watchful, and strengthen the things which remain, that are ready to die: for I have not found thy works perfect before God. Remember therefore how thou hast received and heard, and hold fast, and repent. If therefore thou shalt not watch, I will come on thee as a thief, and thou shalt not know what hour I will come upon thee." He then removed the soiled nightshirt, and exiting the room, closed the door.

By the time the patient awoke, the thermal water had yellowed the passage. Experience had shown that the first thing the patient read was the command on the wall, "Rise up and walk," after which the patient would notice the opened book. Many first read and then tested the functionality of their limbs. Others, and these were the majority, did it the other way around. In any case, their mental processes eventually brought about the insight that they were obligated to hold to the conditions of the agreements signed at the start of treatment. Therefore, the patient did not express aloud his joy at the miracle of his cure, but quietly dialed the number of the medical committee, which immediately dispatched a representative, documented the state of his constitution, and then informed him that he must, after settling his bill, leave at once, which should pose no problem now that no physical infirmity remained. Thanks to the brevity of the treatment and the travel agency installed in the cure center, a seat was already reserved on the next departing airplane. The patient at once had the opportunity to proceed to the foyer under his own power, where he willingly presented his credit card and paid what was due. Then he climbed into the center's own limousine with darkened windows, and an hour and a half later found himself left to his own devices at the international airport of the capital city.

The secret of the special treatment for the seriously disabled, particularly the illusions of the granite room, were known only to the pool attendant, who operated the various devices; the directorate; and the designer who had conceived the décor and the laser effects. The pool attendant was a simple shepherd. He did as he was told, was paid well and regularly, and was indifferent to all the rest. Anna Lévay was listed in the cure center's register as an unskilled worker.

The organizers of the cure center had arranged matters so that the comings and goings of patients aroused little notice in the town. There were few who knew about Anna Lévay's present life. She had informed her colleagues that she had taken on temporary employment at fifty percent higher wages than her teacher's salary, with the added benefit that she no longer had to shout out her lungs; in fact, if she wished, she did not have to speak a word to a single person. She went home at the end of each day only to sleep, and on the weekends to clean house. She had been offered a room in the cure center; indeed, the doctor had suggested that she move there, above all to avoid loneliness; she could sublet her apartment. His friend, the lawyer, would gladly help in this; but Anna Lévay had no desire to move. She had grown fond of too many things, and who knew what sort of tenants she would get and what sort of people they associated with. Most of all, she feared for her books. The idea that someone would read the titles and thereby pass judgment on her literary taste seemed to her the equivalent of being forced to perform a striptease. Thus every morning she made her way to work on foot. She did not wish to be picked up in a car. She called the chauffeur only when it was raining, for then she had no desire to walk. I can use the exercise, she said to the doctor, who argued in favor of the chauffeur: The streets are a dangerous place, not that she would have another accident, did she not remember that she was a very inattentive pedestrian and that once, last fall, in front of the hospital, within the braking distance of his car, had almost walked into that car and been run over by him? Anna Lévay cast a penetrating glance at the doctor, so penetrating that he felt an uncomfortable tingling in his spine, as though his spinal cord had turned into a nest of ants and these insects were strolling along his nerves, dropping their burning poison. His glance became fixed, and he dared not move his neck, lest the crawling vermin go into an uproar. He reckoned on an embarrassing unmasking; indeed, it even went through his head that Anna Lévay knew precisely what he had wanted to say that time. Surely, she saw through him, and was deliberately tormenting him, by first allowing a span of time to elapse and then asking, "That would not have done, would it?" Thereupon the unpleasant feeling left the doctor, and he was able to reply, "No, it would not have done."

Anna Lévay had both her payment from the cure center and her pension deposited directly into her bank account, which grew handsomely. Yet she had no interest in the size of her savings; she usually did not even spare a glance for her statement; her strategy was to live on her pension, the entire amount of which she withdrew once a month. She really had no time to spend money. When she had a rare free weekend, she did her shopping in the store in her building, and because she felt herself in a financially secure position, she often allowed herself an extra container of cream, expensive cold cuts, a better brand of coffee. Otherwise, in her refrigerator were to be found the ingredients for her breakfast, a few tasty morsels of this and that, and butter, more recently margarine, which she spread on bread underneath the rosehip jam. Her midday meal, when she took it, and a snack were eaten in the cure center, after which she had no appetite; she returned home and went to bed.

Three days after the vernal equinox, Anna Lévay had a vision. She lay in bed and had drawn the blanket over the small pillow that was placed so as to lessen the pressure of the halo.

The morning twilight had begun, and the light of the rising sun was reflected in the wall of the neighboring building and shone between the slats of the blinds. She really should have gotten up, but she was unable to move. In the space under her blanket she saw an apparition of light that filled her entire field of vision. She tried to shield herself from it by turning onto her other side, but there, too, she saw it. Then for a while she lost control over her body.

She found herself in a state of paralysis; behind her closed eyelids the light divided itself into seven circles, of which one was in the center; then this central circle of light was covered by something, but the brightness behind it was so strong that she could make out only a contour; it was the contour of a human head. The light broke over the ends of the hairs on the head into small colored points, but she could not make them out precisely, for she was unable to focus her vision. Then a voice, presumably from the mouth belonging to the head, said to her, "Fear not."

She was unable to obey. She wondered only, and that only vaguely, how the vision was possible, for in the shadow she believed that she recognized the departed Dr. János Lévay. In her vision she lay on an operating table like those described by individuals claiming to have been abducted by extraterrestrials, and her late husband was bending over her. Now she felt that she had sufficient strength to move. She threw off the blanket and sat up with a rapid motion. Through the space between the blinds a broad golden ray of light was cast over her haloed head. She could see it in the polished surface of the wardrobe. She thought about the life of the deceased Dr. János Lévay, whether he would have been permitted, after having compromised himself politically, to climb the career ladder, and if so, whether he would have ascended higher than the neurologist.

On this day, she carried out her tasks at the cure center apathetically. She acted like a young maid in love. In the foyer she sang the *Excelsus super omnes* from Handel's *Laudate pueri dominum* and the beginning of the *Gloria* in the original Latin: "*Gloooooooooria Patri, Glooooria Filio et Spiriituuii Saancto.*" She knew not what she sang. With her gaze fixed on a white spot on the red marble cladding of the wall opposite, she raised her voice like that of a real singer, executing even the most difficult coloratura passages cleanly, and the marble walls reflected the sound in a manner wondrous to hear. She sang, oblivious to all around her, and with great richness despite her weakened vocal cords, but then she became aware that a small crowd had gathered about her, and she paused momentarily.

The patients to whom she was on her way to help in their treatment stood still and stared at her. She returned her gaze to the pattern on the marble wall, and again lifted her voice in song.

The manager was informed at once of what had transpired. Not knowing that he owed his existence to Anna Lévay, he walked up to her and placed his hand on her shoulder. "What are you doing here, my good woman?" Anna Lévay awoke with a start from her contemplation of the marble clouds, and when she saw that she was not alone, she immediately stopped singing. An elderly Italian patient, by profession the concertmaster of an orchestra, who was at the center for treatment of a urological disorder, saw in Anna Lévay an artist who had somehow slipped down into the proletarian echelon, and he wished to converse with her to make a public show of support. "Do you like Handel" he said in English. "*Laudate pueri* is my favorite, too." Anna Lévay did not answer, but walked away as though she had heard nothing.

At midday, after the last group had left the pool, she slipped and fell into the men's pool. Fortunately, no one was in the room. She was unable to swim, and instinctively, she turned herself over onto her back and floated in the warm water until the current drove her to the pool's edge and she was able to anchor herself and climb out. As a girl, she had never dared to go into a swimming pool, for her classmates had told her that bathing men were not to be trusted. One could swim innocently in the water and immaculately conceive.

That evening, she was about to leave the building when the porter at the employees' entrance—for the help were not permitted to use the elegant main entry—informed her that the manager wished to speak with her. Like a properly trained animal Anna Lévay turned around, returned to the women's dressing room, removed her overcoat, put on her work clothes, closed the door of her locker, slipped the key to the locker into her pocket, and set out for the manager's office. This was the first time that the manager had wished to speak with her. In the foyer, where the thick red carpet swallowed her footfalls and where she had sung that noon, she stopped before a gold-framed mirror, and like a servant girl who primps before entering a salon, she smoothed her smock with its light-blue pocket flaps and light-blue collar. The gold and red color scheme of the foyer seemed to her more appropriate to a bordello than a sanatorium, but that was none of her affair. But she did find it revolting.

The manager's office was lined from floor to ceiling with precious wood inlay. The carpet on the floor was red, just as in the foyer. Brass shimmered from decorative accoutrements. The manager sat behind an elegant desk and stopped her on her path when she had reached a conference table that seated four. "Have a seat," he commanded, making no attempt to be polite. He then excused himself for coming to the point at once and with no preliminaries, but he was a man of few words, the cure center was a demanding workplace, the product, the cure of the sick, and by no means an inexpensive one! In a brief digression he indicated how long many patients waited until from the farthest corners of the planet they could finally come to the cure center, and how much money it cost them, money that they worked hard for, whoever paid for their treatment at the cure center had the right to said treatment, for which they required peace and quiet. Here the manager made a pregnant pause. Perhaps Anna Lévay suspected something, perhaps she realized why she had been summoned, and would ask forgiveness.

The manager felt that he had not had sufficient opportunity to prove himself in his post, for there was little scope here in the cure center for the application of classical economic theory. And so he felt like a racehorse that had been trained to gallop but now found itself yoked to a plow. In fact, outside of his area of expertise, he knew nothing of the world. He had been appointed manager because he had good references from the mayor and the municipal treasurer, to whom he was indebted for the appointment, and who, as he had learned from a former school friend in the know, had demanded, and received, ten percent of his salary as agent's fee for getting him the job. Therefore, the manager felt the need to assert himself, and to do so had apparently decided upon—through application of the law of least resistance—the area of human resource management.

He waited for Anna Lévay to take the hint and answer for her behavior, but this she did not do. Rather, she continued to sit, looking at him with large eyes beneath her wrinkled eyelids. And so the manager took a large gulp of air, like a pearl diver before taking the plunge, and continued his lecture. A complaint against Anna Lévay had been made, and in fact, several of the patients had complained that in the early afternoon, between twelve thirty-four and twelve forty-five, she had disturbed the peace by loud singing in the foyer. That was impermissible. Such behavior could not be tolerated. He wished most emphatically to make her aware that according to the complaint, she had sung in Italian, Latin, and who knows, perhaps some other language, and to top it off, had sung a song with religious content, thereby violating four fundamental rules for the treatment of foreign visitors.

First: There are guests at the cure center who are not sympathetic to the Latin and Neo-Latin culture; indeed, some exhibit a distinctly allergic reaction to it. Anna Lévay should just think about the harm that would result if a patient from a former Italian colony should take offense and immediately pack up and leave.

Second: She sang a sophisticated religious song, apparently in the Roman Catholic tradition, whereby she may well have given offense to the religious sensibilities of some of the patients; after all, the cure center was not a "Catholics only" facility, one cannot discriminate on such a basis; at present there are Shintoists, Buddhists, Muslims, and Protestants in the center, not to mention adherents of any number of other religions. And then there are the atheists! Good lord, the atheists could stage a revolt, no doubt an even greater one than the religious fanatics. No single employee of the cure center has the right to discuss religious matters without the unanimous consent of all patients present. Such could even be taken as an attempt to proselytize, which is strictly forbidden because it interferes with the right of religious freedom, and the result could be a lawsuit against the center, which would constitute an intolerable situation.

Third: Let us assume that no one had objected to Mrs. Lévay's song and that in future Mrs. Lévay would continue to sing. Now he, the manager, would have his doubts as to whether she did this with no ulterior motive, from pure feelings of amiability and for her own enjoyment, for according to his sources, the level of performance was well above that of an amateur, which is, of course, not to say that critical ears had failed to notice certain errors of intonation and rhythm. He would be forced to conclude that she was after some kind of financial advantage, although he had no intention of suggesting that she had placed a cap or a kerchief on the floor and was begging, no, rather that she was attempting to curry favor with the patients in the hope of a large tip. That was forbidden. Were she to continue such practices, she would be exercising the profession of a performer, for which she would be required to appear before a commission and apply for a business classification and license, register, and pay taxes on her income, not to mention royalties to the writers' and composers' unions.

Here again he introduced a significant pause and waited for an apology, which a second time failed to materialize. After this repeated undermining of his calculations, he was filled not with a feeling of having proved himself, but with one of defeat and embitterment, and he worked himself more and more into a rage.

He had also been informed, he said, that at noon, after the last group had been taken from the pool, she had gone bathing without authorization, and, what is more, in the men's pool. Such actions are specifically forbidden to the center's personnel. The strict hygienic statutes require that the water must now be drained from the pool and that the pool be disinfected out of its regular schedule. Needless to say, the cost of this operation would be borne by Anna Lévay, assuming that she had not taken out employee liability

insurance. Had she not? Well then, the directorate of the cure center cared about its employees, and she could consider herself fortunate that she could repay the cost in twelve monthly installments,
which would be deducted from her pay.

Anna Lévay continued her silence.

The manager continued: In connection with these two regret-
table incidents he had requested a copy of Anna Lévay's contract
with the cure center and learned that she had been engaged as a
temporary worker. He had read about the functions that she was
carrying out and had come to the conclusion that her position at
the center demanded a high degree of responsibility, for she came
into intimate contact with patients, and she had influence over patients' moods and attitudes through her appearance, her speech,
and her behavior; in fact, such work required medical training. She
should not take it amiss, but the fact that one had worked for forty
years in a high school did not necessarily mean that such an individual was suited for such specialized work. Indeed, quite the opposite: The long, monotonous work had probably shattered her
nerves. And to top it all off, she was receiving, as her papers revealed, considerably higher wages for her work than were war-
ranted. He wished to make her aware that nine hundred twenty-five
thousand four hundred seventy-seven unemployed workers would
fold their hands in prayer and thank the Lord if they had such a job
as hers. Moreover, older individuals—begging your pardon, but a
fact is a fact—and particularly pensioners, are not normally engaged
in the tourist industry. What is needed here are young and bright-
eyed men and women. The presence of sullen employees whose appearance—begging your pardon again, but a fact is a fact—is less
than aesthetic would cause depression among the patients. He was
well aware that the doctor had recommended Anna Lévay, on hu-
manitarian grounds no doubt, because teachers are not adequately
compensated, and those living on a pension have every reason to
complain. However, the cure center, and the good doctor would
certainly understand this, was a serious enterprise whose ultimate

purpose was to turn a profit, and was not a social welfare society. It is a fact that up to now no one has had any reason to complain of Anna Lévay's performance on the job, but the singing and the abuse of the pool had shown that her appointment to the cure center was not an unmitigated success.

Again a pregnant pause.

As mentioned, the directorate of the cure center is worker-friendly, and therefore, we would like to reach an agreement with you. If you resign of your own free will and make no further demands on the center, that is, if you state in writing that you will not take any legal action against the center nor any action before the industrial tribunal, then we will forget about the costs associated with the disinfection of the pool. If we cannot come to such an understanding, then we may ourselves be forced to have recourse to legal action.

Anna Lévay asked for a piece of paper. The manager, who by now was completely nerve-wracked, indicated the shelf in the computer desk standing against the wall. Anna Lévay walked over to the desk, took a piece of paper and a pencil, sat down again at the table, and wrote for three minutes. She showed the paper to the manager, then turned and departed without a word, with just the hint of a nod. The manager, nonplussed, remained alone, with no chance to terminate his monologue with a final turning of the screw, which would have finally given him the feeling of having proved himself as well as the opportunity to gloat over Anna Lévay's defeat.

This unspoken final sentence ate at the manager. When he had convinced himself that Anna Lévay was by now far away, he began to shout from behind his padded door. He spoke to himself, called Anna Lévay an idiotic old woman, and paced about the room in circles. In his rage he strode into the chair on which his visitor had sat, twisting his big toe. The pain engulfed his entire foot, ran up his shinbone, ascended his thighbone, and infiltrated his groin. Then it climbed his spinal column and began beating against his skull like a gong. Because he was limping badly, he had to take a taxi home. He did not dare to drive his own car. He might have been able to operate the gas pedal, but he did not trust himself to manage the brake.

Meanwhile, Anna Lévay had gone below to the changing room, taken the key from the pocket of her smock, opened her locker, removed her smock, put on her overcoat, and placed several articles that she had in her locker in a plastic bag: a pair of white leather orthopedic shoes with wooden soles, a terrycloth handkerchief, a bottle of liquid soap, a blouse, an opened package of cough drops, and a Greek Bible that a patient had given her. He had not stolen it, for it was included in the price of the room; but he had one already at home. He was holding it in his hand as he was leaving the room, and he must have seen how Anna Lévay was looking at it with such unambiguous longing, for the patient—after she had exchanged a few sentences in Greek with him in which the retired teacher told him that in her student days she had played Antigone—had expressed his amazement at the strategies of cultural survival behind the Iron Curtain and given the sumptuous volume to Anna Lévay. He was in a hurry: The cure center's automobile that was to take him to the airport was waiting, and the driver had come in looking for him several times, glancing impatiently at his watch. The man had then awkwardly taken his leave, and the car had sped away.

It would have been superfluous to close the locker, and so she left the lock with the key stuck in it hanging from the door. She left her place of work as she had entered. The porter did not notice that her bag had grown larger since her first exit. Anna Lévay walked home. The sky gradually grew dark. She went slowly, and there was peace in her heart. At the bridge she looked back, saw the illuminated yellow water tower, the symbol of the town, and observed the scene of the crutches demonstration in January, but it elicited no emotion from her. Arriving home, she ate a piece of bread with honey, drank a large glass of warm milk, and then attempted to watch television, but the hospital drama gave her no pleasure, and so she lay down and fell asleep.

Again, she had a prophetic dream. Instead of drinking the glass
of milk that she had drunk that evening, she opened the window
and let the milk drip onto the poplar tree under the window, which
she ultimately regretted, for she really wished to drink, and she knew
that there was no more milk in the refrigerator, for she had poured
out the last drops from the last package. Therefore, she took in her
mouth the branch of the tree that beat against her window on windy
nights and sucked in the water of life as though through a drinking
straw. She was consumed with the desire to fly, and she climbed out
of the window. The light branches of the poplar bore her massive
body easily; she climbed upward to the treetop, felt a gentle warm
wind in her face, looked up at the Milky Way, which was clearly visible, fastened to the heavens in the dense undergrowth of darkling
chaos like droplets of milk from a nursing goddess. She desired no
more milk. In her dream she climbed ever higher, wandered among
the stars in their courses, let herself be borne at a crossroads into a
sea of warm milk; on Earth below she saw but a single object, and
that only with her inner eye: the tree into whose branches she must
return. Each time she turned about, she searched for the poplar, for
she feared losing it from her sight and not being able to return. She
drew light into herself, which soon made her feel replete and heavy,
as though the light were matter. Finally, she sank again; now she saw
Earth with her material eyes: the continent, the lake, the town, the
cure center, the district in which she lived, the poplar before
the open window. Good Lord, she thought, I hope a burglar hasn't
seized the opportunity while I was away! Now she was in the treetop;
she sensed the branches scraping against her feet; then she began to
fall at great speed. She had often had such dreams, dreams of tripping and falling down a staircase, but then she would always awake;
this dream was much more serious; she knew that already in her
dream, as she lost her dreaming sense of space and now sped downward with ever greater speed, far longer than the distance from the
top of the tree would warrant. She felt herself on a dark path and
wanted to cry out like a terrified child on a roller-coaster.

When she awoke, the terror had passed. She recalled the events of the previous day, and was satisfied. Since she had nothing to do, she loafed. She spent the entire day in bed, and was able to recover somewhat from the exertions of the previous week. She unplugged the telephone and disconnected the doorbell.

That same day, the manager of the cure center, having spent a wretched night with a painful foot, returned to work. He had to ask his wife to drive him, which she did only grudgingly, for she did not like getting up early. Insufficient sleep resulted in damage to the facial skin, caused rings under the eyes, she would look as if she had spent the night in a whorehouse. Thus spoke the former beauty queen in a tone that seemed a great distance from the eagerness of her honeymoon days, but then she drove him after all.

The manager decided to go with the first group into the pool, which had certainly cured worse cases than his own small sprain. He donned a linen nightshirt, joined the rituals that preceded the immersion, and then let himself float about in the water for half an hour. The vote had been for meditation music of type three. He almost fell asleep, and if there had been room to fall over, he surely would have. He could hardly wait to emerge from the pool cured. The shirt clung to his body, his hair was dripping, streams of water flowed from his hairy legs and disappeared in the cracks between the tiles in the sloping marble floor. But the pain had not left him. Nor had the others been cured, if one could judge by the grumblings of dissatisfaction. And the religious group that followed experienced the same negative results, and all the other groups that day as well.

Soon, a line of disappointed patients appeared outside the manager's office. The manager put on his best poker face and explained that he was sorry, but the patients themselves had, with their own signatures, acknowledged that they undertook treatment at their own expense and risk, that they would bear all negative consequences that might arise, that the cure center bore no obligation with respect to the result of treatment or the degree of cure. You are free to undergo treatment again tomorrow; perhaps your longing for a cure was premature.

On this day, the pool attendant was treating a man in the secret chamber who had a spinal injury. Having heard about the failures in the group treatments, he at once suspected that there would be a scandal if after undergoing the standard procedure the patient were to awake and see the inscription "Rise up and walk." And although he did not know what caused the miraculous cures to take place, he immediately notified the doctor.

The doctor dropped his work at the hospital and rushed at once to the cure center. He looked for Anna Lévay, but could not find her. Nor could he reach her by telephone. He climbed into his automobile and sped to where she lived. He rang the bell, but with no result. He waited for someone to exit the building, then entered and walked up the staircase. He rang the doorbell for a long time and banged on the door, but all for naught. He finally had to conclude that there was no one at home. So he hurried back to the cure center to find out who had last seen the retired teacher. He learned that the treatments on the previous day had all been successful and that Anna Lévay had gone home that evening at seven o'clock. The doctor wished to know the exact time, and so he asked to see the tape from the surveillance camera at the employees' entrance. The porter recalled precisely that the fat lady—for thus he spoke—had left after the seven o'clock news and the sports program had played on his radio. There was nothing to be seen on the tape. A terrible suspicion overcame the doctor. He rewound the tape to the time of the start of the workday, about eight o'clock. He carefully examined the pictures from between seven-thirty and eight-thirty, but there was nothing to show that Anna Lévay had arrived. Witnesses declared that she had already been at the pool at eight-thirty. He fast-forwarded the tape and examined the images at the time of her departure. At five past seven there was a slight imperfection in the image: an oval spot, brighter than its surroundings, like a mathematical drawing of two overlapping circles, an unidentified something that looked like a mandala, or a representation of the vulva.

It then occurred to the porter that Anna Lévay had left twice, that is, just once, actually, but the first time she had been about to leave, but then turned back in order to speak with the manager. He did not say this as a result of the doctor's having initiated him into the secret of his search, but because the doctor had emphatically asked him whether he had noticed anything unusual on the previous evening. The porter thought a long time, said no at first, and only after repeated prompting came up with the fact that indeed, something unusual had occurred, namely, that the manager, who unlike the good doctor normally did not stoop to conversation with mere blue-collar mortals, had wanted to speak with Anna Lévay that evening. The poor woman had to turn around, she was already on her way out, the manager did not show the least bit of human consideration, he could at least pay attention to the fact that her workday was over and speak to her during working hours, it was not good when someone suddenly became such a big capitalist that he would run over his own mother to make a profit. The doctor kept his impatience in check and asked further questions so that the true purpose of his interrogation would not be so apparent, and consequently, he warned the porter that in the future he should pay better attention and forbade him to play the radio while on duty.

Leaving the porter's lodge, he hastened to the office reserved for members of the board of directors, sat down at the desk at the end of the conference table, picked up the telephone, and ordered the manager to appear before him at once.

The manager arrived five minutes later, having come from another part of the building. He was limping badly. The doctor knew that such an injury could be easily cured by the water but that on this day there was no cure to be had. "Why don't you bathe?" he barked at the manager, to which the latter replied that he had done so; perhaps he had not been cured because his personality was too powerful to allow any sort of mass hypnosis to have an effect on him, just as it had failed to work on the rest of the group. About the religious group he knew nothing; perhaps, one should do a study comparing results for religious and atheistic groups. To the question where he had received his injury, the manager replied that one of the employees had caused a scandal, she had disturbed the patients' peace and quiet with her singing, and moreover, this woman had been seen entering the men's pool, and therefore it was his duty as manager of the facility to reprimand her. But the employee had shown no contrition, and so he, in order to maintain workplace discipline and simultaneously to make an example of her, had been forced to dismiss her, which had affected his spirit so adversely that after the woman had left, he had tripped in his agitation over the leg of a chair; since then, he had been in great pain.

After the first sentences, the doctor had realized how the narrative was going to conclude, but he nevertheless took the manager in for an x-ray, which revealed a fracture, which, as the orthopedist reported, could not be completely cured, even with an operation; an operation was superfluous, he would be left with a slight limp if the fracture healed; until then he would place the foot in a plaster cast; he should take it easy and then walk on crutches for six weeks.

Upon their return to the office, the doctor explained to the manager that the implementation of statistical studies and documentation of cures, which required precise information, was a matter for the board of physicians. Experience has shown that those for whom a first attempt at a cure fails will never be cured, but he should not be too upset; a slight limp was a trivial physical imperfection. Then he slowly cleared his throat and began to speak.

He knew—thus began the doctor—how hard his interlocutor worked, also, that this was his first significant managerial position, and that he had good connections, but in the cure center, where issues of health are so delicate, it was simply impossible to have an employee with his foot in a cast or who walked with a limp. Such a situation would greatly harm the enterprise. As an expert in marketing, he, the manager, must know that his presence would suppress profits; if patients were to see him, they would at once begin to doubt the effectiveness of the cure, which, finally—painful though it is to relate—means that this accident has made his further employment at the cure center entirely infeasible. He will certainly find another position, for the mayor and municipal treasurer will be glad to help him; in any case, such a talented professional will always find a place in a market economy.

The manager looked like one who has been caught urinating in a swimming pool. He defended himself: The patients rarely saw him in any case, but there was truth in what the doctor said, and so he would take a leave of absence until he was completely cured; he had not even thought of that before, but he did not believe that his condition should affect his position; he would at once seek out the best orthopedic surgeon in the country, not that he had no faith in the town hospital, but the local orthopedist was the husband of a former girlfriend of his, that is, a personal acquaintance, but not to worry, he would soon be fit as a fiddle again, until then, he requested an unpaid leave, and he would be on his way.

Ostensibly to this end, he made use of the cure center's chauffeur, but instead of proceeding to the capital, he went to visit his patron, the treasurer.

It would appear that the doctor had figured that the manager would do just that, so he drove to the mayor's office, walked in unannounced as usual, and explained the unfortunate situation to him. Although not even the mayor was privy to the secret of the cure, which even the doctor did not fully understand, that is, his information was only indirect, he was nonetheless one of the principal beneficiaries of the center's profits. To remove the roadblock that would amount to an economic disaster for the center, the mayor gave the doctor, who indicated that he had found a solution to the problem, a free hand. He instructed the mayor to telephone the treasurer and tell him that the manager was needed for another, more important, position and that a replacement at the cure center had already been engaged.

That call transpired at exactly the moment at which the agitated manager was limping into his patron's office, who, since he was engaged on the telephone with the mayor, motioned his protégé with a wave of his hand into a chair, so that the manager was compelled to listen to the audible half of the brief conversation. All was now clear to him. He put aside the mask of cool composure that is obligatory in the business world and commenced to threaten to lodge a complaint against those who ran the cure center, for a temporary physical infirmity could not be allowed to act as an obstacle to employment, why, that amounted to discrimination, there was certainly something deeper behind his dismissal, perhaps he had not greeted some local worthy loudly enough, or, and this was perhaps the more likely explanation, the mayor required the position for one of his own protégés. The treasurer urged the manager to be reasonable and informed him that the owners of the enterprise could select as manager whomever they wished to engage and could discharge without cause whomever they wished to let go, he had nothing to say in the matter and should be a good sport and go home and put an ice pack on his leg. When a suitable position became available, he would let him know.

Again, the doctor attempted to telephone Anna Lévay. He let the phone ring until finally a busy signal sounded. He would even have been content to leave a message on an answering machine.

Anna Lévay, however, heard nothing, because the telephone was still disconnected. She lay in bed, lazing in its warmth, and listened, as she had all morning, to the sounds emanating from her building. She heard her neighbors starting their day as usual; they washed, breakfasted, brushed their teeth, then locked the doors to their apartments and went to work. Only one wife stayed at home, who, after her husband had left, set about her housework, singing the while; and a young girl as well, an imaginary invalid perhaps, who, judging by the sounds, had received a visitor shortly after her parents' departure. It was a lovely morning. At noon, Anna Lévay cooked noodles with cheese and poured over them some leftover mushroom tarragon sauce. She had no appetite for soup. Then she lay down again and continued where she had left off before lunch. She suspected that without her presence the activities at the cure center would come to a standstill, and she wanted to wait and see what the consequences would be. She was curious about what would happen, not only because the work there guaranteed her financial independence, but also because she herself was uncertain whether the miracle really came through her alone.

After his fruitless attempt at telephoning her, the doctor rushed over to Anna Lévay's apartment. Her door did not open to his ring. He dared not beat his fists against the door. Behind the door, all was still. As a check he pulled a gray hair from his head, and after making certain that he was not being observed, stuck both ends of the hair carefully, but deeply, into the interstice between the door and the frame, so that a draft caused by the door's opening would waft it away.

The next morning, his attempt at telephoning Anna Lévay brought the same lack of response. The hair was still in its place. The doctor could not keep away any longer from his practice. There was to be a consultation on a patient who apparently suffered from religious delusions. This sort of malady was treated exclusively in the capital; there was a locked ward for just such cases, and the professor of psychiatry in charge had asked that he be notified of every such case. The patient, an organist from a small market town about thirty kilometers away, who together with the priest had visited the town's purveyor of devotional articles for the purchase of some requisite items, was maintaining that Judgment Day was at hand; early that morning, an angel, a harbinger, had walked across the canal bridge, the angel had looked like a normal human being, except that from the bus window one could discern an aura of light emanating from the head, just as in the pictures of saints. The woman—for the angel had appeared as an elderly woman—had looked at him and with her glance informed him that she cured the sick, and the organist told them that as the bus drove by her, he had seen a vision of the saint surrounded by a host of angels in white robes.

The priest did not confirm the vision, he had noticed nothing of the sort, though he had been looking in the same direction. Whenever he came to town, he observed the height of the water in the canal and the color of the water. This time, he had looked in that direction because he had thought of the poor child who had fallen into the water at a place where there was no railing, where its tiny heart had immediately ceased to beat in the frigid water. He added that the organist was of unsound mind, he had taken him only to get him out of the village for a change of air, he had been nowhere in over ten years, his livestock kept him on his farm, in the summer season he was engaged in agricultural work, otherwise, he spent every free minute with his music, was as impassive as a carthorse, and came alive only on Sundays, when he could sit at the organ. The priest defended himself; one knew that the organist suffered from a personality disorder, but he was the only one they had.

The patient described his vision to the professor of psychiatry exactly as he had seen it, the black boots, the legs heavy with varicose veins from long standing, the gray winter coat encompassing her, the cream-colored silk shawl, the bright-green light-engulfed hat of rabbit fur. He described it all with such precision that the professor declared the hallucination to be of the most severe variety, and he wished to transport the patient to his ward in the capital as swiftly as possible. Then the organist began to speak without any apparent coherence. He turned his gaze to the upper left corner on the north side of the treatment room, as though there were someone there, as though his words were part of a sensible communication, and he soliloquized:

I am for peace: but when I speak, they are for war. O keep my soul, and deliver me: let me not be ashamed; for I put my trust in thee. They rewarded me evil for good to the spoiling of my soul. Thus I was as a man that heareth not, and in whose mouth are no reproofs. All that hate me whisper together against me: against me do they devise my hurt. They are all gone aside, they are all together become filthy: there is none that doeth good, no, not one. They gather themselves together, they hide themselves, they mark my steps, when they wait for my soul. Behold, they belch out with their mouth: swords are in their lips: for who, say they, doth hear? Deliver me out of the mire, and let me not sink: let me be delivered from them that hate me, and out of the deep waters. Fill their faces with shame; that they may seek thy name, O LORD. Let mine adversaries be clothed with shame, and let them cover themselves with their own confusion, as with a mantle.

After the first sentence of this monologue the professor added the diagnosis of schizophrenia, and declared that the other sentences indicated paranoid fantasies. Then the organist gave a long discourse on the apparition, to which the doctor listened in its entirety with great impatience and a sour expression on his face, but he could not leave to seek out Anna Lévay, since he would have to accompany his distinguished colleague to the hospital cafeteria for lunch and then to a long kaffeeklatsch in the office of the medical director, who had the reputation of a great skirt-chaser and whose office was resplendent in Socialist-era luxury. It was half past four when he was finally able to get away.

He turned on his cell phone and saw that he had several messages. One was from his wife, that he should call home: There was a problem. Another, also with a message that there was a problem, was from the cure center, from the shepherd turned masseur turned pool attendant. In the third, the deputy serving in place of the dismissed manager gasped into the apparatus that some of the patients were demanding the same treatment as that which produced the miraculous cures, for such was included in the price that they had paid, and until at least one believable report of a new cure was presented, they would use their wheelchairs and walkers to blockade the corridor leading to the office and hold all employees hostage.

The doctor hurried to Anna Lévay's apartment, where he found intact the hair so artfully placed the day before. Neither ringing the bell nor telephoning her produced a positive result. In order to carry out the plan that he was now hatching, he would have to wait until dark. He returned to the hospital, entering through the rear door. Then he lay on the sofa in his office and dozed off. It was quite dark when he returned to the apartment block where Anna Lévay lived. He climbed the poplar tree to her bedroom window, supporting himself on the tree's unpruned branches. Apparently, his ascent went unnoticed; most of the curtains were closed, the glow of light behind them revealing the universal evening activity of watching television. There was even light in the particular window in which the doctor was interested. He could see through the window that Anna Lévay lay in bed. The book resting on her stomach rose and fell regularly in accompaniment to her breathing. Strewn about the bed, and particularly on the pillow, were additional volumes, some open, others closed, some right-side up, others turned over; in short, there was general disarray.

He knocked on the window. No response. He knocked more forcefully. Nothing. He then banged as loud as he dared, hammering at the windowpane again and again. Soon his hand ached, and he felt that the leg that was supporting him on the branch would at any moment be seized by a cramp. The hand that was grasping another branch began to tremble. Then Anna Lévay turned onto her side; the book fell from her stomach, she lifted the blanket, placed her hand under her head, and continued to sleep. Once more, the doctor banged against the windowpane, primarily to express his dissatisfaction with the situation. The window popped open, its wooden frame pushed against the gauze curtains, a breeze entered the room, and Anna Lévay awaked. She walked in her nightgown to the window, shut it, arranged the curtains, and closed the heavy draperies as well. The doctor then pulled himself together, almost, in his fright, plunging the ten meters to the ground, and hammered with his last strength at the window, though he dared not call out, nor even to whisper. Anna Lévay pulled back the curtain, opened the window, and saw to her great surprise the doctor, hanging in the tree branches.

She recognized the comedy in the situation, but she did not cry out, nor even did she laugh. With her finger to her lips she cautioned the doctor to be silent, and then went into the pantry and came back after a moment with the ironing board, whose upholstered side she held to her body while holding out the unextended foot for the doctor to grab hold of, which he did, thereby obtaining access to the room.

Anna Lévay asked for no explanation, and therefore the doctor did not ask why the doorbell and telephone had yielded no result. He said only that a mistake had been made, a fatal error, the manager had not the right to dismiss her, her place was certainly not lost to her, he had had such concern about Mrs. Lévay, for he had attempted a number of times to reach her, but now he was glad that she was all right, she was not offended, he hoped, and would return to work the next day. Then the teacher offered her visitor a chair and a cup of tea. She took honey, butter, sugar, flour, and eggs, and set to work. The doctor asked nothing; he only watched as she mixed together the dark mass, which must have weighed a kilo and a half, floured a wooden board, rolled out the dough to the thickness of a knife handle, and formed small rings. The rings, of which there were about two hundred, were three centimeters across, which is to say that they were tiny. They went into the oven, and after fifteen minutes they came out again, baked to a golden brown. Then she rolled them in apricot jam, then in ground nuts, and packed them individually in paper baking cups. There was room for all of the little cookies in two old tins. Without a word, she gave the boxes to the doctor, who took them, also without a word. He understood what was to be done, but before he left, he asked whether he might visit

Mrs. Lévay the next day. The answer was no. Then Anna Lévay added that she needed to recover, and would return to the cure center when she felt up to it.

The next day, the patients at the cure center received with their breakfast drink a small honey cookie. The drink was terribly bitter, brewed from medicinal herbs, and was served in an alcoholic decoction, about two hundred milliliters per patient. They were told that every last drop must be drunk. The guests, hoping, of course, for a cure, drank it down, but it tasted so bad without any sweetener that each of them then ate the little honey cookie.

Five minutes later, all of the patients, drugged, had laid down their heads on their tables. On that day, there was no bathing. The pool attendant and a gardener transported the unconscious bodies to their rooms. For this purpose they employed carts that were normally used for the transport of supplies within the building. Each body to be transported was loaded onto the small payload area of a cart and fastened to the frame with elastic cords that the gardener had removed from his motorcycle's luggage carrier. The room numbers were easily determined from the patients' meal cards. There was no time to undress the patients; the workers simply removed their shoes and covered each sleeper with a blanket. Later, a cleaning woman and a nurse turned the sleepers onto their sides, so that nothing that might be coughed up would get into their lungs.

The doctor, whom the pool attendant had immediately informed about the mass intoxication—he suspected sabotage; perhaps someone had attempted to poison the guests—had already arrived at the center. He had completed his morning rounds at the hospital, and before that had visited the supply manager of the cure center, to whom he had given the cookies with instructions to serve them that morning as an example of a typical local specialty. He also had requested that the herbal tea be brewed especially bitter, and ordered the extract to be supplemented with the finest dessert wine. The ingredient that had put all the patients to sleep was one that the doctor had added himself. When the guests were in their beds, he ordered that the fifteenth verse of the twelfth chapter of Paul's letter to the Romans be highlighted with thermal water, in the manner that was usual for the seriously impaired. "Rejoice with them that do rejoice, and weep with them that weep." He had selected this verse at random, he had leafed only once or twice through the volume, which the publisher had enhanced by setting verses considered of particular importance in boldface. In his haste, the pool attendant, who carried out the order, was not sufficiently attentive, and so for some of the patients he dampened the verse before or the verse after. The result was that some of the patients, as a result of their search for the significance of the highlighted passage, experienced lifelong manic depression, others, a psychic alteration of a masochistic nature.

That evening, all the patients awoke. A short time later, they streamed into the dining room, since it was dinnertime, though no one felt any particular appetite, and even the usual babel was lacking. Silently, they ate nothing but bread, and drank with it an expensive Tokay. Then they packed their bags, climbed into the awaiting buses, and left without a word of farewell.

No new patients replaced them for three days; their cure had ended much earlier than had been planned. Arrangements for accepting patients into the center had now to be altered. The mayor, referring to the need for promoting tourism, came to an arrangement with the governmental authorities whereby a local airport that had formerly been used for military purposes would now be opened for private air traffic. Those who had applied for admission to the cure center would be quartered in a hotel in a nearby major city and instructed not to leave the hotel grounds, since notification to depart could come at any moment. As soon as a place in the center became available, the next patient on the list would be so informed, and then transported from the hotel to the nearest airport and with the airport's private airplane be flown within a few hours to the local airport; the treatment could begin a few minutes later. Everything would work mutatis mutandis in the opposite direction, and thus the cure center would always be one hundred percent full.

For reasons of security the treatment strategy was altered as well. Two gurus who had come to the center with the desire to assist in curing patients and had emphatically demanded their right to religious freedom were placed under contract, on the assumption that they could do no harm by spending their days alternately sitting silent in a corner of the great hall. The patients, who were told that the two were praying for their health, were required each to spend three hours a day with them, in absolute silence, motionless, for if they moved, then, so they were told, the prayer for their health would turn into its opposite.

When Anna Lévay returned to the cure center, she could not bear the sight of the enfeebled bodies that were encamped on the heated marble floor at the feet of the bald guru. The smell of fifty sweating bodies was unbearable to her. In her worker's smock she climbed over them and opened the window behind the guru, whereupon a warm wind billowed the silk curtain. Anna Lévay stood there in the light, from her hair and clothes wafted forth into the noses of the throng the scent of cheap soap and cheap fabric softener. A breeze ran over the guru's naked backbone, a nervous shivering overcame him; he turned to face Anna Lévay, and then turned again to the front, facing the crowd, which dared not move. Anna Lévay addressed them: "Dear people, arise, go, your limbs are falling asleep here." With these words, she left the room; and the people stood up, cured.

After this manifestation, so that her person would not be brought into association with the cure, she could no longer show herself to the patients. The doctor asked Anna Lévay to count a quantity of incense that had been purchased for the gurus. There were about fifteen hundred sticks in the package, he said, but if Mrs. Lévay had the time, he would like very much to know the exact number, for it was a rather expensive consignment, and it would not be good if some of the sticks were to disappear without being accounted for. From that hour forth a stick of incense always burned in front of the gurus.

Two days later, Anna Lévay was given the task, at the request of the municipal board of health, of taking water samples for testing from the two pools. The doctor then froze this water in a freezer bought for the purpose, and when holy water was needed in the cure center's chapel, he gave the servant of the Lord on duty an ice cube. When the faithful crossed themselves with that water, the healing process took hold in them.

On that same day a crate of matzot was delivered, which Anna Lévay was assigned to place on a shelf in the storeroom. By evening, the entire shipment had disappeared.

11

On Saturday, the fourth of April, Anna Lévay visited a former student, who had herself become a teacher and lived in a nearby village with her large, happy family, whose per capita income was far below the poverty level. They spent the weekend at her family's ancestral vineyard. For supper, there was potato soup from a cast-iron kettle, cheese, homemade bread with lard and bacon, onions, a watered sour wine, a view of the lake, and the noise of six healthy little children.

Anna Lévay gave in to their cordial invitation to spend the night. She paled at the thought of the return trip to the town with its myriad windows, though on the other hand, she did not wish to be a burden to this family, and therefore requested that she be allowed to sleep in the outbuilding that housed the wine press. She would feel comfortable there, she said, there was a blanket, the single sofa cushion would do nicely for a pillow, and the bench around the stove, whose vintage was the end of the last century, would make a wonderful bed. She had not slept on such a bench since her childhood, she would be pleased if they would allow her this bit of nostalgia, she would sleep in her clothes and feel herself the guardian of this noble vineyard, she could get up early the next morning and thin the dew-covered vine shoots. They finally agreed that the family would come up the hill in the morning and they would spend the day there together.

Now she was alone in the twilight. She felt content; she sat down on the hummock at the entrance to the cellar and looked westward. It was a sunset fit for a glossy postcard. The red sunlight colored the blue-green water of the lake a wine-dark purple and red.

The wind had been blowing out of the west the entire day. Dry gusts swirled over the sandy paths, sucking up the dusty earth, which had long seen no rain. On the surrounding hills could be seen the tumult of a sandstorm. Farther away, on the main road, according to radio reports, thirty-five automobiles had collided in a massive pileup after the sudden appearance of a dust cloud. Slowly, the sun sank, but Anna Lévay could not tear herself from the view. She saw the lights from the opposite shore, the water sparkling in its depths, the stars shining with foreboding. She knew the names of none of the stars. Rather, she knew the names, but she could not associate a name with the appropriate star. This made her uneasy. She thought of the Babylonian astrologers, medieval scholastics, free thinkers of the Renaissance, and scholars of the Enlightenment who knew more about these things than today's educated men and women, and she was overcome with the insight, which seemed to her a cold reality, that to each of us, the workings of the world are unfathomable.

She sat with her back to the wall of the cellar, and for some unfathomable reason, she wept. Alone in the darkened yard, she became consumed with anxiety, such as children experience when they are alone in the dark: terror in the face of loneliness, meaninglessness, powerlessness, and the vastness of the universe, through which Earth pertinaciously plies its course. As she sat motionless, a bright star began to wander from one branch of an apple tree to another. As she observed its motion, she was no longer afraid, yet an immeasurable sadness enveloped her, alone in the silent night.

When the family came to the vineyard the next morning, they found Anna Lévay lying on the oven bench. They had arrived in a truck, driven by their neighbor, who was preparing for the spring-time work in the vineyards. Anna Lévay's student had taken the op-portunity to transport some plants that had wintered in her house. She always saw to the transplanting and division of the plants out-doors, and then in winter brought the plants back indoors. When Anna Lévay awoke, she took over watching the children. Calling "Come unto me," she herded them together; then an anxious shud-der came over her, the fear that her nocturnal solitude may have un-balanced her mind, for of course, she knew the quotation. That this sentence had escaped her lips, and that it should have come from her of all people, she took for a bad joke. Only when all the little children were tumbling about her did she finally lose her inner ten-sion, and she sat them down in a circle on a tablecloth outside by the cellar and put slices of bread in their mouths, as the Lord's ser-vants give bread to the faithful, and she told them the tale of the poor man who outsmarted the devil.

At noon, she decided to return home; in vain they asked her to stay. Her student, who had finished with her plants, fetched a flow-erpot with a palm seedling and put it in the hands of her former teacher. It was only with difficulty that Anna Lévay managed to hide her terror. The entire family waved goodbye to her as she de-parted with the plant in her hand in the direction of the town, without luggage, just as she had arrived. She carried the plant before her as though it were a sacred object. She had only six kilometers to walk, so she did not wait for the bus; she walked along the shoulder of the road, and although many cars overtook her, and many of them angrily honked at her, she simply walked on, with the palm seedling in her hand.

The following week, on Thursday, Anna Lévay went to the cure center for a swim. She splashed for half an hour in the yellowish water of the otherwise empty women's pool, calmly, without a thought in her head, then dressed, dried her hair, and went to look for patients.

It was suppertime. They were seated at a long table, eating silently; at the front sat the Indian guru—the only well person in the entire group—and completely self-absorbed, recited verses from the wisdom of his native land.

Anna Lévay walked among them, a silent observer; then she placed two beeswax candles in the guru's hands, one of which he placed at each end of the table. All glances then turned to the candles, half of the company gazing in one direction, half in the other. Thus they sat for about an hour, motionless except for the almost automatic downing of a glass of wine every so often. Then one of the patients stood up, walked up to the guru, and kissed him. The others did likewise. Finally, the Indian urged them to depart.

A quarter of an hour later, the cure center's bus drove up to the gates. All the patients boarded, except for one, who insisted that he wished to remain until Holy Saturday. The new manager had food brought to him that he could reheat himself and led him to the guards' room, now vacated; then the main building was closed up, and all the employees, except for a few guards, departed for the Easter holiday.

Anna Lévay returned to the room where the employees took their break. She was very tired. She undressed to her underclothes, for she had brought no nightgown, and covered herself with a sheet.

In her dream she was placed under interrogation. She wanted to speak, but her mouth would not open; she wanted to write down what she wished to say, but her hand was paralyzed. Unknown beings were touching her, they tormented her body, placed her in a powerful beam of light as bright as sunlight but that came from everywhere at once and from which there was no escape. She closed her eyes, but her eyelids, revealing to her their network of blood vessels, blocked out only a little of the light. And so she placed her hands before her eyes, but between the contours of her fingers she saw a painfully intense red spot. Then nothing.

She awoke the next morning bathed in sweat. Menopause! Her body was stiff from having lain all night, and it was little obedient to her command. Slowly and ponderously, she stood up. She left the room and walked into the corridor. It was dark. The electricity had been shut off throughout the building. Alone, she walked into one room after the other. The last guest had departed, from which she concluded that it was early on Easter morning. She went into the ballroom, sat down in the center, and waited. The morning twilight shimmered. She was not hungry. She waited for the six o'clock bells, when the faithful would be going to church, so that she could walk home unobserved. But then, she did not go home, but to the grave of the late Dr. János Lévay. There she sat on a bench and mused.

She was unable to collect her thoughts, but she reflected on the Resurrection and its symbol the egg, which led her to her late husband's testicles, which in the beginning she had hardly dared to touch. Even later, she had touched them only in the most passionate love nights and then only at János's express bidding, and in the way he wished, but she had always treated them with the delicacy of raw eggs. The memory embarrassed her, and she thought of her son, who was successful with women, and wondered whether what he offered them was like what her husband had given to her. She grew red again, and turned her thoughts to the resurrection of the individual, the continuation of life across the generations, and then to Dr. János Lévay's corporeal reality, until her thoughts became thin and insubstantial.

In the late afternoon she fled the sleet and entered the foyer of the mortuary, then kneeled again at her husband's grave and breathed the fresh scent of earth, filled with the aroma of vegetal decomposition.

In the late evening she walked home.

On Monday, she boarded a train, taking advantage of the ninety-percent discount for pensioners, and rode about the entire day, first to the capital, then to the country's eastern border. She wanted to look around, to see the land with its lovely gardens, to be the traveling companion of families out for picnics, to speak with people, to observe them, just like others, a bit suspiciously, sniffing, like dogs that mark their territory with a lifted leg. The train compartment was filthy. Water steeped in rust had apparently run in rivers over the windows; the water had dried, and the rust was stuck to the glass like the viscous scum of the times, through which she now had to peer to observe the landscape. The fields were green, trees were in flower, grass waved in the wind. Every now and then a few deer appeared, rabbits and pheasants, too. For the first time since her discovery of the halo, Anna Lévay was unreservedly happy, happy because she felt free.

The next day, at eleven in the morning, she traveled home. Upon her return, Anna Lévay decided not to go to the cure center until Wednesday or Thursday.

On Thursday, she was crossing the canal bridge when she heard the squealing of brakes. It was the doctor. He invited her to ride with him, and aside from the usual pleasantries spoke not a word until the padded doors of his office had closed behind them. There, he demanded an account of where Anna Lévay had spent the entire past week. She replied that she had spent the morning and the day before, Wednesday, at home in bed; on Tuesday she had returned home from the eastern border, whither she had traveled on Monday, making use of the favorable train fares; that followed a Sunday spent in a depressive state of mind at the cemetery, from morning till evening. And in the time before that she had been in the cure center, exhausted, where she had slept. As though scolding a kindergartner, the doctor told her to her face that she was lying. No one could have survived at that time in the cure center, for on Saturday the pest control company had been there, for some of the guests had complained. A couple of rats, who lived among the rocks in the harbor, had apparently slipped into the building in search of food, one had even reportedly been seen in the ballroom, and so to avoid such incidents, the directorate had decided to use the Easter holiday to poison the rats with prussic acid, so where, then, had Mrs. Lévay been between Thursday evening and Sunday morning?

Without replying, Anna Lévay walked to the door and left the room. In the employees' room she found everything as she had left it. She took the rumpled sheet and thought of displaying it to the doctor as proof. As she was folding it up, she saw the large yellow spots. She took the sheet into the laundry room, but despite repeated scrubbings could not restore its original whiteness. When it came out of the wringer, the fabric was smooth, but the spots were still there. She did not want to be seen with it. Because of the random checks of employees entering and exiting the building, she could not take the sheet home with her. To be sure, nothing much would happen to her if the laundry service discovered what she had done to their sheet, but she did not want any unpleasantness, and so she rolled up the large red carpet in the foyer, spread the sheet on the floor, and unrolled the carpet over it.

The next few weeks passed with little incident. Anna Lévay went to work every morning at the cure center and remained there the entire day. For her own amusement she thought up the most varied ways of allowing the magical power to do its work, so that no one would be able to figure out the secret of the cure. Like the apparition of the great Wizard of Oz, the cure came to each patient according to his kind. Many could have sworn that healing had taken place in the pool, while for others, it was in the dark marble chamber; yet others said that after breakfast they had been consumed by a great fatigue, and others spoke of an apparition of light. And these were just the standard cases.

In the case of one patient, a believer, Anna Lévay gave him a box on the ear while he was standing in the foyer, saying that she was curious to see whether he would hit back or turn the other cheek. At once, the man recovered his long-lost eyesight. There were no witnesses to this scene, for Anna Lévay had made sure to hit him at a time when the two were unobserved.

Minutes later, the crowd of patients that gathered around him could detect on his face the mark of a feminine hand. The cured man told them that he had clearly heard an angel's voice, but when he opened his eyes, there was no one to be seen. Asked what he had done then, the man replied that like a good Christian—though shaking with fear—he had, of course, turned the other cheek, but he was not struck again.

Anna Lévay's schemes were almost infinite in their variety. One evening, she held a séance. She summoned the spirit of Swedenborg, and quoted extracts from *Heaven and Hell*. No one saw through her stratagem. The quotations had the effect of personal messages to each of those present; this effect was strengthened by the archaic language. One woman fell unconscious, then the next, and finally, Anna Lévay was alone in the room with twenty unconscious individuals, who revived only after she had gone. Each of them told the cure center's psychologist of a wonderful journey to the world yonder.

Fifty days after her lamentation in the cemetery, Anna Lévay received an invitation to a municipal reception. She turned it down, she had to work and had no time for entertainments. One day, when a group of prominent men was scheduled to visit the center, Anna Lévay was standing in the foyer, a slop bucket in her hand, for a patient had thrown up, and she had to clean up the mess. At that moment, two cameramen rushed in to film the arrival of the guests, to capture on video the manager shaking the hand of each visitor and then the procession of the group into the dining room. The two followed the procession with their cameras until the last footfall had disappeared from the stair on which Anna Lévay was standing. The doctor, who was near the head of the group, paused, gave her a friendly pat on the shoulder and asked jovially, "Well, then, Mrs. Lévay, have you thought up a better story?" Then he continued, without waiting for an answer, "Change your clothes and come upstairs with us."

This moment was an important one for the doctor, because he remembered precisely where Anna Lévay had stood on the stair. On the film, which was shown on local television that very evening, there was no Anna Lévay to be seen. The doctor, as a principal supporter of the television station, ran into the editing room and asked that the film be transferred to a videocassette for his personal use. He telephoned the other local station and made the same request. He could have watched the film right then and there, but he did not want others to see his agitated state, and he could hardly send the employees out of their own screening room, for that would also have aroused suspicion.

After receiving the cassette, he chatted a bit with the staff, and then he hurried home. He shut himself in the bedroom and watched the recording, establishing the same result. He saw how he had stopped, the procession had passed him, and then, standing at the end of the procession, he had bent his upper torso a bit to the right, waved with his hand, and apparently conversed with the wall. He watched the video six times more, stopped it with the pause button, measured the direction of his gaze with a ruler that he held up against the television screen. No, he was not speaking with someone outside of the picture; even his characteristic gestures were clear: Under his fingertips he could again feel the fleshy form of Anna Lévay's shoulder beneath the linen smock. But this cannot be, he thought, and a deep sigh escaped his lungs. He attempted to locate in his memory similar cases from his practice, and so he looked for examples in folklore and contemplated mythological data. Then there was a sudden knock at the door.

His wife asked to be admitted. After several more knocks she called out, "Whatever it is, dearest, let me look, too." And she knocked even louder. To make use of the misunderstanding the doctor slipped a pornographic film into the recorder, let his wife in, and apologized, he thought she had fallen asleep and did not wish to disturb her. If she was so curious, then she should come in by all means. They watched the film awhile, then the husband performed his conjugal duty to his wife's satisfaction, and when she was lying in sweet slumber, he slipped out of the room. "No wonder," it suddenly occurred to him, that Anna Lévay had refused to be x-rayed, when at the start of their acquaintanceship she had come to him with her alleged illness. No wonder! The night that she was dismissed, he had also been unable to see her on the surveillance film.

He then recalled the small imperfection in the image that he had seen that time, that oval spot, brighter than the background, like a drawing of two intersecting circles in a mathematics lesson, like a mandala, or a vulva. He returned to the bedroom, put in the cassette again, and watched once more the scene from the cure center. Nothing. That cameraman was a slovenly bungler: The marble wall before which Anna Lévay had stood was too brightly illuminated, and so there was no special patch of light that could be identified.

The doctor spent the next day in a study of the specialist literature. He read about witches and ghosts. He read about women who assumed the bodies of men and the heads of animals, who slept with the devil, who rode on one or another household item that doubled as a phallic symbol, who drank the milk of animals and nursing mothers, who gathered on the sabbath for orgies, who had incisors in their vaginas, who could bind and unbind men's souls, destroy and heal. He knew that most of these things were more myth than fact, but with the vague notion that there might be a kernel of truth behind it all, he searched further. He could not search Anna Lévay's body for wounds that did not bleed and for the devil's brand. Since she had eaten and drunk before numerous witnesses, given evidence of carrying out normal biological processes, was visible by day as an opaque body, and possessed a shadow, one would have to discard all possible variants in the category of ghost. This conundrum would revolve in the doctor's head throughout the entire summer.

In the first week of July, the international folk dance festival was held, as it was every year. In the evening, Anna Lévay stood on the balcony of the library and watched the whirl of the dance on the concrete platform named for the previous chairman of the munici-pal council. At the moment, a group of Armenians were dancing, a charming, graceful collection of adults and children. Among them was a delicately stepping, professionally smiling young beauty. In one step of the dance, all raised their linked hands into the air, shifted their weight to their back legs, and gazed heavenward. Then the delicate beauty fell out of step and left the ring. The others let her go, assuming that she was not feeling well, and continued their program. However, the distressed dancer took two steps forward, stood still, her arms raised toward the darkened sky, and stared at the apparition on the balcony. In the characteristic sounds of her mother tongue she repeated a single word, *angelos, angelos,* which in Armenian, as in ancient Greek, means "messenger," and with her open palm, she pointed to Anna Lévay. The group leader called to her, and the girl returned to the circle. At the end of the dance, as the others were leaving the performance area, the girl remained, rooted to the spot, her face gazing aloft; no one dared to walk onto that space, and all their gazes followed that of the girl, but all they saw was the librarian and Anna Lévay. The group leader returned to fetch the girl, but she would not move. She stood and repeated the word *angelos.*

Only after the doctor had given her an injection did she reveal that an old woman was standing on the balcony enveloped in light, a holy one, an angel, for she had seen the glowing ring around her head, and the woman had looked down on her and, so she believed, said that the dance had pleased her, she had spoken Armenian, she must be the group's guardian angel, please, fetch her from the bal-cony, she must speak with her, she wished to ask whether she would one day become a famous dancer. The doctor went through the routine of taking her pulse, blood pressure, and temperature; then he declared that the girl had apparently suffered a heat stroke, for which she should be treated. She should lie for three days in a cool, dark room, and for added protection, no one should speak with her, she should not be allowed to excite herself. He was soon finished with his examination; then he ran up the stairs as fast as he could, through the passageway on the top floor, where a glass door led to the balcony on which the girl had seen the apparition. He saw no one. The riddle was never solved, and the doctor withdrew, without waiting for the traditional fireworks. He sought a cool, dark place, like the one he had recommended to his patient.

By the beginning of September, the press of tourists had let up. The streets and beaches emptied; at the end of the month, the shop owners and innkeepers would head to southern beaches for their vacations, to rest after the hectic season. The leaves were starting to fall. Every morning, beneath the window of the pensioned high school teacher Anna Lévay, children walked to school.

On Friday, the thirtieth of October, in the morning, before, as she figured, the crowds would be at the cemetery, she made a pilgrimage to the final resting place of Dr. János Lévay. She sat for a while, and then she began to speak. She did not look about her, knew not whether anyone was listening, for at this time of year, vocal manifestations of grief or pain were considered normal. She began her monologue by addressing her husband, "János, János." Then she reproached him for his irresponsibility, as though the departed one were a recalcitrant child that needed to be brought up properly, that he had run out on her just to let himself be shot, that he had left her alone with a child beneath her breast, and she asked Doctor Lévay would he please, if there actually was a world beyond, and if souls there could really travel where they willed, and if such a journey were not too expensive, then would he please look after their son, see what he was doing at the other end of the world, and if it were not too much of a financial burden, could he requisition a guardian angel for him, with whom he—of course discreetly, if possible subconsciously—could talk about whatever it was that troubled his soul. Then she enumerated the difficulties that she had been through since the death of Dr. János Lévay: the moral and financial obstacles of child rearing, the torment of university entrance examinations, the interrogations about the rejection of humiliating compensation payments, which were supposed to compensate for over forty years without a man and the accompanying torment of longing, until she was finally overwhelmed, and shouted, "You have cheated me, robbed me, done me in. In fact, you have completely fucked up my life!"

After that, she felt somewhat relieved. She experienced no regret, nor any particular depth of feeling, only a mild giddiness. She arose like one who has clearly said what was on her mind, and with calm steps walked through the town. At home, she prepared a bath for her body dirtied by dust and ash, which was bathed in sweat from the long walk, a body that had breathed in the noxious atmosphere of the cemetery. Our story would frame a nice symmetry if she had now observed—but no, she did not notice it at all; she did not even think about it; she did everything with routine movements, did not turn on the television, and did not remain long in the water.

It was only the next morning that the suspicion came to her.

The room with the pool was steaming, for the workers on the morning shift had bathed, and she could hardly see. She walked over to the large standing mirror, wiped it off with her sleeve, and saw that she saw it not, the halo, which the day before had shone so bright. Yet she had no sense of loss.

It was a week before the directorate came to the sad conclusion that no more miracle cures were taking place. The lawyer observed that while earlier, such cases had been sporadic, now on a single day three patients had complained that they had not been cured. It was now a frequent occurrence that one had to take out the contract that the patient had previously signed and point out the particular clause, which was perfectly legal, of course, but not particularly pleasant.

The doctor, who decided to view the past week's surveillance films, could not find Anna Lévay on any of them, since the pictures went to the archive on the last morning of the week, and thus he did not obtain the film for the day on which Anna Lévay had become visible. He was not surprised. She could have done her work even if she were not in the pictures. And yet the facts as they now stood gave cause for anxiety. He knew of one way by which he could convince himself of Anna Lévay's magical powers. That evening, he went to her apartment with the intention of inviting her to go sailing, or else out in a motorboat, it didn't matter which, the water was the important element, because if his suspicion was correct, then the circumstances around the fish episode of the previous year would be reproducible. If she possessed magical powers, then Anna Lévay would turn down the invitation, but if she had none, she would accept.

The teacher let him in at once. She was just now occupied in the kitchen. After a lengthy introduction—Why was she not coming to the cure center? Because she wasn't feeling well. Why didn't she see a doctor? She hadn't the time. Why did she not seek any help? She could have it if she wished. She didn't want anyone involved in her private life—the doctor finally came out with the invitation. Anna Lévay gratefully accepted, but with a condition: If she was not feeling well, then they should postpone the outing, she wished finally to make an excursion on a yacht, after all, she clearly had more than half her life behind her and still had no idea what such a voyage was like. They agreed to have lunch together on the following day, and in the afternoon, if the weather and circumstances were auspicious, to go out with a small company aboard the mayor's yacht.

That night, the doctor tossed and turned uneasily in bed. He dreamed that he was sailing on the lake, and silvery fishy bodies were beating against the side of the boat. He dreamed of oil-green water, the scent of wind, and of a net that stretched to the skies. He was sore afraid. Then he awoke. He switched on the lamp on the night table, and about six seconds later, turned it off. He saw spots on the wall, spots the color of eggshells, which moved about and then slowly formed an image, that of Dr. János Lévay. He remembered him well; back then, he had observed him performing an operation. How thoroughly he washed his hands. The Dr. Lévay in the image also washed his hands, but he directed his gaze to the doctor, as though he were the patient to be operated on, the one on whom he must concentrate.

His wife was sound asleep, and he did not want her to know anything about this business. Therefore, he got up and took a sleeping pill, but when he lay down again, he soon saw the image again under his eyelids. Then he was afraid that the image would pursue him in his sleep. He stuck his finger in his throat and spat out the tablet. Then he brewed strong coffee and spent the rest of the night watching videos.

The next day, exhausted, he went to see Anna Lévay and took her to the restaurant at the cure center, which was named for Lazarus of Bethany. He had earlier become convinced that the matzot, the incense, and the ice cubes that he had set aside in case of emergency had lost their effect, and he told the mayor that for a week now their enterprise was no longer a functioning concern, and then he told of the experiment that he had planned. They agreed that regardless of the outcome of the experiment, the lucrative operation of the cure center must be ensured at all cost.

The doctor and Anna Lévay ordered the same thing: forest-mushroom soup and baked zander, the guest adjusting her taste to that of the host. The host seemed tense, the guest, bored. To drive away her boredom, she blew out the middle candle in the three-armed candelabrum on their table. A fresh, sweet breath, like that of a child, wafted into the doctor's face; yet that served only to increase his tension, which he sought to overcome by appearing pointedly relaxed.

And so the doctor turned to Anna Lévay and without circumlocution told her that he knew a joke that was related to their program for the afternoon, and without asking her whether she knew it, he began: A priest, a minister, and a rabbi were good friends.

One beautiful autumn day, the three went fishing together in a boat on the lake. While they were fishing, they drank a bottle of wine. Eventually, the bottle became empty. But without wine, what is the point of fishing? They were about to head for shore, when the rabbi said, "There is no need to weigh anchor and give up our fishing; I will fetch some wine." With these words, he left the boat and walked swiftly upon the water, swiftly, and with determined steps, to the shore. A few minutes later, he returned with a bottle of kosher wine. The trio continued to fish and to drink. Eventually, the bottle became empty. They were ready to quit when the minister said, "There is no need to weigh anchor and give up our fishing; I will fetch some wine." With these words, he left the boat and walked upon the water, swiftly, and with determined steps, to the shore. A few minutes later, he returned with a bottle of communion wine. Eventually, the bottle became empty yet again. The priest considered it his duty to fetch a bottle of wine. He left the boat, disappeared beneath the surface, and was drowned. Then the minister said to the rabbi, "My dear colleague, we are wicked indeed, are we not? Do you not think that we should have told him where the pilings are?" To which the rabbi replied, "I beg your pardon. What pilings?"

Anna Lévay laughed at the joke, but only out of politeness. She knew it already and understood the provocation. Evidently, something supernatural was expected of her, and the unexpected invitation to an outing on the lake was but a pretext for a trial by water. At this juncture she blew out another of the candles, the one on her left, but the result offended her sense of symmetry, so she took the right-hand candle that still burned and exchanged it with the blown-out candle in the middle.

One could see that the doctor was not feeling well. A whole baked zander was brought out, instead of its two eyes, two olives stared at him hypnotically, the fruit of the holy tree. He stared at them while Anna Lévay spoke to him. He heard the syllables, but his brain could not assemble them into meaningful sentences. The focus of his gaze shifted, and instead of the green olives he saw two vague greenish points, in which he thought he could discern two eyes looking at him, two green lidless reptile eyes. Then these eyes began to move back into the deep black background; there were more eyes, many more; he saw stars, and below them a bright light, perhaps it was the light from the candle. He could not free himself from the sight, and in vain he turned his face away. When the external darkness had enveloped him, he addressed the Lord familiarly, and then he thought that he heard with his inner ear, "Who hath eyes to see, let him see," and for a moment he saw before the dark background the contours of Anna Lévay in white, with a halo. Then he came to himself, and again, he saw the olives in the fish's eye sockets, but then the olives expanded, became liquid, began to move, then to shimmer green and slow, like duckweed on a lake. He looked. Anna Lévay was smiling at him; she seemed to be saying that she was one of the pillars, one of the thirty-six, and if he didn't understand, he should think of his girlfriend Éva, or he should try to imagine the number fifty-six as a Roman numeral, LVI. It was a bit clumsy, but nothing is perfect. But the teacher's mouth was not moving. The doctor was incapable of saying a word; he stared into the woman's face with a rigid reptilian gaze, as he had earlier stared at the fish. He no longer saw a halo around the head. A new vision emerged: He saw that the bodies in the room were becoming transparent, the background of the restaurant gradually shone through them, the legs of Anna Lévay's chair glided a bit forward, a cool breeze blew, and all became calm.

The waiter appeared. The doctor asked for the check, and said that he would pay with his credit card. When it arrived, he examined, as he always did, every item. He saw that the check was for only one dinner, and to avoid later awkwardness, told the waiter that he would pay the lady's check as well.

The waiter asked whether the lady would be arriving later, and he asked the doctor to describe her. The doctor lost his temper and began to shout. The waiter was not an idiot, the woman with whom he had arrived had just left. The waiter began to argue with him, telling him that he had come alone, but the doctor then swore at the waiter, and in a fit of democratic feeling, shouted that he had no wish to be an exception, this wasn't the Diner's Club, two meals for the price of one, he had no desire to pay for only one dinner when he had ordered two, the waiter should simply add up the check properly. Then he asked the waiter where the lady had gone. The waiter replied that he had seen no lady, which brought another round of cursing from the doctor; the waiter should quit talking nonsense, if he was accusing him of madness, there would be serious consequences. Then the headwaiter, the former Latin teacher at the high school, walked over to the table and mollified the doctor. The woman had of course gone out through the door, to the right, over to the main building, and he grinned mischievously, as though he were letting the doctor in on an intimate secret, as though he were initiating him into a marvelous adventure, and he obediently wrote up a new check, for two dinners, which the doctor proceeded to sign. The headwaiter begged the doctor's pardon, it was simply discretion that resulted in a check for one dinner being written, the doctor's good wife, when she saw the statement, to avoid possible questions, in this business discretion is the first principle, but if this is how it is to be, then I beg your pardon, the young waiter is still in training.

The doctor ran out in search of Anna Lévay.

The headwaiter cleared the table personally, with the waiter's assistance. They piled the expensive hand-painted porcelain plates silently on the serving cart. When they came to the serving dish on which the fish had been served, the headwaiter nodded toward the door by which the doctor had just exited, and whispered to his assistant, "Let him alone, my boy. Can't you see that he is mad? And he was considered such a good physician." With that he blew out the middle candle and observed, "*Sic transit gloria mundi.*"